"HOW MANY MEN HAVE YOU KILLED, GANNON?" TRANE YELLED.

"I ain't but twenty-two years old, and I bet I've killed twice as many."

Jake eyed the man for some time. "Why did you come here, Trane?"

"I came here to kill you."

There. Those were the words Jake wanted the witnesses to hear.

Trane continued, "I bet every man I ever shot was faster than you are, Gannon."

"Did you plan on talking me to death, Trane?" Jake interrupted.

The young man started to say something, then went for his gun.

GANNON

DOUG BOWMAN

A TOM DOHERTY ASSOCIATES BOOK
NEW YORK

This is a work of fiction. All the characters and events portrayed in this book are fictitious, and any resemblance to real people or events is purely coincidental.

GANNON

A Tor Book
Published by Tom Doherty Associates, Inc.
175 Fifth Avenue
New York, N.Y. 10010

Tor® is a registered trademark of Tom Doherty Associates, Inc.

ISBN: 0-812-53452-2

First Tor edition: April 1994

Printed in the United States of America

0 9 8 7 6 5 4 3 2 1

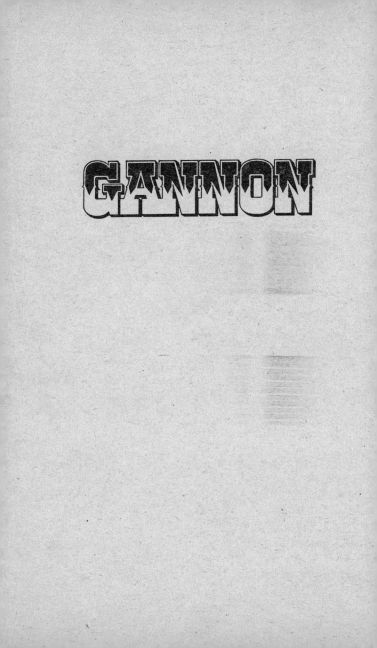

GANNON

One

Jake Gannon sat beside his campfire, roasting a rabbit over the gray coals. Not enough heat, he decided; he must scrounge around for more fuel. He tramped around in the darkness for a while and gathered enough wood to finish his supper and boil his coffee in the morning. As he neared the fire, he could see that his camp had been invaded by two bearded men.

Cradling a rifle in his arm, the taller of the two stood at the fire eating the half-cooked rabbit, while his partner rummaged through Gannon's personal gear. Gannon quietly laid the wood on the ground and stood watching, standing outside the faint glow of light, where the men could not see him. The interlopers themselves, however, made perfect targets around the dying campfire.

Jake had seen enough. Easing his Peacemaker from its holster, he called, "Did you fellows lose something?"

The big man dropped the rabbit and fired his rifle at the sound of Jake's voice, while the man who had been on his knees going through the saddlebags clawed at the gun on his hip. Gannon fired two shots, killing both men instantly. Then he slowly backed away into the darkness.

No amount of money could have hired Jake to walk into the glow of that campfire just now, for unless the men had been downright stupid, there would be someone else out there on watch. He walked into the brush and made himself a bed of leaves behind some mesquite bushes. He heard no sounds during the night.

He awoke at daybreak and could plainly see the horses of the dead men. A dun and a big piebald were tied to a bush two hundred yards from his camp. Catching his own horse and mounting bareback, he circled the area till he was convinced that no other horse had been near his camp. Then he rode forward to look the men over.

Both wore heavy coats, and Jake wondered why. This far south the weather almost never turned cold enough to be uncomfortable at this time of year. Searching the men, he found that their pockets were filled with plunder. The smaller man even carried a doorknob in his coat. Both men carried money, but no identification. Jake took a dollar from the big man to pay for the rabbit, and as compensation for his having to go to bed without supper.

Gannon sat wondering what he was going to do with the bodies, pondering the many possibilities. He cared little whether or not they received a proper burial. Anyway, he had no tools to dig a grave with.

The men had been stupid, all right, and Jake wondered how they had managed to get as old as they appeared to be. They probably could have taken him easy enough, if one man had come into camp and held his attention while the other got the drop on him. They had obviously thought they had come upon easy pickings. Perhaps they had mistaken him for a pilgrim. Jake Gannon was neither a pilgrim nor easy pickings.

Jake had been exposed to violence at an early age, and could well remember the day the Union forces rode into Franklin after overrunning General John Bell Hood's Confederate defenders, with which Jake's father had served. Two weeks later, Hood's army was soundly defeated at the Battle of Nashville. More than three months had passed before Jake learned that his father had been among the first to fall during the two-day Nashville conflict.

"The Yankees rode into Franklin jist like they owned the place," Jake had often heard his mother say. "They didn't treat us kindly, neither; jist took anything they wanted. A lot of the young girls claimed they done worse."

Jake had been twelve years old at the time. He could not say what did or did not happen with the girls, but the soldiers had not mistreated him. They did ride to his crib and ask that they be given corn for their horses. Fearing that they would take it all if he did not share with them, young Jake had sacked up several bushels. The soldiers had thanked him politely and continued on their way.

Shortly thereafter, Jake and his mother had abandoned their farm near Franklin and moved to Kentucky, where they had relatives. Though leaving his birthplace and the only home he had ever known was upsetting to the youngster, he had hitched up the team and driven his mother north without complaining. They were soon settled in a well-built cabin with several acres for planting.

The new homestead had been given to them by Clare Gannon's older brother, a man said to be involved in many illegal activities. At any rate, Jesse Ride was a man of means, and the fact that he took care of his own was well known throughout the Cumberland Mountains. A giant of a man, he was known to pay all debts, be they debts of gratitude or revenge, and few men dared to trifle with him.

Young Jake soon had a large garden growing and several acres of corn planted for horse feed. Clare Gannon spent much of the summer canning vegetables for winter. Jake kept the table supplied with plenty of fresh meat, for wild game was abundant in the mountains, and he was an excellent shot with the long rifle.

Mother and son lived well indeed, and stayed on the homestead for five years. During the winter of 1869, Clare took to her bed with pneumonia, and a week later she was dead. At age seventeen, Jake was alone in the world. That was when Aunt Rose told him that he had had a twin brother who disappeared before his first birthday.

"Them hogs et that baby jist as shore as I live an' breathe," the tottering old woman had said. "Seb'm ub'm in 'at pen, an' it wouldna took 'em more'n one minute ta eat ever' trace o' that child, flesh hair'n bone.

"Yer pa always thought he crawled off somewhere'n a painter got 'im, but I know better. No leb'm-month-old baby couldna made it all th' way over ta them woods, an' I shore ain't never heerd o' no painter crossin' no plowed field ta git nuthin'. Weren't no use in lookin' fer scraps o' cloth, th' baby weren't a-wearin' no clothes.

"Anyhow, yer brother disappeared 'at mornin' an' nobody ain't saw hide nor hair o' 'im since. Yer pa an' ma both wanted ta wait till ya wuz growed afore tellin' ya, but it looks ta me like yer 'bout as growed as yer gonna git."

Unwilling to trust the old woman's memory, Jake had questioned other relatives and learned that he was indeed the survivor of an identical twin. The accepted story was that while Clare Gannon had been busy bathing Jake, his twin had disappeared, never to be seen again. Uncle Jesse added the information that Jake himself had almost died a year later when he "et a bait o' crab apples that swole in his stomach."

For several years after his brother's disappearance, Jake's mother had kept him with her at all times, seldom letting him out of her sight. He did, however, attend school at Franklin, where he learned to read and write very well. After moving to Kentucky, he never saw the inside of another schoolhouse, though he did continue his education by reading every book he could find.

After the death of his mother, he turned the small farm back to nature and spent most of his time pursuing his first love: hunting and trapping along the mountain streams. He sold meat and hides to anyone who would buy in order to sustain himself. Occasionally, he did odd jobs for his uncle, such as hauling whiskey around the mountains on the backs of mules.

Jesse Ride owned several thoroughbred racehorses, and had given Jake a mare named Princess that Ride considered too old for racing. The mare had won several small races but never finished in the money in any race that Ride thought to be of consequence, always running somewhere in the middle of the pack. Ride was fond of saying that Princess had the speed but not the heart to be a champion.

Uncle Jesse owned a stallion named Big Sir who certainly had the heart. The animal had won so many races that people refused to bet against him, but not before Ride had cleaned up in both money and property. Nowadays, the horse spent his time idly grazing in the pasture when he wasn't breeding mares for a fat fee. If Princess ever came into heat while Uncle Jesse was away on business, Jake intended to let her "jump the fence" to Big Sir, for he desperately wanted a colt from the big stallion that many men were calling unbeatable.

Jesse Ride died in 1872, done in by a Tennessee man's hunting knife. Some men had brought the body home, and there was talk of organizing a party to hang Ride's killer. Jake had refused to join them. Though he did not say so, he suspected that the Tennessee man had used the knife to protect his own life, for Jesse Ride had been a large and overbearing man.

Even as his uncle's body lay inside the big house, Jake led Princess through the pasture gate. She was in her breeding cycle, and showed little resistance as Big Sir made short work of the chore. A few days later Jake rode through the Cumberland Gap and headed west, never to see Kentucky again.

"You look jist like yer daddy," Aunt Rose had said to Jake the morning he left, "same build an' ever'thang." And just like his daddy, Jake stood six-foot-three in his socks and weighed more than two hundred pounds. He was a handsome man, with his father's black hair and his mother's deep blue eyes. And though he had been involved in all of the usual scuffles during his growing years, he had lost none, for Jesse Ride had taught him self-defense early on. Later, Ride had schooled him equally well in the use of weapons, insisting that his nephew would be the best fighting man in Kentucky.

Jake had roamed the west for seven years, traveling as far north as Montana and as far west as California, performing a wide assortment of jobs. A few years ago he had come back to Texas. Texas had it all, he had decided.

The horse he rode these days was a thoroughbred chestnut gelding, the colt dropped by Princess. The son of Big Sir was a dead ringer, and Jake had never seen a finer animal. Now six years old, the horse's speed and stamina had literally saved Gannon's life on at least one occasion:

On a bright morning in North Texas three years ago, Jake had been attacked by a party of Comanches. He had sent three braves to the happy hunting ground with his fifty-caliber Sharps rifle, and his horse had outrun the rest.

In a chase that lasted for more than an hour, Big Red had run the Indians' mustangs to a quivering standstill, then had stood on the hilltop prancing for all to see. Jake thought that the Comanches had been more interested in capturing the horse than getting their hands on its rider.

Jake Gannon was both quick and deadly with any type of firearm, and plenty tough. Though he had seen hand-to-hand combat many times, he had never fallen to another man's fists.

Indeed, the would-be robbers who now lay dead a short distance away could have chosen an easier mark.

Moving the rocks that had encircled his campfire to a location several yards away, he built a fire and filled his coffeepot. He decided to carry the dead men to the town of Mission and turn them over to someone in authority there, for he certainly did not intend to haul them all the way to Laredo.

He had eaten the last of his cold biscuits and was sipping his coffee when he noticed three specks on the eastern landscape, specks that he soon determined were riders headed in his direction. They traveled very slowly, as if tracking.

Then, perhaps seeing the smoke from his campfire, the riders put their horses to a canter. As they neared the horses of the dead men, the three stopped for a conversation. From his sitting position on a large rock, Jake watched as one man rode forward to inspect the horses, while the remaining two eyed Gannon steadily from a distance of three hundred yards. Shortly, the men rode into his camp.

A tall, bearded man who sported a deputy sheriff's badge was the first to speak. Pointing to the dun and the piebald, he said, "Them your horses?"

"Hardly," Jake said, pointing. "Used to belong to those fellows lying in the bushes there." The deputy's eyes followed Jake's point to the men's booted feet, which were in plain view.

The lawman rode to the bodies and dismounted. A few minutes later he returned, saying, "Did you shoot 'em?"

"Uh-huh," Jake said, nodding.

"Mind telling me why?"

The smallest of the riders chose this time to speak. "He shot 'em because the sonsofbitches needed shooting, Hack."

The lawman stared at the blond-haired man beside him. "Do you know this man, Whitey?" he asked.

"Sure, I know him, been knowing him for years."

Jake had recognized Whitey Compton immediately, but held off offering a greeting, for reasons that he learned the hard way. Sometimes a man did not wish to be recognized. As he got to his feet and walked forward with his right hand extended, Gannon spoke to the small man.

"Good to see you again, Whitey," he said, grasping Compton's hand. "Pardon me for not speaking up before, but I didn't know what name you were traveling under this year." Then, speaking to all three, he added, "Get down and rest yourselves. I don't have any food, but there's warm coffee in the pot."

After dismounting, the deputy quizzed Gannon further, seeming satisfied with his answers. In a short while, the lawman began to explain the reason behind his manhunt:

Three days ago, the deputy had dropped in on an old friend who owned a small spread forty miles to the east. The friend was getting on in years, and was sick much of the time. Two bearded men, one much larger than the other, had robbed old man Lewis in broad daylight. The larger of the two had held the sickly man down on the bed while the other ransacked the house. They had taken money, weapons and everything else of value, then calmly rode away on a dun and a big piebald.

"Them horses are standing right out yonder, mister," Deputy Hack Evans said. "Tracking them was no problem at all."

"I'm sure you've found your men, Deputy," Jake said. "The horses are right where their owners tied them."

"Well, I don't reckon they killed anybody," Evans said. "What I can't figure out is why they left old Lewis alive, knowing damn well he could identify them."

"They didn't get any smarter by the time they got here," Jake said. "Tried to rob my camp while I was out gathering firewood."

The third member of the deputy's party, a brown-haired man maybe thirty years old, spoke now.

"It's like you said, Hack. The men we've been trackin' ain't killed nobody, but this fellow admits that he has. How do we know that it happened the way he says?"

Whitey Compton spoke quickly, almost shouting. "This man's name is Jake Gannon, Sid! Calling him a liar ain't nowhere near the healthiest thing a man could be doing. Besides, it's his word against theirs. They ain't saying much!"

"Jake Gannon?" Sid faced Whitey and raised his eyebrows. "I've heerd o' him lots o' times."

Whitey nodded.

"Ain't been no ambush here," the deputy said. "One of 'em was shot in the throat and the other one damn near between the eyes."

"Well, I didn't know all that," Sid said. Then, turning to face Jake, he added, "I'm sorry, Mister Gannon, I didn't know who you wuz. I shore ain't callin' you no liar, neither."

Jake nodded and reseated himself on the rock.

The deputy announced that the county would take charge of the dead men and their horses, and he was soon busy going through their gear.

As Evans walked toward the thieves' horses, Whitey Compton trotted up to him. Speaking softly, he said, "That horse of mine is more'n fifteen years old, Hack; how much does the county want for that piebald?"

The deputy looked around, making sure he was out of earshot of the others. "How much you got?"

"Ain't got but six dollars."

Looking over his shoulder once again, Evans said, "Gimme the six and switch your saddle."

Compton complied and led his new horse away from the others. The deputy loaded the bodies, and, with Sid at his side, departed for Mission. Compton had elected to sit on the rock with Gannon and talk for a while.

The two had known each other for several years, had even made a couple trail drives together. Through no effort of his own, Jake had run into the small man at least once a year since then. It seemed that no matter where Gannon went, Whitey eventually showed up.

Compton was twenty-five and weighed no more than a hundred twenty pounds, and still possessed most of his mischievous boyhood ways. He could always be counted on to find some way of getting into trouble. Though finding a man that Whitey could handle in a scuffle would have been extremely difficult, he was forever picking on larger men when he was drinking. Jake had seen him in at least a dozen fistfights, but had yet to see him win one.

One of their mutual friends had said to Jake, "I once saw one of Whitey's drunk Mexican girlfriends stand toe to toe with him in El Paso. She slugged it out with him, Jake. She whupped his ass, too. Bein' clobbered by a woman didn't seem to bother him at all. He jist had another drank and went off huntin' some big man to pick on. I thank Compton's crazy."

Though he carried a thirty-six-caliber Navy on his hip, Whitey was a slow draw and a worse marksman. He seemed to realize this, for he never challenged any man to a gunfight. Jake considered that to be the prime reason for Compton's continued good health.

Whitey sat now with his legs crossed, smoking a cigarette. "Been a while since I saw you, Jake. How you been?"

"Just surviving," Gannon said, "moving around a lot."

Whitey walked to the piebald and began to pet the big horse. "I bought him from Hack, Jake; what do you think of him?"

"He looks mighty good to me. Of course, he wasn't the deputy's horse to sell, but I suppose he belongs to you now. I would have made him write me a bill of sale, though."

"He wouldn't have done it. He's dumb, but not that dumb. He's got to cover his tracks. We saw him put the money he took off them thieves into his own pocket, but I'll bet that when he gets the bodies to Mission the men will be broke, and Hidalgo County will have to bury them."

"Maybe so," Jake said. "I guess that's one of the hidden benefits of being a lawman."

Pointing to the piebald's hip, Whitey asked, "Did you ever see that brand before?"

"I don't think so. Looks like an ox yoke."

"Yep, I believe that's what it is."

The men sat on the rock trading stories for some time, bringing each other up to date on what they had been doing since they had last worked together. That job had been on a spread in northern New Mexico Territory, and had ended a year ago when the owner sold out.

Grinding his cigarette out beneath his boot heel, Whitey said, "Don't know where you're headed, but if you're not in too big a hurry I've got part of a smoked ham in my saddlebag."

Gannon chucked softly, wondering where Whitey had managed to steal a ham. "I suppose a fellow with a smoked ham would be welcome around anybody's campfire, Whitey. The fire's still hot and I'd be glad to furnish the skillet." Gannon added grounds and water to the coffeepot, and soon both men were eating heartily.

As Compton sat gnawing the last of the meat from the bone, he explained that old man Lewis had given him the ham for the trackers to eat on the trail. Whitey had refrained from mentioning it to his riding partners.

"Where you heading now, Jake?" he asked, tossing the bone into the brush.

"Going to Laredo to look up a man named Frank Indio."

"Well, Indio sure ain't hard to find; owns the biggest saloon in town."

"That's what I've been told," Jake said. He saw no reason to divulge the details of his present mission to Compton, a mission that had taken every waking hour of his time over the past several weeks:

Last winter, Jake had been riding along Old San Antonio Road near the town of Nacogdoches when he overtook a wagon driven by a middle-aged man who was accompanied by his wife and teenaged son. Andy Ledbetter had introduced himself and his family, and invited Jake to tie his horse behind and join them in the wagon. Being saddle-weary and starved for conversation, Gannon had accepted the ride.

The Ledbetters owned a small spread twenty miles from town, and within the hour Andy had offered Jake employment for the remainder of the winter. Having only a few dollars to his name, and tired of sleeping in a different place each night, Jake had taken the job. Though the family was on hard times and could afford to pay only twenty-five dollars a month, the food and living conditions were excellent. That the couple had originally come from Kentucky had been another contributing factor in Jake's decision to work for them.

Though Andy had painful back problems, he was a hard worker, and his son, Tony, did as much as he could after school each day. And in addition to her cooking and housekeeping chores, Sarah Ledbetter spent at least half of each day working outside. Jake had been happy enough with the job, and had even built the family a new barn. Two months ago he had decided to leave on this mission after a long discussion around the supper table.

"Fellow claimin' his name was Hite was the first one to show up," Andy was saying. "Rode out here three times tellin' us what a good deal it was. Started out wantin' three thousand dollars for a hundred head of purebred cows and three prize-winnin' bulls.

"Brought Frank Indio with him the last time, and Indio talked us into givin' him two thousand dollars, all the money we had in the world. Said he'd deliver the cattle within one month, but that's the last we ever heard from him."

"How long ago did this happen?" Jake asked.

"Be two years next month. We went to the sheriff with it, but he ain't gonna do nothin'. Didn't even write down what we told him."

"It's mostly my fault," Sarah Ledbetter said softly. "I believed every word Indio said, and I guess I sort of helped him talk Andy into it. It's just that we wanted a start with some purebred cattle so bad, Jake."

"Did you get a receipt for the money, Andy?" Jake asked.

"Sure, I got a receipt, but that's all I ever expect to get." Andy walked to another room and returned, reseating himself at the table. Pushing the handwritten document across the table to Jake, he said, "I took the money out of the bank in Nacogdoches and handed it over like a good little boy." Andy dropped his fork in his plate noisily. "What I got in exchange was that damned worthless piece of paper."

Jake Gannon had come from good stock. His parents had been honest, law-abiding citizens, and had instilled those same values in him at an early age. Though some folks might call him rough-and-ready, he was an honest man who had never taken another man's dollar without giving fair exchange. He had little patience with liars, and none whatsoever with thieves. Later, he lay in his bed thinking long and hard about the man who had swindled the kindhearted, hard-working Ledbetters out of their hard-earned money. When he came to breakfast the following morning he announced his decision.

"I'm gonna be riding this morning, Andy. I intend to start looking for Frank Indio."

Ledbetter did not answer, and the room was quiet for some time. It was Sarah who finally broke the silence.

"Are you going to try to get some of our money back, Jake?"

Gannon was busy buttering himself a biscuit. "Gonna try to get it all back. I'll be needing that receipt, though."

Andy handed over the yellow piece of paper, saying, "I guess you've made up your mind, Jake, so I'll make you a deal: get back all or any part of that money, and I'll halve 'er with you."

"I couldn't let you do that, Andy," Jake said. "It's too much money."

"I'll be damned if it is!" Andy said, raising his voice. "I've done without it so long that gettin' back half of it would seem like a windfall to me. That's the way I want it and that's the deal I'm makin'. We split 'er right down the middle."

Jake nodded in agreement, and the men shook hands.

Within the hour, Gannon saddled Big Red and loaded his pack horse, then headed for Fort Worth.

He had traveled around central Texas for more than a month asking questions, then headed south. Last week he had arrived in Brownsville, where he learned that Frank Indio was running a saloon in Laredo. Now, sitting on a rock in the lower Rio Grande Valley, Jake knew that he must be on his way. He said so to Whitey Compton.

"Think you might need some help in Laredo?" Compton asked.

"No, no, I'm just gonna be taking it easy."

"Well, I guess I'll be riding on into Mission," Compton said. "Gotta leave for Houston in the morning."

"I'll ride as far as Mission with you. I need some grain and a few other things."

Pointing to Jake's animals, Whitey noted, "I see you're still riding that big thoroughbred."

"For sure," Gannon said, beginning to put his pack together.

Two hours later they rode into Mission, and Compton stopped at the first watering hole.

"I'll be leaving you here, Jake, good luck to you."

"Same to you," Gannon said, knowing that if his life followed its usual pattern, he had not seen the last of Whitey Compton. As Jake rode away, he noticed that the deputy's horse was tied at the saloon's hitching rail. The thieves had been carrying more than enough money to pay for their own burial, but Gannon agreed with Whitey's prediction that the county would have to bury them. Nor would the money taken from old man Lewis ever be returned to him.

Gannon stocked his pack with enough food for several days and loaded a sack of grain on his pack horse. Soon he was following the muddy Rio Grande northwest toward Laredo.

Two

Keeping close to the river was no easy task. There were places where it was impossible to ride through the dense brush and saplings. Nor could a man lead a horse through. The thickets contained the tallest mesquite trees Jake had ever seen, many of them reaching a height of sixty feet or more. He circled around them to the north, and after a five-day ride, he arrived in Laredo.

Founded by Spaniards in 1755 and named for Laredo, in Santander, Spain, the town stood on the bank of the Rio Grande, opposite Nuevo Laredo, Mexico. Seat of Webb County, it had become an important frontier post in 1848, when the river was established as the boundary between Mexico and the United States.

As he looked down the hill into the bustling settlement, Gannon could see that a large portion of its inhabitants were of Mexican descent. He led his horses down the hill to the livery stable and requested that they be stabled and fed. Then, with his saddlebag lying across his left shoulder and his Winchester cradled in his right arm, he began to walk around the town.

"Can you direct me to the Silver Dollar?" he asked of a man who was standing in the doorway of a barber shop.

"Walk up the hill to the corner, then turn south. You'll see the sign."

Jake was soon sitting in the saloon sipping a beer. The building was large, even by Texas standards, and had a bar at least fifty feet long. A potbellied stove stood in the center of the room, around which were scattered tables and chairs of various shapes and sizes. Farther back, several tables were set up for gambling, and beyond those was a small dance floor.

A white-haired man sat on a piano stool, nonchalantly sipping a drink, as if waiting for someone to ask him to play. Two doors opened off the rear of the building, no doubt leading to cabins where the saloon girls sold their favors. To the right of the gaming tables was a door made of heavy hardwood, which Jake supposed led to the office.

Only five men were in the establishment, all of them seated at the far end of the bar. Jake took the first stool inside the front door.

As he served Gannon's second beer, the balding bartender said, "Haven't seen you before. You just passing through?"

"I've got some business with Frank Indio and a man named Hite," Jake answered.

"Hite's been dead for over a year, mister, but Frank's in the office. Should be out pretty soon. The cook's fixing him a steak right now."

Moments later, a woman came from the kitchen bearing a large tray of food. She set the tray on a table and knocked on the office door, then returned to the kitchen.

Indio appeared in the doorway, his green eyes darting around the room. He nodded to someone sitting at the bar, then walked to his table. He was a fat man of medium height, with a pale, sallow complexion, reflecting the fact that he spent all of his time indoors.

Gannon finished his beer and walked to Indio's table. "I came from East Texas to talk to you, Indio."

"Well, make it brief," Indio said around a mouthful of beef, "and it better be good."

"I intend to make it brief, Indio," Jake said, pulling up a chair for himself with the toe of his boot, "but I can't make it good. You see, I'm from the Jake Gannon Collection Agency."

"Jake Gannon?" Indio asked quickly. "I've heard of him."

"It's a one-man agency," Jake said.

"Then you must be Gannon."

Jake nodded, then continued. "You talked a friend of mine in Nacogdoches out of his last dollar, Indio, and the cattle you promised to deliver are two years overdue. Of course, you remember good old, gullible Andy Ledbetter. The money you owe him is half mine, mister, and I'm here to collect!" Pointing to Indio's plate, he added, "The only way I'm gonna let you keep eating big steaks like that and breathing this good South Texas air is for you to cough up two thousand dollars, along with two years' accumulated interest."

Indio's pale face turned whiter. He sat with his hands folded in his lap. "You cannot goad me into a gunfight, Mister Gannon. I am no gunfighter."

"Well," Jake said, chuckling, "that should make my job a little easier."

"Besides," Indio said, ignoring Jake's remark, "I do not have that kind of money."

Gannon was on his feet now. He leaned forward, looking Indio squarely in the eye. "That's not my problem," he said. "I've got a receipt that says you had it when you left the bank in Nacogdoches, and you damn well better find it again. Hear me, Indio, and hear me right: I'm giving you ten days to put the money in my hand. If you don't, I will kill you."

Then, continuing to glare, he poked his finger into Indio's soup bowl, stirring it round and round. "Soup's a little thin today, ain't it?" he said. Then he walked through the front door.

He registered at a hotel on the same block, deliberately taking a room on the top floor of the three-story building. He had a good view of the street and the front portion of the Silver Dollar. From the window, he soon saw the bartender, minus his apron, walk from the saloon, stroll casually to the corner, and turn west. He was quickly out of sight.

Directly across the street from the saloon was a hardware store. After a while, Jake was standing underneath its wooden awning, leaning against the building and staring at the saloon. Nothing that might happen at the Silver Dollar was of interest to him. He was merely hoping that his presence might unnerve its owner. Patrons going into the saloon paid Jake no mind. But when they came out they looked him over good, a sure sign that Indio knew he was there. When darkness came, he returned to the hotel and went to bed.

The following morning, he had scarcely taken up his position in front of the store when the owner opened the door and handed him a nail keg.

"Take this," he said. "If you turn it upside down it makes a pretty good seat." Gannon accepted the keg and was about to speak, when the man stepped back inside and closed the door. A short while later the door opened again, and a small cushion landed at Jake's feet. He was soon sitting on the soft seat with his back against the wall.

At noon, he walked next door to a billiard hall, which also served food. After eating, he sat on a bench watching two men play the game. One of them seemed to be very good at it. The other might have been, Jake was thinking, if he would take that cigarette out of his mouth so he could see the balls. The man looked silly to Gannon, who had never smoked a cigarette in his life. As a small boy he had promised his mother that he would never smoke till he was a grown man. Now he did not smoke because he knew it would shorten a man's wind, and maybe his life. Shortly, he finished his coffee and returned to the nail keg.

He continued the same routine for six days, and this morning a man entered the hardware store and spoke to him from behind the closed door.

"You've got bad trouble comin', Gannon. Indio sent to San Antonio for Johnny Trane nearly a week ago. Trane might already be in town, for all I know."

"Thank you," Jake said, then added, "I can't help but wonder why you're telling me this."

"Because Indio is a crook, and Trane is a murderer."

Gannon remained seated while the man walked back into the street and disappeared around the corner.

Jake was somewhat relieved to learn that he might have to fight only one man, and was not surprised that Indio had hired a gunman. Gannon had expected no less of the swindler, for he knew that the man who would give up two thousand dollars without a fight was rare.

Jake had never seen Johnny Trane, but had heard the name many times. It was said that he had killed as many as a dozen men in gunfights. Gannon had also heard that many of them were novices and drunks, among them a sixty-year-old man and a sixteen-year-old boy. Johnny

Trane himself was said to be a youngster, barely into man-hood.

The store owner had already put out the keg when Jake arrived at the store the next morning. Pushing his hat to the back of his head, Gannon took his seat and leaned his shoulders against the building.

An hour later, the saloon door opened and a handsome young man walked through. Though he wore no coat or hat, he was expensively dressed, with finely tooled boots and a silk shirt that buttoned at his wrists. His neatly combed blond hair grew to his shoulders, and appeared to be slicked down with some kind of grease. A pair of pearl-handled Peacemakers rode low on his hips in holsters that were tied to his legs with rawhide. Gannon had no doubt that he was now looking at one Johnny Trane.

Standing on the plank sidewalk in front of the saloon, the young gunman pointed across the street to Jake, shouting, "I've been hearing all that stuff you've said about me, Gannon, all them threats you've been making!"

A faint smile began to play around Jake's mouth. The oldest scheme in the book, he was thinking, keeping his seat.

Trane then walked into the street at an angle, stopping forty feet to Gannon's left.

"Get out into the street, fellow!" Trane shouted. "Let's see how good you are."

Jake said nothing, and stayed where he was. He was in no hurry; he wanted witnesses. When a sizable crowd had gathered on each side of the street, Gannon got to his feet, his body bent slightly forward and his legs spread apart. He had no intention of walking into the street and becoming a target for possible hidden guns. Here, under the awning with his back to the wall, he felt that his only problem was in front of him.

"How many men have you killed, Gannon?" Trane

yelled. "I ain't but twenty-two years old, and I bet I've killed twice as many."

Jake eyed the man for some time. "Why did you come here, Trane?"

"I came here to kill you!"

There, now; those were the words Jake wanted the witnesses to hear.

Trane continued, "I bet every man I ever shot was faster than you. I bet—"

"Did you plan on talking me to death, Trane?" Jake interrupted.

The young gunman exploded. "Why you—"

Trane never finished the sentence, for Gannon killed him. A shot to the mouth sent him to the ground instantly, where he quivered once and lay still. Trane had no more than cleared his holster when he died. Indeed, he had been nothing close to a match for the quick-handed Gannon.

Jake took a few steps backward and reseated himself. Two men were now removing Trane's body from the street, and Gannon could see Indio poking his head through the doorway of the saloon. He quickly removed himself when he caught Gannon's eye.

Within minutes, the town marshal was on the scene, and, without speaking to Jake, he circulated among the crowd. He spoke with several witnesses at length, then crossed the street to Gannon. He was a short, muscular, dark-haired man about forty years old.

"Open and shut case, Gannon," he said. "Every man here says you acted in self-defense."

"Trane informed me that he was about to kill me," Jake said, getting to his feet.

"I know," the lawman said, nodding several times, "been told all about it. I knew Trane was coming to town, and I knew why. Not much happens around here that I don't know about.

"The fight ended exactly like I thought it would, 'cause I knew about you planting Buzz Busby up in Fort Worth a while back. Busby was plenty fast, and I figured any man who could outdraw him wouldn't have no trouble putting Johnny Trane away." He pointed toward the saloon. "I suppose you know where your main problem lies. I've tried to close the crooked bastard down several times, but I never could make nothing stick. I'll be gone in a few minutes, and if you decide to go over there and finish the job, I won't be around to stop you."

"It hasn't come to that yet," Jake said.

The marshal turned to walk away, saying over his shoulder, "Good day, sir."

Today was the tenth day, and Jake brought his horses from the livery stable. He tied them to the hardware store's hitching rail, and sat on the keg with his rifle across his lap. He had decided to give Indio until noon.

At ten o'clock an old man came from the saloon and walked directly to Jake.

"Frank wants to know if you intend to carry out your threat," he said.

"I didn't make a threat." Jake shooed a fly away from his face. "I made a promise. I keep my promises."

The man hurried back across the street. In twenty minutes, he returned. "Frank says you can come into the saloon and pick up the money."

Jake shook his head emphatically. "No! Tell him I want the money delivered to me right here, and remind him that he's running out of time." Jake got to his feet and moved to a position that put a post and his horse between himself and the saloon, then jacked a shell into the chamber of his Winchester.

At ten minutes to twelve, Indio's messenger crossed the street again, this time carrying a brown paper bag.

"The money's in here," he said. "Frank wants a receipt."

"How much money's in the bag, old-timer?"

"Twenty-two hundred. I helped him count it."

Taking the bag and peeking inside, Jake tucked it inside his shirt, then handed the old man the yellow slip of paper.

"Here," he said, "I'll give him back his own receipt."

Keeping his horses between himself and the saloon, he led them to the end of the block and turned the corner. Then he mounted Big Red and headed northeast. At the top of the hill, he sat watching his backtrail for half an hour. No one followed. He counted the money, then transferred it to his saddlebag, keeping the paper bag to start his next campfire. He had a long ride ahead, a distance of more than four hundred miles.

The Texas sun was hot in the middle of June, and the trip to Nacogdoches took almost two weeks. Out of consideration for his horses, Jake let them set their own pace, and neither animal seemed eager to expend a lot of energy during the day. Gannon rode mostly in the cool of the morning or late afternoon, or, when he was in an area that he knew well, at night.

Sarah Ledbetter was standing in the yard scattering corn to the chickens when Jake rode into view. Flinging the remainder of the grain to the ground, she trotted to meet him, a wayward strand of her salt-and-pepper hair waving in the breeze.

"Lord, we've been worried about you, Jake, are you all right?"

"Yes, ma'am, just hungry."

"Well, I can sure fix that; Andy butchered a calf just yesterday." As Jake stabled and fed his horses, Sarah stood in the yard pulling on a rope that was attached to a huge bell, a signal to the men in the fields that they were wanted at the house for whatever reason.

"Andy and Tony are out in the field," she said, as Jake walked to the porch. "They've done enough for today, anyhow." She headed for the kitchen as Jake seated himself on the doorstep. Minutes later, Andy and Tony came trotting across the hillside. Their pace slowed to a walk when they spotted Jake.

"Didn't have no idea what we'd find when we got here," Andy said breathlessly. "When she rings that bell at this time of day it means to come running." He grabbed Jake's hand, patting him on the back. "I've been asking about you each time I saw somebody, but nobody'd heard anything. I don't know when I've been so glad to see a man."

"Pa mentions your name at least once every hour," Tony told Jake. Then, to his father, he said, "I'll go back to the field and get the horses, Pa."

Opening the saddlebag that lay across his knee, Gannon handed the money to Andy.

"Two thousand dollars," he said, "and two hundred interest."

Andy stared at the money, speechless. He was soon in the kitchen, where Sarah was busily preparing a meal.

"Look at this, Sarah," he said, waving the money in front of her eyes. "Jake got back every dollar. Made Indio pay interest on the money, too."

"Jake's a good man," she said, "I hope you didn't forget to give him half."

"No, no. Gonna do that right now." Andy took a drink of water from the gourd dipper and returned to the porch.

"I'll be putting this to good use," Jake said, when Andy had divided the money equally. "There's a little place that lies along the Brazos River out near Waco that I've had my eye on for a long time. This should be enough to buy it and put it in top shape."

"Six-Shooter Junction, huh?"

"Well, that's one of Waco's nicknames, but I doubt that the town fathers call it that. Anyway, the place I want is several miles out of town. I wouldn't be spending much time in Waco."

"Wouldn't think you'd want to. That place is known all over Texas as a den of thieves, cutthroats and gunslingers. I wish you luck, but you'd better keep an eye on what's yours."

"I will, Andy."

Gannon spent the remainder of the week with the family, then headed west to the Brazos. Though he had become extremely fond of the Ledbetters, and was leaving with some regret, he knew that if ever his dream of owning his own place was to be fulfilled, he must begin now, while he had the money.

Andy's concern that Jake was riding into a dangerous area had been well taken. And though he feared no man, Jake was well aware of the fact that he had made some enemies over the years, men who would not hesitate to attack under cover of darkness, or from just around the bend. As far as he knew, however, no one in Waco had reason to dislike him. Though he had passed through the town several times, each visit had been brief, and he could not call a single man's name who lived there. If he could make a deal with Handy for the river property, Jake intended to spend most of his time at home, for there would be much work to do.

He reached the Angelina River just before sundown, fording where the water was only a few inches deep. Picketing his horses on the west bank, he soon had his own bed made. He kindled a small fire for coffee, then extinguished the flame. Sarah Ledbetter had made sure he had enough ready-cooked food for the trip. After eating, he climbed atop his bedroll, using his blanket for a pillow.

The warm temperature of the June night made a covering for his body unnecessary.

Lying beneath the stars and the rising half-moon, Gannon spent some time thinking about his recent manhunt. He felt no remorse whatever about Johnny Trane. Young though he was, the man had surely understood the rules of the West: raw justice. And that justice was usually meted out by the citizenry, for many of the lawmen were little better than the scum they were paid to police. Bent on becoming known as the fastest gun around, Trane had traded his life for a chance at the notoriety to be gained by outdrawing Jake Gannon. As far as Jake was concerned, the young man had committed suicide. There would always be somebody like Johnny Trane. And there would always be somebody faster.

And there would always be men like Frank Indio. Jake had not been surprised that the sheriff of Nacogdoches County had made no effort to apprehend the swindler. Nor had he passed Indio's name and misdeed along to other lawmen around the country. Nevertheless, Gannon believed that Indio would eventually get his comeuppance, most likely from the man he least expected to fight back.

Gannon had never called upon the law for anything. He was a man who fought his own battles, and occasionally those of others who had been put upon or cheated. Though the mere size of Jake Gannon was often enough to deter would-be troublemakers from trifling with him personally, he had more than once felt obliged to step in when a ruffian attempted to run roughshod over a smaller man. At other times Gannon had been able to bring such things to a halt with his deep, commanding voice. The scars on Jake's knuckles told the story. A wise man read that story and gave him a wide berth.

He was back in the saddle at sunup, his favorite period of the day. It had long been his habit to rise at the first suggestion of dawn, sitting motionlessly as he watched the wonderment of night turning to day. Then the giant fireball seemed to come out of the ground no more than a few miles away. Some worshiped it as a god, while others cursed it for its searing heat. Though Jake himself had been guilty of the latter, he knew that the ball was the giver of life, and tried to let it shine on him for a few hours every day. Today it would shine on him longer.

At noon, he stopped at a spring that was shaded by two large oaks. He stood for a few moments watching the vein boil sand up from the bottom of the spring, then helped himself to a tin cup that some thoughtful soul had left hanging on a broken branch nearby. He watered his horses, then unburdened their backs and picketed them on good grass.

After eating his fill of beef and biscuits, he leaned his back against one of the oaks and relaxed while his horses grazed. He would allow them to eat for at least two hours. Sitting on top of a small knoll, he had a good view of the area around him. Texas must surely be the best place on earth for raising cattle, he was thinking. With abundant perennial grasses, plenty of shade, and an ample supply of water, central Texas was a cattleman's dream.

The country was big, raw, and wild, however, and no place for the fainthearted; a message that had been driven home to more than one Easterner who had thrown up his hands and gone back home to his mama. It took a certain type of man to make it on the frontier, and for every one who made it, a dozen failed.

Gannon had worked for several successful men over the years, and noted that each possessed the same qualities:

the ability to see farther ahead than one season, the determination to stick with his idea come hell or high water, the love of hard work, and the guts to take a chance. Gannon believed that he himself possessed all of these same traits, and was right now on his way to the Brazos to buy some property.

Three

The following week, Jake bought six hundred forty acres of land from a man named Henry Handy. The section lay north of Waco and south of the new settlement of Whitney, which had been established just this year and named for Charles Whitney, of New York, a major stockholder of the Texas Central Railroad which had recently brought rail service to Hill County. A few miles farther to the north was the town of Hillsboro.

Fifteen miles west, on the Bosque River, was the town of Clifton, which had been settled by Norwegians in 1854. A dozen miles to the south, situated on the Chisholm Trail, was Waco, notorious for the low moral character of many of its inhabitants. Thieves, gunslingers, and con men of every stripe found refuge there, and seemed to be at least tolerated by local law enforcement.

The Brazos formed the western boundary of Jake's

newly acquired section, and yesterday Handy had shown him the corners of his property. And though it sagged at the roof, a livable cabin stood on the hill a hundred yards from the river.

"That cabin'll stand for another hundred years, Jake," Handy said. "Ain't a damn thing wrong with it but that roof. Here's what me and my boys will do: for just fifteen dollars, we'll split the shingles and put a brand-new roof on it. I guess you might want to build a bigger place one of these days, but till you do, that cabin is plenty solid."

"You've got a deal, Mister Handy, the sooner the better."

"We'll be starting in the morning." Handy returned to his own home a quarter mile away.

The cabin, built of foot-thick logs and consisting of two large rooms and a small porch, was indeed sturdy. Gannon saw no reason to build a house at this time; the cabin would do nicely. Tomorrow he would go to Hillsboro and buy a team and wagon. He also needed some tools, a stove, bedding, and curtains for the windows. Then he would start to build a barn and corral for his animals. He had already chosen the spot, a hundred yards south of the cabin. At sunset, he picketed his horses on good grass and carried his bedroll into the cabin. Within the hour, he was sleeping soundly.

When he returned from Hillsboro the next afternoon, he was driving a wagon loaded with everything he needed for his homestead. The large pile of shingles lying beside the rock chimney was evidence that the Handys had been at work. Gannon unloaded the stove and fitted several joints of stovepipe into the flue. He soon had a fire built and a pot of beans boiling for his supper.

The following morning, he rode the length and breadth of his property, never once pushing his horse above a walking gait. Then he crisscrossed the square-mile area till he was totally familiar with the lay of the land. No spring, ditch, or dead tree in need of cutting escaped his attention.

Afterward, he stood beneath a large oak on his east boundary, gazing down the grassy, sloping plain toward the river, visualizing at least a hundred head of Herefords grazing there. And it was going to happen, he promised himself, nodding at his own thoughts. For many years he had dreamed of owning his own place, and now it had come to pass. No one could take it from him, for it had been bought and paid for. Lock, stock, and barrel, as the old saying went.

Jake had discussed the property with Henry Handy more than a year ago, but had been unable to raise the money to buy it. Finding a section of land anywhere in Texas that was more ideally suited for what Jake had in mind would have been extremely difficult. Ringed on three sides by trees of various types and sizes, the timber abruptly gave way to unruffled plains that sloped gently to the river, three quarters of a mile away.

The Brazos itself, aside from being a neverending source of water for any number of cattle, was beautiful to the eye. Snaking onto the property like a long train, its depths ranged from two to fifty feet, and its banks were relatively clear of all but a few cottonwoods. Immediately after passing Jake's cabin, the river made a sharp turn to the east and disappeared into the timber. Right at the bend was where the deepest water was, according to Handy.

When Jake began to ask questions about the land adjoining the river on the west bank, Handy spoke quickly. "Some bunch in England owns that property," he said. "For miles and miles. Don't look like they ever intend to do anything about it, nobody ever even comes around. Everybody around here sort of looks on it as community property. Not that anybody's ever tried to graze it. A fellow might hear from somebody pretty quick if he did that."

The barn and corral materialized quickly, thanks to Henry Handy's two teenaged sons, John and Henry Junior. The boys were good workers who knew what they were doing, and Jake paid them men's wages.

A few rows of corn, beans, tomatoes and onions grew alongside the cabin, and though the small garden had been planted late, Jake expected it to produce vegetables before the first frost. Yesterday he had shot a crow and hung the dead bird on a stake in the garden, hoping to deter others from pecking at the young vegetation.

Today was the first day of August, and the weather was hot. Jake saddled Big Red early, for he had business with a banker in Waco. The Brazos separated Waco east from west, and was spanned by a suspension bridge that, when built in 1870, was the longest and widest in America and thus became a vital avenue over which passed much of the great Western movement.

Coming into town from the east, Gannon had no more than crossed the bridge when he spotted a big piebald standing at a saloon's hitching rail. Looks like Whitey Compton's mount, he thought. Sure enough, when Jake rode forward he could read the familiar brand. Shaking his head and chuckling silently, he tied his own horse and headed for the bank.

When Gannon returned to the hitching rail, Compton was standing beside his horse. A white bandage was wrapped around his head, and much of his face was discolored.

"What happened to you, Whitey," Jake asked, extending his right hand for a shake.

"An old sonofabitch named Red Jordon hit me in the face with a buffalo gun. They say he was about to cut off my ears while I was unconscious, but somebody talked him out of it. Do you know him, Jake?"

"Nope."

"Well, you sure don't want to either. That old bastard had just as soon kill you as look at you."

"What did you do to him?"

"Nothing! Absolutely nothing. I was just talking, maybe funning around a little."

"Some people don't have your sense of humor, Whitey. Come on, I'll buy you a drink."

Jake soon learned that Compton had traveled to Houston from the Rio Grande Valley, but had been unable to find work there. When told that Gannon had bought his own place, he said, "Maybe you could use me, Jake. You got any work?"

"I doubt that I have anything you'd care to do."

"Care, hell," Compton said, finishing off his drink, "it ain't a matter of caring anymore. I'm down to three dollars; I'll do whatever you've got."

"I need a winter's supply of wood cut for the stove and fireplace. I also need a well dug and a rock curb built around it. Are you game?"

"Nothing I ain't done before; I'm your man."

"We'll be leaving as soon as I buy a few things." Jake drained the last of the beer from the mug.

They arrived at the cabin before dark. Whitey spent the first few minutes walking around, commenting about how beautiful the place was, especially the way the trees north of the cabin abruptly yielded to the lush, green grass in a straight line.

"Looks like somebody just stretched a string up through there," he said, "planting trees on one side and grass on the other." This was not the case, of course: many years before, the land west of the trees had been cleared for farming. When cultivation ceased, the grasses had quickly taken over, and any young trees that attempted to grow there had been eliminated with ax or hoe—a process that Gannon would have to continue.

Jake walked down to the river, where he extracted a four-pound catfish from a line he had baited and dropped into the water this morning. The fish, along with beans and biscuits, provided supper for them.

"Hell, Jake, you're living good out here," Whitey said, slurping the bean soup from his bowl. "You gonna put cattle on this good grass?"

"Of course. That's what I talked to the banker about this morning. He says he knows all about this place, and he agrees that it'll support a hundred head easily. Says if I need financial assistance, that's what he's there for."

"A few years back you could have rounded up all the cattle you wanted for nothing. The Big Thicket's still full of them, for that matter."

"They're more trouble to get out of there than they're worth, Whitey. Even if a man had them, he'd still have the job of driving them several hundred miles. They're wild and mean, and they'll try their best to kill you at every turn. Besides, I believe that longhorns are on their way out. I think that within the next few years, Texas ranchers will be producing nothing but purebred cattle."

"You're probably right," Compton said, lighting another cigarette, "and you're not the first man I've heard say that. Several other breeds are probably better eating, but they're not as easy to raise as longhorns. They'll eat briars and brush when there's no grass."

Jake explained that he was in no hurry to buy cattle, that he intended to spend the remainder of the summer fishing and taking things easy.

"Mister Handy's building a boat for me now," he said.

"I built one once," Whitey said, "but I never could stop it from leaking. Spent more time bailing water than row-

ing." Compton snuffed out his cigarette in an empty to-
mato can, and was busy rolling another.

"I'm gonna have to ask you to do most of your smoking
outside, Whitey," Jake said, motioning to the open door.
"This cabin ain't very big, and the smoke interferes with
my breathing habit." Compton said nothing and walked
into the yard, where he sat down on a chopping block beneath the giant cottonwood. Jake followed, dragging a
chair behind him. They sat for a long time listening to the
bullfrogs and other night sounds, and speaking very little.
Finally, Compton broke the silence.

"Did you ever shoot Fred Ryan, Jake?"

"Never saw him again after the trail drive ended."

"Well, somehow I expected you to do him in as soon as
they paid us off. I mean, it wasn't right the way he kept
going out of his way to ride you all the time."

"Ryan had lots of problems, Whitey. I think most of
them were in his head. Unless he changed his ways, somebody probably has called his hand by now."

The next morning, they set about digging the well on
the east side of the cabin, and on the tenth day, they struck
a good vein of water. Then, using a mixture of sand, clay
and water, and stones the size of a man's head, they built
a four-foot curb around the top.

Then they cut and hauled firewood till they had a stack
half the size of the cabin, which Gannon thought was
surely enough to get him through the winter. Although
central Texas winters seldom brought snow, the weather
could get downright miserable and stay that way for weeks
at a time. With the well dug and the wood neatly stacked,
Jake paid Compton a month's wages, saying he had nothing else for him to do.

"You're welcome to stay as long as you want, Whitey,
it's just that I have no more work for you."

"No, I'll be moving on. Gonna go out around Big

Spring and see if I can sign on with somebody for the winter."

"Well, try not to run into that Red Jordon again," Jake said, joking. Whitey's face had healed nicely, with only a small scar visible across his nose. He saddled the piebald and rode south, following the river toward Waco.

At noon, Jake was eating his dinner on the porch to escape the heat of the kitchen when a visitor rode into the yard. A seventy-five-year-old man named Tom Handy, father of Henry, reined his buckskin to a halt and dismounted spryly.

"Been wantin' to meet ya," he said. "I see ya got things lookin' purty good around here."

Jake stepped into the yard, where the men shook hands and introduced themselves.

"Folks jist call me Pop," the old man said. "Henry said ya wuz a strappin' feller an' he wuz right. I swear, ya look to me like a man that could shore carry his own end of the log." Pop sat on the corner of the porch and continued the one-sided conversation.

"We're settin' right where the original house stood. I put the old buildin' up in forty-eight, and she burnt down in sixty-one. That's when I built this cabin. I lived in it fer three year, while I wuz buildin' the big house on the other side of the hill. Couldn't work on the new house but jist once in a while, too busy tryin' to make a livin'.

"We settled in this area in forty-seven, me an' my two brothers did, God rest their souls. The Meskins weren't all we had to fight, neither. We fit white men and Comanches, too. I always thought it wuz the Injuns that burnt the house down. No way of knowin' fer shore, weren't nobody here when she went."

Getting to his feet, Jake said, "Want something to eat, Pop? Or some coffee?"

"Nothin' to eat, might have a dab of coffee." The old-timer was soon sipping the strong liquid, occasionally blowing air into the cup to cool it.

"Did Henry's boys put the new roof on fer ya?" he asked.

"Henry worked on it, too," Jake said. "His sons just about built the barn and corral, though."

"Henry's done a fine job with them boys," the old man said proudly. "They ain't scared of hard work an' they both know that ya don't git sump'm fer nothin'. Either one of 'em can build anything Henry can. Or me either, fer that matter." Pop filled his pipe with tobacco and, through a cloud of smoke, continued to talk about his family.

"We had a daughter that wuz four years older'n Henry. Pore little thing drownded right down there in that river. I reckin she wuz jist playin' along the bank an' fell in. Me an' my brothers drug the river fer two hours an' finally fished her little body out. I always thought that wuz what killed her mother. She shore never wuz the same after that. She din't want no more children, neither. I guess Henry wuz jist a accident."

Unable to think of anything to say, Jake attempted to refill the old man's cup.

"No, no, Mister Gannon. One cup at a time is all I can handle. Of course, if ya wuz passin' around a whiskey bottle, then that there'd be a little bit different."

"I'll try to have some next time you stop by," Jake said, chuckling.

Mounting his tall horse with the agility of a much younger man, Pop headed over the hill at a hard run. Gannon stood in the yard smiling, and shaking his head. He'd have to remember to get a bottle of whiskey next time he was in town.

Two hours later, he saddled Big Red and began to ride the boundaries of his property. No reason for a man to ever go hungry here, he decided, after riding for a while.

He had jumped two deer, a turkey, and half a dozen rabbits within the first hour. He was proud of the beautiful square-mile area, and though he knew it would never make him wealthy, he believed he could raise enough cattle to earn a good living. The banker in Waco had expressed the same opinion. Although Jake thought the small ranch would support at least a hundred head, he might buy only half that number, trusting the natural instincts of the cattle to increase the size of the herd.

Darkness found him back at home, sitting on the east bank of the Brazos under a full moon. Watching the big river rush silently by on its southeasterly journey to the Gulf of Mexico, he was thinking of how small and insignificant a man really was in the grand scheme of things. In the big picture, a man probably meant less than a single pebble. A man walked on earth for only a short time, then nature would erase every sign of his passing. A pebble, in one form or another, would be around forever.

At times such as this, Jake often thought of his twin. What kind of man would he have been had he lived? Would he be the same size as me? look like me? Would he be known as a fistfighter and gunman? Of course, those questions would never be answered, and, as he had done a hundred times before, Jake pushed them from his mind.

Henry Handy's wife, Eunice, sold milk to Gannon for the neighborly price of ten cents a gallon, and he always kept a jug in the river, attached to a small rope. The cool water flowing around the jug kept the milk fresh for three days, by which time he had usually consumed the entire gallon. Tonight, he pulled in the rope and carried the milk to the cabin. Crumbling leftover cornbread into a large bowl, he poured the milk over it and sat down to his supper.

Lying on his bed, waiting for the early evening temperature to get cool enough for sleeping, he made a decision:

he would wait till spring to buy cattle. Winter would soon be upon the land, and the lush green grass would turn brown. Winter would also kill these damned mosquitoes, he thought, slapping at his neck.

There was still another reason for his waiting until spring: he had a friend and former employer near Jacksboro who knew next to everything about cattle. Jake had made two trail drives for the man and had spent one winter on his ranch, in North Texas. Gannon would visit Cap McGill and seek his advice.

The Handys had extended an invitation to Jake to leave his wagon team in their corral any time he needed to be away for a while, where they would be fed and cared for. Tomorrow, he would deliver all of his spare horses to his neighbors. He would need no pack animal on his trip to Jacksboro, which was only a four-day ride.

Four

The settlement had first been known as Lost Creek,
later Mesquiteville, and now Jacksboro. Seat of Jack
County, the community had begun in 1855, and was
served by the Butterfield stage line. Nearby Fort
Richardson, which had been abandoned by the army only
last year, had been the most northerly of a line of federal
posts established in Texas after the Civil War to halt Indian depredations. Among the regimental commanders had
been Colonel Ranald S. Mackenzie, whose Fourth Cavalry
unit had become widely known as "Mackenzie's Raiders."
The fort now stood deserted, with tall weeds growing between its buildings.

When Jake had first come to this area, buffalo could be
seen grazing everywhere. It had been estimated that sixty
million of the wooly creatures roamed the Great Plains
from Canada to Mexico, and North Texas seemed to have

more than its share. Hide hunters had thinned the herds pitifully in recent years, and in some areas wiped them out completely.

The buffalo had been central to the existence of the Plains Indians, who used them for food, shelter and bone implements. Their dried dung, known as buffalo chips, was used by both Indians and white men as fuel for fires. This morning, Jake came upon a small herd of buffalo cows accompanied by a large bull. Standing near the wall of a shallow canyon, they had somehow escaped the hunters' rifles.

The old bull was very frail. Breeding bulls lost more than two hundred pounds during July and August, for they had little time for eating. Buffalo made grunting sounds to communicate with each other, and warned off intruders with a loud snort. The aggressive, guttural roar was most often heard during the rutting season, when mature bulls went looking for cows. The roar had a distinct purpose: to ward off all rivals for the privilege of mating.

But as Jake rode closer, the animals made no sound and stood still, as if quietly accepting their designated fate of long-distance slaughter by some mysterious source associated with humans. The scraggly herd had nothing to fear from Jake, for though he had taken many buffalo for food over the years, never had he shot one for its hide. Nor would he ever. He circled the sorry herd and rode on.

The noonday sun was at its zenith when he rode down the dusty street. The town had changed little in five years. The same two-block-long plank sidewalk still spanned the entire length of the wide street's north side, and the livery stable still stood at the west end. A few new buildings had been constructed on the south side and a few more upgraded, but with the exception of a new three-story hotel, the overall appearance of the town was the same.

Gannon saw no evidence that the buffalo hunters remained. He had been told that the hide men, along with most of the sporting crowd, had moved to Fort Griffin, a hell-raising town in newly organized Shackelford County.

Seating himself at the bar in the Palace, Jake ordered a beer.

Pushing the mug along the bar in front of him, the bartender came to a halt when he reached Jake's stool. "New in town?" he asked.

"Not exactly. Been gone a few years, though."

"Well, I guess you were here when the town was alive. It's as dead as Crockett's nuts now; all the good spenders have gone to Fort Griffin."

"They'll leave there too when they finish off the buffalo," Jake said, sipping the cold beer. "And if they go at it like they have everywhere else, they'll wipe them out pretty quick." The bartender nodded, and went about rearranging some tables and chairs in the center of the room.

Gannon was on his third beer when a man he had known for several years stepped through the door. A six-footer, Bunt Cofield had been on the McGill payroll for most of his adult life. After standing just inside the door for a few seconds to adjust his eyes to the dim lighting, he rushed to the stool where Gannon sat.

"Didn't think I'd ever run into you again, Jake," he said, holding up two fingers to the bartender. "Damn, it's good to see you."

. Gannon was on his feet, grasping Coefield's outstretched hand. "Same here, Bunt, and I've thought of you often."

Cofield was smiling broadly, shaking his head. "I thought I recognized that horse outside. Ain't that the colt that was following that thoroughbred mare you rode off on?"

"One and the same."

"What did you do with the mare?"

"She was getting on in years. I traded her for a new Winchester."

They sat at the bar for some time, drinking beer and talking of old times. They had worked together on both of the trail drives Gannon had made for McGill, and knew each other well. Slim, trim and tough as rawhide, Cofield was a thirty-year-old native Texan who just happened to be exceedingly handsome. His shoulder-length brown hair, long eyelashes, well-shaped mouth and fine features gave his face a somewhat girlish appearance. More than one man who had mistaken Bunt's pretty face for femininity had received a rude awakening. He was an excellent scrapper who would fight at the drop of a hat. He would also furnish the hat.

Though known for his moonlight rides with the ladies, Cofield seemed happy enough as a single man, and content with life on the McGill spread. Jake remembered times when he had seen goggle-eyed females literally following Bunt around in the various cattle towns they visited. Cofield always appeared not to notice, and went his merry way.

Bunt had been born in a dugout less than thirty miles from where he was now sitting. He had never known his father, who had died after a fall from a horse. His mother had remarried a year later, and Bunt had been given the surname of his stepfather. Aside from his travels with trail herds, he had spent his entire life in North Texas, and knew the vast area like no other man Jake could name.

"How's the old man?" Jake asked after a while. "It's gonna be nice seeing him again."

"If you recognize him," Bunt said. "Cap admits to two-seventy-five, but I think he weighs over three hundred pounds. He's been walking with a cane the past year or so; rheumatism, the doc says."

Curt McGill, now known locally as "Cap," had been in

the area for thirty years, and was one of its most prosperous ranchers. When Texas cast its lot with the Confederacy during the Civil War, McGill had attained the rank of captain, although, like most Texans, he had been involved in little or no actual fighting. Throughout the war, Texas functioned primarily as a supply source, and suffered far less than other southern states.

In like manner, Texas fared relatively well during the Reconstruction period. Racial and political tensions were high and problems were many, but a Republican government, imposed by the victors, ruled generally with moderation and sometimes with vision as prosperity slowly returned.

At war's end Cap McGill turned to ranching and over the years had acquired a great expanse of land. Now nearing seventy years of age, he was liked by most who knew him.

"You're gonna spend the night out at the ranch, ain't you?" Bunt asked, buying a bottle of whiskey for the road.

"I planned on staying more than one night," Gannon said, "if you don't mind."

"Mind? Cap won't let you get away nohow. Besides, after you taste our cook's vittles, you ain't gonna be wanting to leave."

They covered the ten miles to the ranch in less than two hours, arriving just before sunset. After stabling their horses, they took the steps two at a time and stood in the hall that cut the house in two. Bunt began to knock on the door, calling to McGill.

"Come on out, Cap! I've got a new man I want you to meet." Leaning forward, with much of his weight resting on a cane, the white-haired McGill soon stood in the doorway, a pair of eyeglasses perched on his nose.

"Well, I'll be damned," he said, his lower lip quivering slightly, "I thought you'd be back in Kentucky by now."

"Nope," Jake said, "don't have any reasons to go back." He crossed the hall and grasped the old man's shoulders. "A pleasure to see you again, Cap. You're looking good."

"I've got mirrors in the house, Jake. I look like hell. You know it and I know it, but I am trying to lose some of this weight so it won't take but six pallbearers. Come on into the house. I've got some of that good Kentucky whiskey."

They followed Cap through a well-stocked library and into his den, the walls of which were generously ornamented with the heads of wild animals. Two large bearskin rugs lay on the floor near the fireplace.

"This whiskey is straight from Bourbon County, Kentucky," Cap said, pouring generous amounts into three glasses. "The label says it's seven years old. More like seven months, I suppose."

"Or less," Jake said, accepting the glass.

A three-sided conversation lasted for an hour, then Cofield excused himself, saying he had chores to perform. Upon Bunt's departure, Cap began to speak softly.

"I've been thinking about you for more'n a year, Jake, even thought about sending somebody to Kentucky to look for you. I wake up hurting in a new place every morning; that is, when I manage to sleep at all. Something is slowly eating at me, and I ain't too damn long for this world.

"As you may or may not know, I have no heirs. I've been sitting in this den trying to run this ranch for the past three years, but it's actually Cofield who keeps the wheels turning. He's a good cattleman who knows what he's doing, but he damn sure didn't write the book on how to handle men.

"Bunt gets mad too easy, and he's not the clearest thinker in the world when he's that way. Even so, he's been with me half of his life; the most dependable and trustworthy hand I could ask for, and I've got to look out for him.

"The two of you always respected each other and got along well. Your presence seems to have a stabilizing effect on his heavy-handedness. What I'm gettin' at, Jake, is this: I plan to turn the whole shebang over to Bunt next week. If you'll stay around for him to lean on till next spring, I'll give you twenty head of Herefords and a good bull to take back to the Brazos with you. I'll spell that out in my will in case I'm not around."

Cap reached for the bottle and poured himself another drink, adding, "This stuff eases the pain some. I don't feel like dressing myself in the morning till after I've had a few."

Jake sat quietly, looking at the once lively and energetic McGill. The grossly overweight man's eyes held a vacant stare and his complexion was a pale yellow, as if no blood circulated beneath his skin. Indeed, he had the look of a beaten man. Only a few years ago, Cap had been no more than a social drinker. Now, if his round-the-clock consumption of whiskey eased his pain somewhat, Jake saw nothing wrong with it. And since Cap had no descendents, Gannon thought he was correct in treating Cofield as an heir.

McGill had married a young Mexican woman shortly after the Civil War. The union had produced no children, for she had quickly tired of ranching life and run off to California with a piano player. Cap had never remarried.

"I doubt that you're as close to leaving us as you seem to think, Cap," Jake said, refusing another drink by placing his hand over his glass. "You might outlive every cow you own. About Cofield, it could be that he's a little brash at times, but he knows what needs doing and he'll get it done. One way or another he'll get it done, Cap. And I guess you can count on me to stay around till spring. I

sure don't know of any way that I could earn the cattle between now and then. I appreciate the gift, sir."

"Gift, hell, you'll earn everything you get. I promise
you that."

At this moment, several horses could be heard approaching the house. "The hands are coming in," Cap said.
"I guess you'll be wanting to say hello to the ones you
know and meet the ones you don't. Mickey and Bake are
both still with us."

Jake walked into the yard and on to the corral, where a
dozen riders had dismounted. Mickey Barnes, who
weighed little more than a hundred pounds, ran toward
him with his hand out.

"Hey, big'un," he said, laughing loudly, "I see nobody
has shot you yet."

Jake took the small man's hand, remembering a time
during the summer of '74 when Mickey had saved his life
by shooting a Comanche off Gannon's back. Barnes was
an excellent shot and a good ranch hand. Well aware of the
fact that he was not as strong as the larger men, the diminutive cowboy played it smart: he let his rope and his horse
do the work.

Jake next said hello to Bake Mellon, a six-footer from
New York who had been on the ranch almost as long as
Cofield. Mellon had come west the same year he began to
shave his face, and had gained employment on the McGill
spread shortly thereafter. He was a man who went about a
given task methodically, and usually had little to say. He
was especially appreciated for his horsemanship, a natural
talent that he had honed to perfection on this very ranch.

Gannon met and shook hands with the other riders,
many of them showing visible signs of having heard his
name before. In the old days, when any tree or rock might
conceal an Indian, a man would not have even considered
riding the range unarmed. Unlike in the old days, none of

these men wore sidearms, though Jake had seen rifles on a few saddles. His own ingrained habit of buckling on a gunbelt when he put his pants on each morning had saved his life more than once, and he had no intention of changing his custom.

At supper, Jake quickly understood what Cofield had meant by his remark about good vittles. The long table was lavishly set with platters of beefsteak and ham and, in the center, a large pot of chicken and dumplings. Large bowls contained beans, mashed potatoes and fried okra. Sourdough biscuits, cornbread, and lighter bread baked in long loaves were there for the choosing, along with cakes and pies. Jake sampled most of it, and thoroughly enjoyed the meal. Back in the yard, he mentioned the quality of the food to Cofield.

"Marie's the best damn cook in the world," Bunt said. "She cooked at the hotel in Jacksboro for years, and a lot of us used to ride into town just to eat there. Cap was in the hotel restaurant the night she quit, and he hired her on the spot." Bunt went on to explain that a drunken cowboy had mistaken Marie for a whore and was in the process of showing her how things were going to be, when someone shot him in the neck. The cowboy recovered, but Marie quickly said good-bye to the hotel management. She had now been on the ranch for three years. Though overweight and middle-aged, the auburn-haired Marie was nevertheless a striking woman, and Jake could easily understand how the inebriated cowboy had become aroused.

They sat on the porch talking till late in the night, long after the hands had gone to bed. Jake told Bunt of his place on the Brazos, and the things he had done to improve it.

"I'd like to see it, Jake. Did you get any work out of Whitey Compton while he was down there?"

"Yeah, he did all right; stayed till I didn't have any more work for him."

"He's been by here a couple times in the past few years; always works a month or two, then rides on. I never could quite figure that fellow out, Jake. He's smart as a whip about some things, and crazy as a loon about others. Picked a fight with little Mickey Barnes the last time he was here."

"Really?"

"Hell, yes. Mickey whipped his ass three times in one day, and Whitey still didn't believe it."

Slapping his knee and laughing softly, Gannon said, "That's Whitey, all right."

Later, in the bunkhouse, the two men went to bed side by side in the same corner where they had slept years earlier. Gannon felt as if he had come home again, and went to sleep thinking of the good food he had eaten. Perhaps some day, if he had a wife, he could eat like that all the time.

Jake had not mentioned Cap's intention of giving the ranch to Cofield, nor would he. Discussing another man's business was not good policy. Though Jake himself had always gotten along well with Bunt, he had at times seen the man treat others with disdain. Like the time a new hand had innocently let the rope slip from his hands while attempting to draw water from the well. Both the rope and the bucket had wound up at the bottom of the well, and Cofield jumped on the young man with both barrels. Only a few well-chosen words from Jake had saved the youngster's job.

McGill had been correct about Cofield's quick temper and lack of tact, and Gannon supposed that many of the hands disliked Bunt because of it. They tolerated his methods, however, because they knew that they could not win an argument with Cofield as long as Cap was the judge.

Cap would simply send them packing if Bunt said so, and year-round ranching jobs were difficult to come by.

Shortly after breakfast, wanting to let his own horse rest for a few days, Gannon roped a big buckskin in the corral. He was soon headed north, riding alone. Barnes and Mellon stood in the yard, watching as Jake rode over the hill.

"There goes one hell of a man," Mellon said.

"I don't know a single man that I believe could stand up to him," Barnes said. "But like most big men with nothing to prove, he don't push people."

Gannon rode for hours in an area he had seen many times in the past. Though no more than a hundred fifty miles from his own place, the difference in terrain and vegetation was remarkable. Except for stunted mesquites, and a few scattered pecans where moisture accumulated, this area was treeless. His own acreage hosted tall oaks, sweet gum, pine, and an assortment of smaller trees that he could not name. And it was well that Cap laid claim to a large territory, for it might take as much as fifty acres in this area to produce one cow, while the same sized plot on his own place would probably produce ten times as many. And his own prairie grass would bring cattle through a hard winter in much better condition.

As he neared the north boundary, Jake turned east, then south, to approach the ranch house from a different direction. All morning he had been thinking of his commitment to Cap, and wondering just what all it would entail. He felt that his job, as far as Cap was concerned, was simply to ride herd on Cofield. Tomorrow, he would begin to stay close to the man, for as all men do, Bunt had changed much in the past five years.

Sunday morning, Jake was in the bunkhouse with the Abbot brothers, whose job was farming and taking care of the hogs. The younger Abbot sat at a card table, and appeared to be writing a letter.

Of no one in particular, he asked, "Does January come after September?"

Jake sat quietly for a while, then deciding that the man was serious, told him where in the sequence of months January fell. After writing a few lines, the man laid the pencil aside and walked outside. The older Abbot, who was sitting on his bunk shuffling a deck of cards, began to laugh.

"That brother o' mine shore is dumb," he said, "don't eeb'm know when January comes. I bet I could name ever' month in th' year if'n I really put my mind to it."

Making light of another man's ignorance was not Gannon's nature, but the smug look on Abbot's face as he spoke triggered an uncontrollable urge. Jake hid his smiling face behind his jacket as he left the bunkhouse.

Five

Cap McGill died the following week, two days after officially turning the ranch over to Cofield. Marie had found the rancher's body in bed when she attempted to serve his breakfast. From all appearances he had been dead for several hours, perhaps since early evening.

When Cap's will was read it failed to mention Jake's name or the agreement he had with McGill. Gannon thought that the old man had simply been too sick to put anything in writing, but had surely instructed Cofield to carry out his wishes. Two mornings after the burial, Jake was standing in the yard drinking the remainder of his morning coffee. From the doorway of the bunkhouse, Cofield could be heard barking orders to the ranch hands. Shortly, he was beside Gannon, watching the men saddle up to ride out to their various jobs.

"What are you gonna do now, Jake?" he asked. "You

gonna go back to the Brazos, or do you want a job here?"

Gannon stood quietly for some time, organizing his thoughts. "Cap didn't tell you why I'm here?" he asked, dashing his coffee grounds into the yard.

"Just said that you'd be around for a while. I assumed that you were taking a vacation." Cofield walked across the yard to hold a short conversation with one of the riders, then returned.

"Why are you here, Jake?" he asked.

Gannon explained his arrangement with McGill, carefully omitting the fact that his main job had been to keep an eye on Cofield himself.

"Well, Cap didn't write that down anywhere," Bunt said, "and he sure didn't say anything about it to me. I'm gonna be making some changes around here, too many deadbeats on the payroll. I intend to make this the most profitable ranch in Texas, and I sure can't start by giving away cattle."

"I see," Jake said, turning to carry his empty cup back to the dining room. "I'll be riding in a few minutes," he said over his shoulder.

Jake led his horse from the corral, and stood tying his bedroll behind his saddle. Cofield followed him there, continually shaking his head and chuckling.

"It's not that I'm doubting your word, Jake," he said. "It's just that I'm having a hard time imagining what the hell Cap thought you could do between now and spring that would be worth twenty cows and a bull."

Jake stepped into the stirrup and threw his leg over the saddle. "I know this might come as a shock to you," he said, "but your generous benefactor thought you might need a little looking after." Keeping his voice low, he added, "Cap hired me to keep your ass in line." Gannon kicked his horse in the ribs and was quickly off the premises.

At the saloon in Jacksboro, he had scarcely ordered a beer when Cofield slid onto the barstool beside him.

"I couldn't let you ride away mad," Bunt said. "We've been friends for too many years."

"I'm not mad, Bunt, and we're still friends. I understand your situation, and I realize that each man has to do things his way."

"Well, you just come on back to the ranch. I'll give you the cattle when the time comes."

Jake smiled. "No, no, Bunt, we can't do that. Not now. You'd be paying a man to keep you from being yourself. Besides, I've got enough money to stock my place when I'm ready."

"All right, but you can sure buy your breeders from me cheaper than you can anywhere else."

"I'll remember that, Bunt. Have another beer."

Cofield spent two hours in the Palace, then headed for the ranch. Gannon stayed in town all day, and registered at the hotel just before dark. A short while later, he was in the hotel dining room for supper.

Looking around the room, he could see only one vacant seat. A man maybe fifty years old sat at a corner table. Seeing Jake standing alone, the man crooked his finger and gestured to the empty chair, pushing it away from the table with his foot. Gannon walked forward and seated himself.

"Haven't seen you in a month of Sundays," the man said, as Jake sat down. "Been back to Lordsburg lately?"

"I've never been to Lordsburg," Jake said firmly.

The man cast his eyes downward and continued to eat his food. When Jake had ordered his meal, the man spoke again.

"Do you mean to tell me, young fellow, that you're not

the man I talked with for at least an hour out in Lordsburg a couple years ago?"

"As I said, I've never been to Lordsburg."

"Well, I'll be doggone. I'd have bet my britches that I talked with you out there."

"They say that everybody has a look-alike somewhere."

"Hell, this fellow don't just look like you, he is you. I mean, he walks like you, talks like you, even sits like you. Same height and weight, and just like you, he carries a Peacemaker hanging on his right leg. I tell you, if you ever look him in the face you'll think you're looking into a damned mirror."

Without ever introducing himself or asking Jake's name, the stranger pushed his empty plate aside and left the table. At the front door, he turned to look at Gannon once more. Then, smiling broadly and still shaking his head, he walked from the building.

Jake suddenly wanted to know more. He hurried to the door and called after the man, "Do you happen to know that fellow's name?"

"Sure do!" the man yelled, continuing to smile. "He said his name was Josh Reenow."

Jake returned to the dining room to finish eating his supper. He sat thinking of the things the man had said, all of which Jake had heard before. He had been told by many men in the past that he resembled another man they had seen or talked to. His mind went now to a time in the lower Rio Grande Valley when a Mexican had mistaken him for another man. The Mexican had even called him by that man's name—Josh Reenow. As he ate his dessert, Jake was thinking that he undoubtedly resembled this Reenow, but he soon dismissed the matter from his mind.

In his hotel room, Gannon lay on his bed thinking till late in the night. Other than the fact that he had been on hand when his friend Cap McGill died, he had accomplished little on his trip to Jacksboro. He had had no chance to discuss the business of ranching with Cap, for the man had been too sick.

Jake certainly intended to buy his cattle from Cofield in the spring, given that he had been promised a discount on the price. Then, if he still had money, he would try to buy another section of land, doubling the size of his spread. He had decided to call his place "Cottonwood," in honor of the large trees that grew in the yard. Someday, he would build a home where the cabin now stood. Pop Handy had chosen the location well: close enough to the river to be convenient, yet far enough up the hill to be safe from high water when heavy rains caused the Brazos to jump its banks. That had happened many times in the past, according to Pop, but never had the water reached the cabin.

The following day, Gannon was sitting in the saloon when Mickey Barnes walked through the door. He stopped at the bar to purchase a beer, then walked to Jake's table.

"I was hoping you were still in town," he said. "I took the day off. It's been more than a month since I've had one." He seated himself at the table and continued to talk. "I've been over at Casey's place listening to him brag about that quarter horse of his. I'd give a month's pay to see somebody beat that animal just once, and shut Casey up."

"Anybody ever beat his horse?"

"No. Casey's even brave enough to lay two-to-one odds nowadays, but nobody ever takes him up on it. He calls his horse Rocket, and that's about the way the animal runs a quarter-mile race."

Jack ordered two beers and turned the conversation to other things, soon learning that Mickey was unhappy with his job at the McGill ranch. Only this morning he had had words with Cofield when he requested the day off.

"Bunt's all right most of the time," Barnes said, "but sometimes he can be impossible to please. I've been on that ranch almost as long as he has, and I know my job. I don't appreciate being talked down to like a damned greenhorn. When you get that place of yours going to the point that you need some help, I'd like to hitch my wagon to yours."

"You've got it, Mickey," Jake said, knowing that he could not find a better man. "Be next spring, though." Gannon sat in silence for some time, as if contemplating some kind of difficult decision. Then, laughing softly, he said, "Two-to-one odds, huh?"

"Oh, Casey? Yeah, says he'll lay two to one against any man's horse for a quarter mile. You think that horse of yours can beat him?"

"I haven't the faintest idea, Mickey, but I sure like Casey's odds. I know that quarter horses can be moving at top speed after only a few jumps. Big Red never has had to run that way; he's always run for the long haul. He can move out from a standstill mighty quick, though."

Barnes poured himself another glass of beer, his smile turning into a chuckle. He was clearly enjoying the thought that Casey just might finally be about to lose a race.

"Want me to ride Big Red for you?" he asked.

"Are you saying you're a better rider than me?"

"Hell, no, but I'm saying that I believe your horse will notice that I'm a hundred pounds lighter, and I can ride as good as the next man."

Jake broke into laughter. "Just joking, Mickey, of course I want you to ride him. Just remember that quarter-mile races are won or lost at the starting line, and try not to lose too much ground on the getaway. I've never known a horse that could run beside Big Red on a straightaway, not unless it would have been Big Sir, his daddy back in Kentucky. Anyway, if you can manage to be even with the quarter horse at the halfway point, I believe you can wave Mister Rocket good-bye."

"That would be a pleasure, Jake."

Barnes was soon gone across the street to Casey's bar to set up the race. When he returned, he announced that the race would take place at ten o'clock tomorrow morning; that Casey would indeed bet two hundred dollars to Jake's one hundred.

"I made him cover my ten dollars, too," Barnes said.

A straightaway racing course a quarter mile long had been measured long ago, beginning at a starting pole erected outside of town. All races ended at the hitching rail of Casey's bar, so the town's inhabitants could view the results.

Gannon wanted to see the course, and with Barnes at his side, he walked the entire distance, looking for anything that might spook the horses. Jake decided that it mattered little which side of the course his horse ran on, because it was level, and completely free of rocks and holes.

Later in the afternoon Jake talked with Casey, confirming the race. When Barnes asked Casey if he had ever seen the animal he was about to race, the man said he did not care how the horse looked, "as long as it ain't got more'n four legs."

Mickey headed for the ranch to spread the news about the race. Cofield was enthusiastic about the contest, and allowed the hands to cut "high card" from a poker deck. Men with the lower cards would remain on the ranch, while the high-card holders would ride into town to watch the race. Barnes, being Jake's rider, was excused from the drawing.

"You mean Jake thinks his thoroughbred can beat Casey's horse in a four-hundred-forty-yard race?" Cofield asked.

"He don't know," Mickey answered, "said he was gonna find out."

"Well, if you were to run a couple miles I believe you might have a chance," Cofield said, "but I'll bet Jake never has seen just how quick Rocket can cover a quarter mile."

"He ain't," Barnes answered, beginning to fashion a cigarette, "but he's seen how quick his own horse can do it."

In this part of the country, the man was rare who would not ride a few miles to watch an outstanding horse perform. The men in the bunkhouse at the McGill ranch were no exception. Deals were made long into the night, with low-card holders using money or other compensation to exchange places with men who had drawn higher cards.

News of the upcoming event spread through town quickly. Several men sought Gannon out to inform him that he stood little chance of beating Casey's swift animal in a short race. Cap McGill himself had run the best horses he owned against Rocket, but had lost all three times.

"I don't expect to win," Jake told the doubters. "I'm just trying to create a little excitement around here." Privately, however, Gannon had not accepted the idea that he was going to lose. He fully expected Big Red to give Rocket the run of his life.

Jake spent the night at the livery, taking no chances that someone might attempt to tamper with his horse. At daybreak, he fed the animal a very small portion of grain so he would not be running on a full stomach. Afterward, he walked to the restaurant for his breakfast. He had just finished his meal when Cofield and a few of his riders showed up.

"I hear you're running a race today," Bunt said, taking a seat at the table. "Do you really think you've got a chance of winning?"

"I wouldn't be running if I didn't."

"Well, I have no doubt that your chestnut is fast, but he ain't coupled right for a short race. I think you're gonna lose, Jake, and I'd bet money on it."

"I already bet a hundred," Jake said, "can't afford to bet more than that."

Cofield left the table and walked to the street. Probably in search of a bet, Gannon thought.

At nine o'clock Jake led his horse from the stable, Mickey Barnes sitting in the saddle. Men and boys lined both sides of the street, and a few women were quietly present. Jake spoke to no one as he led the animal to Casey's hitching rail, where Rocket was already saddled and waiting. A small man held the reins as he stroked and petted the horse. Though smaller, and shorter coupled than Big Red, the muscular Rocket was a beautiful piece of horseflesh, and Jake would have known without being told that the animal could move out.

"You gonna ride him?" Jake asked the man. The rider nodded his head and did not speak, though he was looking Jake's horse over admiringly.

"Well, normally I'd be wishing you luck," Gannon said, turning to lead Big Red away, "but not today."

On a borrowed horse, Jake rode out of town beside Mickey, passing the many men on horseback who lined both sides of the racing course. Two men who would act as judges were already at the starting pole. When loud cheering broke out among the spectators, Jake knew that Rocket was also making his way down the course. No one had spoken to Gannon, and no one had cheered his horse.

Indeed, it seemed that both Jake and his horse were friend-less at this stage of the game.

The horses now stood side by side, one on each side of the starting pole. After a nod from each of the riders, one of the judges fired the starting gun. The race was on.

As expected, the quarter horse broke quickly, and after a few jumps was in the lead. Barnes hit his mount hard with the whip to get his mind on what he was doing, and as soon as the big beast found his feet he closed the gap quickly. The horses were neck and neck at the halfway point. When Barnes went to the whip again, the chestnut pinned back its ears and stretched out, moving ahead by a full length. Remembering Jake's words, Mickey raised his arm and waved good-bye, then bent over the horse's neck and whipped it toward town.

The spectators stood silently, in awe, as the big thor-oughbred galloped past Casey's hitching rail four lengths in front. Then, a trickle of cheers slowly turned into thun-derous applause, as the son of Big Sir came prancing back up the street sideways, as if knowing that he had beaten the renowned quarter horse at its own game.

Barnes dismounted at the hitching rail and petted the an-imal that had carried him to victory.

"Never been on anything like him before," he said, loud enough for everyone to hear. Then, speaking to Casey, he added, "Don't guess you'll be wanting to race this one again."

"I suppose not," Casey said, taking a roll of bills from his pocket. He paid off his bets and disappeared inside the bar. Shortly thereafter, he announced that drinks would be on the house for the next half hour, a tried-and-true method of filling a saloon to capacity in short order. The joy that Barnes had expected to experience by beating Casey was short-lived, because the saloon owner seemed quite jolly about the matter.

"I'm sure you all saw me get my tail tucked in just now!" he yelled to the crowd, laughing. "The fact is, between my racing losses and all this free whiskey you fellows have been drinking, I've had a pretty bad morning. The free-drink period is over, and I expect you to buy something." Most of the men did.

Deputy Sheriff George Hinkley, a man seldom seen inside a saloon, stopped by Jake's table for a drink. He congratulated Gannon on the race, and offered a few words of caution.

"There's at least one man in here who's unhappy about the way the race turned out, Jake. He lost two hundred dollars and refuses to pay up; says you brought a Kentucky racehorse in here and put one over on the whole town. He's already killed a couple of men in Fort Griffin this year. His name is Pete Hale, and he's sitting a few tables behind you. Be careful." With that, the deputy was gone through the front door.

Gannon walked to the bar and bought a drink, then seated himself at a table where he was facing the man. A medium-sized man with black hair, Hale wore a red flannel shirt and a brown felt hat, with the brim pulled low over his eyes. Jake watched as Hale poured himself a drink from his bottle with his left hand then lifted the glass to his lips. All the while, his right hand had remained beneath the table. Not liking the looks of the situation, Gannon was quickly on his feet, headed for the door. He had taken only a few steps when Hale's voice stopped him.

"Hey! Don't go running off there, fellow, I ain't registered my complaint yet!" Hale was on his feet, kicking a chair out of his way.

Looking Hale straight in the eye and standing very still, Gannon knew exactly what was about to happen.

"How many races you won with that horse?" Hale asked, a smirk on his face.

"Now that you ask, I believe he's won every race he's ever run," Gannon said, positioning his feet and leaning forward. "I never did run him for money before, though."

"That's a damn lie," Hale said. Then, as if not realizing that speaking those four words was enough to get him killed, he continued. "I don't appreciate being shystered out of my money by some joker trying to pass a champion racer off as an ordinary horse. You're gonna make good on my losses!"

"Send your complaint to Washington," Jake said, now in position for his fast draw, "and ask them to pass a law against a man owning a good horse."

When a few men laughed, Hale exploded into action. He was still grabbing for the gun on his hip when Gannon shot him in the nose. The heavy caliber knocked him completely loose from his weapon, somersaulting him beneath a table. He was dead.

Deputy Hinkley was on the scene quickly. After walking around the room talking with several of the eyewitnesses, he ordered the body removed from the premises. Then, never once looking at Gannon, Hinkley spoke to the bartender.

"Did you see the fight, Hank?"

"Well," the bartender began, pointing to Jake, "this gent here made one of them kind of draws that you don't actually see. But I'll swear that Hale called him, and Hale moved first."

Hinkley nodded, seeming satisfied with the bartender's testimony. As he passed Jake's table on his way to the door he winked, saying, "Good day, Mister Gannon."

Small knots of men were gathered in various parts of the saloon, each cluster engaged in its own muted conversation. Mickey Barnes was saying to Cofield, "Did you see that draw, Bunt? I didn't even know Jake had his gun in his hand till I saw the flame."

"I never saw but one man empty a holster that quick before," Cofield said. "A fellow named Sam Curtin used to travel around with a medicine show doing six-gun exhibitions. . . ."

Six

Jake was back at his own place a few days later. He was up early this morning and had picked a mess of vegetables from his garden. Shortly after he put them on the stove to boil, he was visited by Pop Handy.

"Saw the smoke comin' from your flue," the old man said. "Welcome home."

"Good to see you again, Pop. I've been gone a little longer than I expected."

The chaff from the beans Jake had shelled was still lying on the porch. Pop nodded his head in that direction, saying, "I put a hoe to your garden a few times to keep the weeds from eatin' it up."

"I could see that somebody did. I appreciate it, Pop." Jake walked inside the house and returned with a bottle of whiskey. "I brought you a present."

Pop shook his head, and did not accept the bottle. "It's

too early in the day for that. Besides, I've got to go over to Henry's and he'd give me hell about it. He says I'm too old to drink." Pop chuckled, and lowered his voice. "I'll tell you what. I'll come back about dark and we'll polish 'er off together. By the way, I picked all your scuppernongs 'cause it was pick 'em now or lose 'em. Eunice made jelly out of 'em and said she was gonna send you some."

"Good. That'll solve one of my breakfast problems."

Pop mounted and rode away, promising once again to return in the late afternoon. When he did return he was already half drunk. No telling how much whiskey the old man had hidden around the area, Gannon thought.

Pop told Jake many stories about the days when he had first homesteaded along the Brazos. The original plot had included the very spot where Jake's cabin now stood. As young men, Pop and his two brothers had fought Indians, Mexicans and white men alike to maintain their holdings. They had later bought several additional sections of land, which Pop had inherited when his brothers expired. Ten years ago he had deeded half the land to his son, Henry. Pop still owned the section adjoining Cottonwood on the north.

Jake intended to discuss buying the property, but not while Pop was drinking.

They talked till midnight, at which time Jake's bottle ran dry. Getting to his feet unsteadily, Pop announced that he was going home. After several unsuccessful attempts to mount his horse, and refusing any help from Jake, the old man wisely led the animal to the cabin and stepped directly from the porch into the saddle. He rode away at a slow walk, and for several minutes Jake could hear him humming an old tune.

The storm hit two hours before daybreak. Gannon was sound asleep, but gradually awakened as the distant thun-

der came closer. Sitting on the side of his bed and looking
through the window, he could see the lightning bolts lighting up the area as bright as day. When a sharp crack
sounded, followed by a clap of thunder so loud it shook
the cabin, Jake knew that the lightning had struck something close.

He opened the door and stood looking toward the barn
for a time, but could see nothing burning. After a while
the wind blew the storm down the river, and all was quiet.
Jake returned to his bed and was soon asleep.

As was his lifelong habit, he was up before sunup and
headed for the barn to feed his animals before preparing
his own breakfast. Before he reached the barn he could see
his prized saddle horse lying in the mud just inside the
corral gate. He knew instantly that Big Red was dead, for
the animal would never lie down this early in the day. He
also knew that the loud crack of lightning that had shaken
his cabin was the one that struck the horse down. Inside
the gate, he shooed the other horses away; they had been
standing in a semicircle, staring down at the stricken thoroughbred. Much of the hair had been singed from the
horse's hide and its hooves were the color of charcoal, as
if they had caught fire and burned. Big Red's eyes had
popped from their sockets.

Jake had not shed a tear since he was a child. Nor
would he now, though he could feel a huge lump in his
throat. He fed the other horses, then walked to the cabin,
where he sat down on the doorstep. There would be no
breakfast for him this morning; he felt as if he might be
sick.

He sat staring at the river as the reality of his loss tore
at his very soul. He had watched Big Red come into the
world, and had even helped with his birthing. He had
picked the skinny colt up and talked to him when he was
only a few minutes old. The colt had grown into the fast-

est and most sure-footed animal Jake had ever seen. He had also been Jake's friend, and had been treated accordingly. Gannon had sometimes talked to Big Red as if he were human, and at times it seemed that Big Red understood.

Only a week ago, the animal had been the talk of Jacksboro. Jake had refused Casey's seven-hundred-dollar offer to buy him, enough money to stock his place with cattle. He had known that he could never live with himself if he sold the horse that had saved his life. Sell Big Red for the sole purpose of winning races for a boasting saloon owner? No, thank you, Jake had said.

Gannon walked into the yard and emptied his Peacemaker skyward to frighten off the buzzards that were already circling overhead, well out of handgun range.

He hitched his team to the wagon and dragged the carcass to a place far below the cabin, where the water table was known to run very deep. There he set about digging the hole that would be Big Red's final resting place. It took him most of the day to dig the excavation, but only a few minutes to fill it in. When he had patted the earth into a mound, he returned to the barn and made a cross out of two large boards.

At the cabin, he heated the metal rod that he used for poking his fire to a bright red glow, then burned an epitaph into the wood: BIG RED—1879. Once he had erected the marker at the grave, he saddled the horse that he normally used for packing and headed for Waco. He would eat supper in town—if he could.

In Waco, he had no problem wolfing down a large plate of Mexican food: enchiladas, burritos, tacos, and a bowl of Mexican beans topped with strong cheese and hot sauce on the side. The Texas saloon served the best in town, prepared by Mexican cooks.

Jake had put out the word at the livery stable that he

was in the market for a saddle horse, and had been in the saloon less than an hour when a man approached his table.

"My name's Wink Farmer," he said. "You the fellow that's looking for a horse?"

"I mentioned it to the liveryman, but I sure don't buy horses at night."

Farmer continued to stand, not having been invited to sit. He was a tall, skinny man, almost bald, with hands that looked like hams hanging from his shirt sleeves.

"Mind if I sit?"

"Not at all," Jake said, pushing out a chair with his foot and signaling the bartender to bring another glass.

Farmer seated himself and readily accepted a drink when the glass arrived. Gulping it down and helping himself to another, he said, "Don't have no horse for sale myself, but my brother-in-law does. He's got a three-year-old gray that wouldn't have no trouble a-tall carrying a big fellow like you around." Gannon refilled Farmer's glass and the man continued. "The horse ain't plumb broke and he's dumped my nephew a few times, but he's big and he's purty, and he can damn shore run. If you look him over, I believe you'll make an offer on him."

"Is the horse in town?"

"No, he's out at Bud's place, halfway between here and Hillsboro. It's the Wilson farm, just after you cross Wolf Creek. Just stick with the wagon road and you can't miss it." Farmer was on his feet now, pouring another drink from Jake's bottle. "No use making too big an offer. Bud's on hard times."

"I wouldn't take advantage of a man just because he's down on his luck, Mister Farmer," Gannon said, with slight irritation. "I've been broke most of my life. I appreciate the information, and I will look at the horse."

Farmer gulped the drink, set his glass on the table, and left the room.

It was close to midnight when Jake returned to his cabin. He fed his horses by lantern light. After a good night's sleep he was back in the saddle at sunup, headed for Wolf Creek.

A pair of black-and-tan hounds announced his arrival at the Wilson farm, and a one-armed man wearing faded overalls walked from the dilapidated shack and quieted the dogs. About fifty years old, the sandy-haired farmer was tall and thin. With a smile that revealed half a row of yellow teeth, he said, "Howdy, my name's Wilson. Can I help you?"

"My name's Gannon, and I met a man in Waco who says you have a horse for sale."

"Got a gray geldin' that I could be persuaded to part with," Wilson said, flashing his teeth again. "Traded a travelin' family a milch cow fer 'im three years ago when his mammy wuz tryin' to wean 'im. That mare weren't havin' no luck with that weanin', no sir. The colt wuz always right under her feet, or tryin' to git in the traces with her. The people wuz mighty upset with 'im, 'cause that mare had a wagon to pull, an'—"

"Could I see the horse?" Jake interrupted.

The farmer motioned toward the barn, and led the way. Two large mules scampered away from the corral gate as the men entered.

"They're scairt I'm gonna put 'em to work," Wilson said, opening a stable door with a bridle in his hand. A few moments later he led a beautiful animal into the corral.

Jake checked the horse's teeth and feet, then slowly walked around it. A fine animal, he quickly decided. It stood close to seventeen hands at the shoulder. Its forelegs, mane and tail were black. The remainder of its body was a speckled gray, with few spots larger than a dime. The near-perfect conformation of its head and ears suggested

Arabian ancestry, and the big, bright eyes held a look of intelligence. Gannon liked what he saw.

"Have you got a saddle handy?" he asked.

A short while later he was astride the big gelding. The animal made a few feeble attempts to unseat Jake, but its heart was not in it. Gannon headed him down the road at a canter. Half an hour later he brought the gray back up the hill at top speed. The beast slid to a halt at the gate and snorted once, then breathed normally. Big, strong lungs! Jake was impressed.

Still in the saddle, he asked, "How much do you want for him?"

Wilson produced a plug of chewing tobacco and bit off a large chunk. "What'll you give?"

"Put a price on your horse, Mister Wilson," Jake said, his voice businesslike. "I'm not gonna do it for you."

Wallowing the tobacco around in his mouth as if in deep thought, Wilson spat on a rock, then said, "Is ninety dollars too much?"

"Nope. Write me a bill of sale and I'll switch my saddle to the gray."

Ten minutes later Gannon rode the gray down the hill and out of sight, well pleased with the transaction. Last night, in Waco, Wink Farmer had led Jake to believe that the horse needed breaking. The only thing the gray needed was lots of riding. The animal was smooth gaited and fast, and no doubt had plenty of bottom for the long haul.

By the first week of November, the weather had turned cold along the Brazos. Usually bundled in heavy clothing, Jake spent many of the daytime hours fishing in the fast-moving river, the source of much of his food. Catfish and bream, and, now that the water temperature had cooled somewhat, an occasional bass were there for the taking.

This morning, he had been sitting on the bank for more

than an hour feeding worms to an elusive school of bream. As was frequently the case, when inactivity allowed his mind to wander, he began to reminisce about his childhood back in Franklin, Tennessee. He remembered November 30, 1864, with clarity. He and his mother were huddled in the storm cellar, covered with quilts, while the Battle of Franklin raged outside.

Though Jake had not personally witnessed any of the shooting, he had heard much of it. He recalled the feeling of his mother's quivering arms around him, no doubt more concerned for her young son's safety than her own. Both mother and son had heard frightening stories of the things Northern soldiers did to helpless civilians when they conquered a Southern town.

He remembered the Yankees riding into his yard and requesting corn for their horses. They had not spoken unkindly to him. Nor had they insulted his mother. At Carnton, a home on the edge of Franklin, the bodies of five Confederate generals were laid out on the back porch. Many operations had taken place, and young Jake had later seen the blood stains on the floor.

Harrison House had been used as a Confederate command post. At another home, family members had blindfolded their horses and led them to the third-floor ballroom to hide them from the invading soldiers.

Jake had listened to many conversations concerning the battle. The consensus was that General Hood's forces had simply been outsmarted by the Yankees, who had slipped past them during the previous night. Enraged and embarrassed, Hood had ordered an assault on the massive Union army, only to be badly beaten.

Jake's memories of his father were indelible. A farmer and part-time blacksmith, Mark Gannon had provided well for his small family. Jake supposed that the Battle of Nashville had more or less been a repeat of the conflict at

Franklin, for the Union forces had won overwhelmingly. His only information had been that his father died during the first few minutes of fighting.

Now, tired of rebaiting an unproductive fishhook, Jake returned to the cabin. He was soon sitting on the porch, cleaning and oiling his weapons: revolver, rifle and shotgun. He knew as well as any man that the action of a gun must be clean and well oiled at all times. Otherwise, it was likely to fail when it was needed most.

He had tried most of the short guns on the market, but had settled on the six-shot revolver that he now held in his hand. Like all good gunmen, he knew that making your own first shot do the job was more important than speed. However, it was a rare man who did not work over or tinker with his gun in an effort to give himself an edge in getting off a shot quickly. And almost invariably that gun would be the Colt single-action revolver, sometimes known as the "Frontier Model" or "Peacemaker." The design of the gun gave it perfect balance, easy to draw and handle. Its large hammer made for easy cocking, and the grip would fit almost any hand.

Always seeking an advantage, most gunmen altered their weapons in one way or another: filing off part of the trigger guard or tying it back, or replacing the trigger with a Bisley Colt hammer for better thumb traction. Some weakened the hammer spring, and removed the front sight to keep it from snagging in the holster.

Jake had filed the front sight from his own Peacemaker; otherwise, the gun remained as the Colt company had manufactured it. As for tying the trigger back and fanning the hammer, Gannon considered it a foolish thing to do, for a man could not hope to be on target even half of the time. He had never known a serious gunman who used the fanning method. It was showy, but the risk was simply too great when a man's life was on the line.

Though the Peacemaker was deadly and possessed tremendous knockdown power, it was not the most feared weapon in the West. That distinction was held by the ten-gauge shotgun. Usually these double-barreled weapons were sawed off to a length of eighteen or twenty inches and loaded with buckshot. They were devastating at close range, by far the meanest handheld weapon known to man.

Even the most skillful gunfighter would think long and hard before risking a showdown against a sawed-off ten-gauge. And if a quick-draw gunman did get lead into a shotgun man first, the odds were high that the shotgun man would live to pull the trigger, spraying his opponent with at least one barrel of buckshot. Even the bravest of the gunslingers usually backed down from such a weapon and waited for another day.

Jake gave his Peacemaker a final swipe, and reached for his ten-gauge.

Seven

Gannon was busy rearranging some things in his cabin when he heard someone shouting from the yard. Opening the door, he was happy to see Mickey Barnes sitting astride a big roan. Crossing the porch and jumping into the yard, Jake held out his right hand.

"It's good to see you, Mickey," he said. "Get down and rest yourself."

Barnes dismounted and tied his animal. "Had another run-in with Cofield," he said, "and I told him what he could do with his ranch. Now that he's both foreman and owner, he's become impossible to get along with. Five of the hands have already quit, and several more are talking about it." He kicked a small stone toward the river and sat down on the porch.

Gannon had listened quietly, nodding sympathetically. "Knowing Bunt's nature, Cap thought it would probably come to that," he said, "and I had my own doubts that he could handle it. Bunt's been poor all his life, with very little say-so about what went on around him. I suppose the sudden jump to a position of power was too much for him."

"It damn sure was. He's even started riding Bake Mellon, and you know yourself that everything Bake does is right. I've been on that ranch over twelve years, Jake, and Cofield only gave me thirty dollars when I left." Gannon listened, but did not comment further on the matter.

Barnes rolled and lit a cigarette, then, through a billow of smoke, said, "I wasn't sure this was your cabin. I didn't see Big Red anywhere."

"Big Red is gone, Mickey." Jake told him the details of the animal's demise, and of his purchase of the gray as a replacement.

"I saw the gray in the corral. Is he as fast as Big Red was?"

"Nope. He's got the same kind of stamina, though." They talked till late afternoon, at which time Jake prepared a supper of fish and potatoes."

"Nothing like what you're used to," he said, pushing a plate across the table to Barnes, "but it's what I have."

"I'm not picky about food, Jake. I'll eat whatever the cook dishes out."

After eating, they continued to sit at the table, and Jake produced a bottle that he had been saving for a special occasion. As they sipped the whiskey, Barnes continued to talk.

"I was hoping to stay here with you through the winter, 'cause there ain't no use in me looking for work at this time of year. Of course, you wouldn't have to pay me anything. I've got enough money to take care of myself till spring. Then, if you're gonna be getting some cattle, I suppose you'll be needing me." Pointing to his rifle leaning against the wall just inside the doorway, Barnes added, "I can keep meat on the table with that." The rifle, a Spencer, was known throughout the West as a powerhouse. Firing three-hundred-sixty grain fifty-six caliber ammunition, the weapon had enough shooting power to bring down any animal on earth.

"You can stay here as long as you want," Jake said. "I enjoy your company, and I'm sure I'll have plenty of work for you next spring. I've got some two-by-fours down at the barn. Tomorrow we'll build a bunk for you along that back wall."

Barnes was already preparing breakfast when Jake awoke the following morning. Gannon headed for the barn to feed the horses. He poured an extra portion of oats for Mickey's roan, for the animal had been on the trail for several days. Soon he was seated at the table enjoying his morning meal.

"Better biscuits than I ever baked in my life, Mickey. I guess you should be the cook from now on."

"That's fine with me. I'm sure I can find a lot of things that need doing. You just come and go like you've always done; I'll take care of things here." They finished breakfast in silence, then sat on the porch talking.

"You know, Jake," Barnes said after a while, "I read somewhere that there are a million and a half people in the state of Texas. Where in hell are they? Sometimes I ride for two or three days without seeing anything bigger than a damn ground squirrel."

"I suppose somebody just made an estimate," Jake said, "because an accurate census would be next to impossible. A few towns like Houston, Dallas, San Antonio and El Paso are teeming with people. Even Fort Worth, Austin and Calvert are spreading out all over, and East Texas is filling up fast with farmers and timbermen. But this is big country, Mickey. Who in the hell is gonna ride fifty miles to count five people? In my opinion, nobody has the faintest idea how many people are in Texas."

A week later, Mickey Barnes was in the Hill County jail. His problem began when he volunteered to drive Jake's team and wagon into Hillsboro for much-needed supplies. After making his purchases, he tied the team to the hitching rail of a run-down saloon, intent upon having a few beers. He had scarcely lifted the beer to his lips when a large, ugly redhead tapped him on the shoulder.

"You're sittin' on my stool, shorty," the man said through clenched teeth. "I've been sittin' there all day, jist walked next door to take care of some business." Barnes, never one to invite trouble, picked up his beer and moved to the next stool.

"That one's mine, too," the man said quickly. "Been savin' it fer a friend."

Situations of this sort were not new to Barnes. All of his life it had been that way. There was one in every crowd, always some overgrown bastard who had to satisfy his ego and warped sense of humor by running roughshod over the smaller man. Determined to avoid trouble if possible, Mickey moved his beer farther down the bar, this time skipping several stools. Chuckling, as if proud of his actions, the man seated himself at the bar. As he sipped his drink he continued to stare at Barnes, laughing and shaking his head. Deciding that he should be somewhere else, Mickey slid from the stool and headed for the door.

"Hey!" the redhead shouted. "That Peacemaker shore looks big hangin' on a squirt like you. Ain't you afraid you might drop it on your toe?"

Barnes had had enough. "Never dropped it on my toe," he said, facing the man squarely, "but I've dropped a few loudmouthed bastards like you with the business end of it."

The big man was off the stool quickly. "Them's fightin' words, feller," he said, reaching for the gun on his hip.

They were fighting words indeed. Just as the redhead brought his gun into firing position, Barnes shot out his right eye.

Half an hour later, despite the bartender's insistence that Mickey had been goaded into the gunfight, Barnes was arrested and charged with murder.

Jake had been unconcerned when Mickey failed to return to Cottonwood before dark. After all, Barnes liked a drink as much as the next man; might even spend the night in town if a woman winked at him. Gannon ate his supper early, then went to bed.

When Barnes had not returned by ten o'clock the next morning, Gannon saddled the gray and headed for Hillsboro. He was now convinced that Mickey had been delayed by something beyond his control. Although the narrow trail was the shortest route to Hillsboro, Jake stayed with the wagon road, thinking that maybe the wagon had broken down.

It was past noon when he rode into town. Before he reached the stable, he saw his wagon parked out front. As he rode closer he could see his horses in the corral. A gray-haired hostler walked forward as Jake dismounted.

"That wagon and those horses belong to me," Gannon said, pointing. "Know where the man is who drove them here?"

"Sure do, he's in jail. The marshal says he killed a man yesterday. I picked up the horses and wagon 'cause it's what the marshal told me to do."

Town Marshal Bo Shula was sitting behind a large desk when Jake entered the office, but was quickly on his feet. Fat, narrow shouldered and of medium height, the balding lawman wore a Peacemaker on his right hip. A full cartridge belt circled his waist, and Gannon immediately wondered how he managed to keep it there. His midsection was as round as a billiard ball. Shula crossed the room to shake hands.

"Hello, there," he said. "I already know who you are. I've seen you around town a few times. It's not every day that I get a visitor with a reputation like you've got."

"Forget the reputation, Marshal, I'm here to talk about Mickey Barnes."

Shula returned to his desk and seated himself behind it. He put a match to a half-smoked cigarette that had been lying in the ashtray, then spoke through a cloud of smoke. "Didn't you buy up some of that Handy land over on the river?"

"Yes. What does that have to do with Barnes?"

"Well, the judge set his bond at two hundred dollars this morning. You being a property owner and all, I guess you could sign it and take him with you, if you're of a mind to."

"That's fine," Jake said, walking to the desk. "Show me where to sign, and trot him out here." Shula produced the document, and Jake attached his signature.

"I sure hope you don't blame me for this," the marshal said. "All I know is that when I walked into that saloon I found a dead man and a smoking gun. Barnes don't deny the shooting."

After retrieving the team and wagon from the livery, Gannon and Barnes stopped at the saloon. Jake wanted to talk with the bartender.

"Hell, yes, he pushed this man into a gunfight!" the bartender barked when asked if he saw the shooting. "The sonofabitch answered to the name of Sid Goff. He's run over half the men in this town at one time or another, always throwing his weight around after a few drinks. If this man hadn't shot him, he'd be dead hisself right now."

Jake ordered a drink for himself and a double for

Barnes, who had spoken very few words since being set free. Perhaps he felt that the less he said, the better off he would be. The bartender, who introduced himself as Cliff Blake, poured the whiskey.

Pushing money across the bar, Jake asked another question. "Are there any good lawyers in this town, Cliff?"

"None that ain't gonna kiss the prosecutor's ass and sell you out. If you want a lawyer that'll wake them bastards up over at the courthouse, get Shannon Page. His office is above the bank, in Waco."

"He's good, huh?"

"He's better'n that. Half the prosecutors drop their charges when they learn that they've got to face Page in a courtroom. Losing cases and being embarrassed ain't good for their records in case they decide to run for something else. I tell you, that Page beats all. I watched him operate right here in Hillsboro two years ago; heard him spoonfeed a jury for close to three hours, ranting and raving back and forth. Every man up there was hypnotized, and they rendered a verdict in his favor without ever leaving the jury box. Most of them were still in a trance when they left the courtroom. I tell you, Shannon Page belongs on the stage somewhere."

Jake emptied his whiskey glass and waved away the bartender's attempt to refill it. "Sounds like Page is the man we need to talk to," he said to Barnes.

Just as the bartender had said, Mister Shannon Page maintained an office in the bank building in Waco. When Jake knocked at the office door he was greeted by Page himself, a handsome blond-haired man who stood six-foot-seven.

"Come in, fellows," he said, shaking hands with his visitors, who introduced themselves. Page invited both men to take seats in heavy-cushioned chairs. "What can I do for you?"

Gannon pointed to Barnes, who was clearly uncomfortable in these fancy surroundings and appeared to be suffering from lockjaw. "My friend, here, has a problem," he said, touching Barnes on the shoulder. "Tell him the story, Mickey."

Page listened attentively as Barnes relived his visit to Hillsboro and the harassment that led to the shooting.

"Were there any witnesses?" Page asked.

"The bartender," Barnes said. "Two other men were in there, but they were sitting at a card table in the back of the room. I believe they were out of earshot."

Page got to his feet and walked around the room, pausing to put a chunk of wood in the heater. When he returned to his desk, he said, "If the bartender will testify in your favor, it sounds like they have a weak case, Mister Barnes. I'll go over to Hillsboro the first of the week and see if I can help you."

"I'll appreciate that, Mister Page," Barnes said. "Of course, I'm concerned about what this is gonna cost."

"Cost?" The attorney chuckled. "I think you should be more concerned about what it will cost if you don't get help. That bunch in Hill County will ship you right off to the state pen in Huntsville. I won't know what it will cost till I get over there and see what I have to do. Just give me fifty dollars now, and that will get me started."

Barnes did not have that kind of money.

"I'll have to go downstairs to the bank for the fifty," Gannon said.

Several times during the afternoon and night Barnes expressed his gratitude for being bailed out of jail, and for Jake's retainment of Attorney Page. Mickey promised to pay back any money Gannon spent as quickly as possible, if he did not go to prison.

The following morning Gannon saddled the gray early. He intended to talk to Pop Handy about another section of land. The weather was very cold. The old man was busy chopping wood when Gannon rode into his yard. Pop quickly laid the ax aside and invited his visitor into the house.

"What brings you out this early in the mornin'?" Pop asked, handing the younger man a hot cup of coffee.

Jake enthusiastically outlined his idea of stocking his place with purebred cattle in the spring. He needed more land, he said, for he had decided to start with a hundred head of Herefords. "I'm hoping we can make some sort of deal on that section joining Cottonwood on the north."

"I don't want to get shed of that land, Jake. Anyway, unless you've got lots of money, you'd be better off takin' it on a long-term lease, somethin' like thirty years."

"Don't know if I'll have enough money, Pop."

"Hell, you'll have a calf crop; give me ten percent. I won't be around no thirty years and Henry probably won't, but the grandsons will. They'll honor any agreement I make with you."

Jake thought the proposition over for only a few seconds. The price seemed fair, and Pop's section had the best grass of any place on the river. He grasped the old-timer's hand, saying, "You've got a deal, Pop. I'll get the papers drawn up in a few days."

Despite the cold, Gannon was in no hurry to get back to the cabin. He spent the morning riding about the property he had just bargained for, as comfortable as could be expected. Never one to concern himself with what was popular, Jake leaned more to the practical, and had a reason for buying every item of attire that he owned.

His hat was a brown, wide-brimmed Stetson. His topcoat was the same color, loose fitting and fleece lined. His vest was a version of the Mexican short jacket, that left his arms free and provided pockets in which to carry things, unheard-of in a shirt. He wore choke-barreled canvas pants made by Levi Strauss in San Francisco.

His boots were loose and comfortable, with a low walking heel. In his own opinion, the tight, ornamented boots with underslung heels that all but crippled a man on the ground had no excuse except vanity. Though the tightness made the foot look trim, and the heel made the man a little taller, cutting the heel under did nothing except interfere with walking. The old story of the high heel preventing the foot from slipping through the stirrup would not wash with Gannon. Those heels started when cowhands still rode with the ball of the foot in the stirrup.

Texas spurs, too, were chiefly ornamental; their rowels, though large, were blunt, and a horse seldom felt them. Jake wore no spurs on his boots, yet his horses had always responded well to a gentle kick.

Gannon and Barnes spent the next several days building fences. They used small poles when they were handy, and at other times split logs into rails. By week's end they had built pens for separating cattle and begun fencing the upper meadow for growing hay. Today was Friday, and Barnes had been unusually quiet all morning.

"I think we should ride into Waco and see what Page has found out," Jake said, as they pushed the last rail into place.

"I'd sure like to know," Mickey said, smiling for the first time today.

When the men climbed the stairs at the bank building, Page was in the process of closing his office for the day. Seeing them, he unlocked the door and motioned them inside.

"There isn't going to be a trial," he said, seating himself behind his desk.

"You . . . you mean I'm free?" Barnes blurted.

"As a bird." Page shuffled some papers around on his desk. "The prosecutor decided to drop the charges."

"He dropped the charges?" Mickey shook his head from side to side. "How in the world did you accomplish that?"

The attorney just smiled broadly.

"That's mighty good news, Mister Page," Jake said, speaking for the first time. "I suppose you'll be expecting some more money."

"Can you stand another hundred?"

"Barely." Jake handed over the money, then asked the lawyer to draw up a thirty-year lease on Pop Handy's property.

"I'll take care of it tomorrow," Page said. "You can pick it up anytime after then."

During the moonlight ride to Cottonwood, Barnes promised once again to reimburse Gannon for the money paid to Page. "Best I can figure, it comes to about six months' work," Mickey said. "Just furnish my keep and buy my smoking tobacco."

Eight

In the early days of the open range of Texas, an un-branded yearling calf belonged to any man who could rope and brand it. Soon, to protect the four-footed property, thousands of brands—initials, numerals and emblems—were registered. A man named Samuel Maverick, who refused to brand his calves, lost a lot of cattle. He also gave his name to the language, as a synonym for a nonconformist. Though Gannon owned no cattle, he had already registered his brand, JGC, and had several branding irons in the barn.

It was now the middle of February, and time for Jake to have another talk with Bunt Cofield. Taking a three-day supply of grub, he saddled the gray and headed for Jacksboro. He carried extra blankets and a tarp behind his saddle.

Sometimes riding through rain, sleet and, as he progressed farther north, a smattering of snow, he arrived at the McGill ranch on the fourth day. He nodded to several men as he passed the bunkhouse, but saw no one he recognized until Cofield himself walked into the yard.

"Hey, Jake!" Bunt yelled, hurrying across the yard. "It was only last night that a few of us were talking about you. Come on into the house, where it's warm."

Cofield ordered Marie to prepare a large breakfast for his guest, which was pleasing to Jake. He had not eaten since yesterday afternoon. Cofield had taken over Cap's den, and Jake ate his meal sitting beneath the many animal heads that adorned the walls. Bunt walked around the room while Gannon finished off the food.

"Been a lot of changes around here, Jake," he said. "Mickey Barnes even left a few months ago."

"I know," Jake said.

"Yeah? Did he come by your place?"

"He's down there now, been there ever since he left here." Jake saw no reason to mention the fact that Mickey had been involved in a gunfight.

"Well, I don't know what he told you," Cofield said with a frown, "but I'll bet he didn't tell you the whole story."

"I didn't ask for the whole story, Bunt. He just said that the two of you didn't see eye-to-eye anymore. Things like that happen all the time between people. I didn't care to hear the details then, and I don't now."

"All right," Cofield said, shrugging his shoulders, "all right."

As was frequently the case when two men engaged in a long conversation, the talk soon turned to horses. Cofield had noticed that Jake was riding a different animal, and mentioned the fact. Gannon related the story of his horse's death, and the lightning bolt that had hastened it.

Bunt wanted to show Jake two horses that he had recently acquired, and invited him to the corral. Gannon leaned against the gate, watching as Cofield paraded the big Appaloosas around the enclosure. Beautiful animals indeed.

"Won 'em in a poker game two weeks ago," Bunt said.

"Then I'd say that was your lucky day," Jake said, moving in for a closer inspection.

"Yep. The fellow was just too proud of his three aces. I hit him with a full house: nines over fours."

Back in the den, Jake refused the drink he was offered and turned the conversation to cattle, saying that he had acquired another section of land and was now interested in a hundred head.

"Does the new section border the river?"

"Uh-huh."

"Then you can handle a hundred head easily with grass to spare, and you've got the whole Brazos River to water out of. It's like I told you last year, I'll sell to you cheaper than anybody else will. I don't know exactly what breeders are going for right now. Whatever the price is, I'll give you a twenty-percent discount. I've got to assume that all of my cows are pregnant, they've been running free with the bulls. It'll take more men than just you and Barnes to get 'em off their home range, though. You'll need two point men, two press men and two men riding drag. I'll lend you the four extra riders."

"That's nice of you, Bunt, and I really appreciate the break on the price. Can we find out in Jacksboro what the going rate for breeders is?"

"That we can do, and if I were you I'd get the cows on down there before they get too heavy with calves."

Finding that a hundred head of pregnant Hereford cows and four bulls were worth two thousand dollars, less the twenty percent discount, Jake now had a figure to take to his banker in Waco. After spending the night at the ranch, he headed home, carrying an ample supply of food for himself and a small sack of grain for the gray.

He moved his herd down to Cottonwood range in the middle of March. Prodded by six able cowhands, the cattle moved along slowly, taking more than two weeks to complete the drive. Bake Mellon had been among the riders provided by Cofield; Gannon had specifically asked that the lanky New Yorker be included.

After fording the river in a tight bunch, the cattle were herded onto the upper meadow. The next day, they were driven singly into a narrow chute at the corner of the fence. While standing, they were branded and ushered out onto the open range. Gannon himself saw to the fire and heated the irons, while Barnes handled the small amount of roping that was necessary. Every man present was an old hand at branding, and the operation went smoothly.

Cofield's riders stayed on Cottonwood for several days, helping to acquaint the cattle with the new surroundings. Although the river provided an artificial barrier on the west, only harassment from mounted men would prevent the animals from straying too far in other directions. Being creatures of habit, once the cattle had settled down and become familiar with their own range they would not stray far enough to become a problem.

The riders—Mellon, Chambliss, Williams and Travis— had slept in Jake's barn since their arrival at Cottonwood. They had now finished their work, and would be leaving tomorrow.

"Sorry about you men having to sleep in the barn," Jake said to Mellon, "but as you can see, my cabin's pretty small."

"Hell, the barn's a big relief from the bunkhouse I've been sleeping in, smelling Rufe Jackson's stinking feet."

"Well, at any rate," Jake said, smiling, "this being your

last night, I think we should ride into Waco and drink to a job well done. The fun's on me."

"Cofield ordered us not to take any money from you."

"I'm not offering you money, Bake, just a good time. Invite the others to saddle up and I'll buy them all a plate of the best Mexican food in Texas."

Inside the Texas Saloon, the men pulled two tables together and seated themselves. Several saloon girls—blondes, brunettes and redheads—stood around staring seductively as the men sat down. After informing the bartender that he would pay the tab for the entire evening of merrymaking by his men, Gannon ordered food and drink for all.

After eating, the men quickly became involved in the frolicky activities, dancing with the girls to the music of a trio consisting of piano, fiddle and guitar.

Joe Chambliss, the handsome dark-haired son of an East Texas lumberman, seemed to be enjoying the evening more than anyone else. He had danced several times with the same red-haired woman, and was now allowing her to lead him up the back stairway. He was halfway to the top when a loud voice stopped him.

"Hey, you! Where do you think you're going?"

Chambliss turned to face a tall, dark man of maybe thirty, standing at the bottom of the stairway. The girl ran quickly to the top of the stairs and disappeared down the hallway. Chambliss stood very still, and did not answer the man's question.

Mellon poked Gannon in the ribs, saying, "That fellow may be biting off more than he can chew. Joe's hell with that six-gun."

Halfway up the stairway, Chambliss stood frozen, watching the man as a hawk watches a rabbit.

"They's my own private stuff you're tryin' to hump, fellow," the man yelled. "I'd say that's a shootin' offense."

Chambliss silently widened his stance. Looking the man squarely in the eye, he answered with a curt nod. In a flurry of action, both men drew and one shot rang out. The man standing on the floor dropped as if he had been hit with a sledge, shot through the head. Chambliss holstered the gun and walked around the body to join his fellow cowhands at the table.

In a short while, the town marshal appeared. Ignoring the men at the table, he walked to the corner of the bar, where he held a muted conversation with the bartender. Then, ordering some men to remove the body from the premises, he approached Jake's table.

"Hope you men don't let this little fracas spoil your evening," he said, casting his shifty eyes around the room. "That fellow never spent no money in here. Can't think of a soul that's gonna miss him. The bartender says you're all having a good time, so drink up and enjoy yourselves." Then he was gone through the front door.

"Beats all in the hell I've ever heard," Mellon said, after the lawman had disappeared. "He didn't even ask who did the shooting."

"He didn't give a damn," Jake said. The marshal's actions only confirmed the rumor that Gannon had heard from more than one source: his fortunes were directly related to the prosperity of the Texas Saloon. John Bisco had been Waco's marshal for more than three years, and it was widely believed that he had bought the job. Where he came from no one seemed to know. He had merely shown up in town a few years ago and had quickly begun to spread himself around. Believed by most to be short on nerve, the forty-year-old, overweight marshal had early on revealed a policy of letting men settle their own disputes. The fact that he was despised by county officials, including the prosecutor and Sheriff Dave Dubar, was well known.

Gannon learned from the bartender that the dead man's name was Dewey Eason, that he had killed several men and had few if any real friends. As the marshal had said, it was very unlikely that his passing would be mourned.

During the ride to Cottonwood, Barnes, who had been quiet most of the evening, rode beside Gannon.

"You know, Jake," he said softly, "that fellow Eason was just as fast as Chambliss."

"I know," Jake said. They rode for another mile, Gannon and Barnes leading the way. The others rode far behind, talking and sharing a bottle they had bought for the road.

Barnes puffed on his cigarette. "You see, Eason had to raise his gun high above his head to get a shot up them stairs. All Joe had to do was clear his holster and shoot straight down. He owes his life to the fact that he was standing above the man. That is, providing that Eason was a decent marksman.'

"You saw it right, Mickey, but let's give Chambliss a little credit. I figure he knew the stairs gave him an edge." They whipped their horses toward Cottonwood.

Summer came early to central Texas this year. It was now the first week of May, and already the weather was hot. Barnes had left for Waco early this morning for supplies. Gannon sat beside the tree nearest his cabin, mending a hole in his sock with needle and thread. Pop Handy had long ago proclaimed the giant cottonwood the "Studying Tree," saying that every correct decision he could recall making had been made while sitting under its canopy.

"Maybe it's a charm of some kind, Jake," the old man had said. "Every time I've had a whole lot of problems that needed studyin' on, I've sat under that tree to do it. The right answers just come to you. Try it, you'll see that I'm tellin' you right."

Gannon sat under the tree often, but for more obvious pleasures: shade and the cool breeze from the river that usually played around its huge trunk.

When Pop Handy rode into Jake's yard a short time later, he was carrying a weapon that appeared to weigh him down. The favorite gun of the hunting range was the massive fifty-caliber buffalo rifle manufactured by the Sharps company, one model of which weighed sixteen pounds. The "Big Fifty" developed two thousand foot-pounds of muzzle velocity, and its average operating range was five hundred yards. Many hunters preferred to dismantle the three-inch cartridges and augment the ninety-grain powder charge, sometimes adding up to twenty grains. Then, sighting through a twenty-power telescope, a hunter could drop a buffalo from a distance of three quarters of a mile. Today, Pop Handy held such a rifle in his hand.

"Hunting buffalo or elephant?" Jake asked.

"Just thought I'd shoot this old fifty a time or two," Pop said. "It's been hangin' on the wall gatherin' dust since I don't know when." He dismounted and handed Jake his TH-2 branding iron. "Guess you'll be brandin' calves any day now. I'd appreciate it if you'd touch mine with this iron."

"Sure will, Pop. I haven't been able to get a good count, but I'd say you've got five or six head coming. Far as I know, we've only lost one calf, and it was born dead."

"Every cow I've seen's got a calf, Jake, and they look mighty good." Pop stood around for a while, then disappeared over the hill.

After a few minutes Jake heard him blasting away. I hope he's shooting that damn cannon into the ground, Jake was thinking, concerned for the safety of his cattle that roamed freely in every direction.

When Barnes returned from Waco he had a spool of

barbed wire in the wagon. He intended to build a fence from the corral down to the river so the horses could water themselves.

Barbed wire, praised by some and cursed by others, was beginning to be widely used by cattlemen. Jake felt that it was only a matter of time before every rancher in Texas would be stringing it, himself included. Though fences might sometimes inconvenience travelers, gates could be built wherever necessary. The wire would eliminate a lot of hard riding and offer the rancher the choice of moving his cattle from one pasture to another to prevent overgrazing. Gannon intended to fence his entire holdings when he could afford it.

With the help of the Handy boys, the hay meadow had been plowed and planted. Jake had had to reinforce the rail fencing three times to keep the cattle form trampling the growing hay, another problem that would be solved by barbed wire.

"Livestock ain't gonna challenge this wire many times, Jake," Mickey said, as he unloaded the spool beside the corral. "Just handling it will cut you to pieces if you're not careful." The wire was called "Baker's Perfect," named for the man who invented it. It had a two-point barb made of flat wire that looped around one strand of the two-strand wire. The barbs were sharp enough to discourage man or beast. Barnes dug holes for the posts till dark. To-morrow they would sink the posts and stretch the wire.

In addition to their cattle duties, most ranch hands were expected to perform other chores. To be referred to as a "good hand" or an "all-around cowboy" was a compliment in itself, but the one-word description that carried the highest regard was to simply call a man a "hand." Mickey Barnes was a hand, and Gannon felt fortunate to have him at Cottonwood. He was small, but smart, and could be counted on to solve most any problem.

As a teenager, in the spring of '67, Barnes had ridden a mule from North Carolina to Texas. His father and older brother had been killed in the Civil War, and his mother had died the following winter. He had been unable to find work of any kind in the mountains. The once abundant supply of meat in the forest had shrunk to precious little, for the war had diminished the wild game drastically. Mickey had just turned fifteen when he mounted the mule and headed west, carrying only a change of clothing, two blankets and the cooked remains of a small pig he had stolen from a neighbor.

Two months later, he was in Jacksboro. He slept in the livery stable for several weeks, cleaning stalls, swamping in the saloons and taking any other odd jobs he could find. It was in one of the saloons that he met Cap McGill. With a bucket and mop in his hands, young Barnes walked right up to the rancher's table.

"I hear that you hire a man out at your ranch every once in a while, Mister McGill," Mickey said, looking Cap straight in the eye, "and I'm needing a job."

Unimpressed with the appearance of the small, ragged youngster, some of Cap's friends began to laugh. A stern look from McGill quieted them.

"What do you know how to do?" Cap asked, his eyes fastened to Mickey's worn-out brogans.

"Nothing special, just know how to work hard." Barnes stood stiffly, a look of determination on his face that suggested he might wait all day for an answer if need be.

Cap finished his drink and slowly poured himself another, staring into the glass and biting his lip as if in deep thought. Finally, raising his eyes to meet those of Barnes, he asked, "Do you have a horse?"

"No, sir, just got a mule."

"Do you know where my place is?"

"Know which direction it is. I can find it."

"Well, you do that." Cap took a sip of whiskey and drummed his fingers against the table. "Look up a man named Beeson and tell him I said to find something for you to do."

"Yes, sir," Mickey said, dropping the mop into the bucket and heading for the door.

Thus began an association and friendship that would last until Cap McGill died almost twelve years later. Barnes learned the duties of a ranch hand quickly, and eventually participated in several cattle drives north to the rails. McGill was heard to say many times during the ensuing years that Barnes was the best hand on the ranch, despite his small stature. Cap was especially impressed with the young man's prowess with a rope, and sometimes asked him to perform for the entertainment of visitors. Mickey was only too happy to oblige, for it usually meant that he was excused from work for the day.

Now, living and working at Cottonwood, Barnes was more contented with life than at any time since the happy days of his early boyhood. Here, he was treated as an equal, and he intended to remain on the premises as long as Jake had a need for his services. At this point the ranch was no more than a two-man operation, and was likely to remain so unless Jake acquired more land and more cattle.

In fact, now that the branding was done and the cattle had settled down somewhat, only one rider was needed to keep them on Cottonwood range. The lush prairie grass was abundant, and, even in winter, maintained its nutrients as it dried on the stem much like hay. Though the cattle would eat the winter grass eagerly, once it was grazed over, the dry stems would not reproduce as they did in spring and summer. It was then that the hay from the upper meadow would be needed. Next month Mickey would be in the field for the first cutting, for he could handle a

sickle as well as the next man. He owed Jake Gannon a
debt that only hard work could repay.

The following afternoon, Barnes drove the wagon to
Henry Handy's place to buy grain for the horses. When he
returned, he had eggs, butter, several jars of jelly and a jug
containing his favorite beverage. When told the contents
of the jug, Gannon curled his upper lip, as if smelling a
foul odor.

"You just don't know what's good, Jake," Mickey said
with a laugh. "Nothing in the world tastes as good as cold
buttermilk."

Nine

Gannon's gray developed into an excellent saddle horse, but the animal showed little inclination toward working cattle, seeming to think it was beneath his dignity to chase after cows. Jake decided to use the big horse only for transportation, for, like virtually all cowboys, he preferred smaller horses that were quicker on their feet, and of a solid color—no paints. Though seldom if ever used by working cowboys, paints seemed to be the favorite of Indians and writers of Western fiction. Jake had never seen an animal of such coloring that was an outstanding cow horse.

Last week he had bought four small black horses from a rancher who lived north of Hillsboro, declining Handy's offer to sell him some of his "Northern-bred" animals at a cheaper price. While the average Texas cow pony could not compare with his Northern brother for looks, he was a far superior animal when it came to hard work. He was quicker, tougher and better adapted to the long, hot days under the saddle. Barnes was pleased with Gannon's purchase and tested the entire string on the first day, proclaiming them all to be well trained and in prime condition.

"We're well fixed for horseflesh now, Jake," Mickey said, joining Gannon in the shade of the Studying Tree. "If you've got somewhere you need to go, just do it. I can handle everything here."

"I'm sure you can, Mickey. Truth is, I've been thinking about taking a ride over to Groesbeck to check on an old friend."

"Groesbeck? How far is that?"

"A hard day's ride; two days, the way I'll be going at it."

Groesbeck lay forty miles directly east of Waco. It had been dedicated as a townsite in 1870 by the Houston and Texas Central Railroad and named for one of its directors, becoming the seat of Limestone County in 1873.

The town's one claim to fame was its proximity to Old Fort Parker. The fort had been established in 1834 by the Silas, James, and John Parker families to protect the settlement of eight homesteads. In 1836, a surprise attack by several hundred Comanches overran the fort, killing five members of the Parker family and carrying five people into captivity, including Cynthia Ann Parker, who was nine years old. She grew up, married a Comanche chief and lived with the Indians until she, along with her two-year-old daughter, Prairie Flower, was captured by white men twenty-four years later.

Cynthia Ann never became reconciled to her forced return to her white kinsmen, and tried several times to escape. Unhappy, and virtual prisoners, both she and her daughter died within four years after being separated from the wild, free life of the Comanche. Prairie Flower went first, then Cynthia Ann starved herself to death.

Gannon arrived in Groesbeck during a downpour. He had ridden in the rain for the last few miles and was wet from head to toe, though he had managed to keep a change of clothing dry by wrapping it in his slicker. He saw no one on the street as he rode through town toward the livery stable. There, he cared for his horse and changed into the dry clothing.

"Seen Hurley Stewart lately?" he asked the hostler.

"Don't never see 'im. He's been dead nigh on to three years."

"I'm sorry to hear that," Jake said. "I worked out on the Lazy S a few years ago, and Hurley was a good friend."

"Well, I guess Ab's runnin' thangs out there now," the man said sourly. "Don't nobody I know have nothin' to do with them people since they brought in them damn sheep."

"Sheep? On the Lazy S?"

"Hell, yes. I hear they got thousands of 'em runnin' up an' down th' river, eatin' ever'thang but th' bark on th' trees."

Hurley Stewart had come to Texas from Georgia in 1848, and homesteaded along the west bank of the Navasota River. He acquired a herd of longhorns, and though buyers for beef were nowhere to be found, there was a ready market for tallow and hides. A man of vision, Stewart correctly forecast the day when the free grazing of public lands would be reduced drastically. As his fortunes improved he began to buy up land in all directions.

By the end of the Civil War, Stewart's domain reached for several miles along both sides of the river. He was joined by his much younger brother, Abner, who moved his growing family onto the Lazy S. Ab proved to be both eager and adept at ranching, and Hurley had been heard to say more than once that Ab's farsightedness had been responsible for much of the ranch's expansion. The Lazy S was now considered one of the best ranches in central Texas.

Gannon rode into the ranch house yard just before sunset and was greeted by Ab Stewart, who was standing beside the water well. A beefy, red-faced man who stood more than six feet tall, Stewart stuck out his hand.

"Well, I'll be damned, Jake," he said, smiling broadly, "I wouldn't have thought of you for a hundred dollars."

"It's been a while, Ab," Jake said, dismounting and taking the man's hand. "I heard about Hurley being gone. I sure am sorry."

"Been about three years, now. Of course, it didn't ketch us by surprise. He'd been ailin' for a long time." Stewart turned his head toward the house, shouting, "Come here, Dory! Come lookee what the cat drug in."

A moment later, Mrs. Stewart walked onto the porch. She was no more than five feet tall, and her shoulder-length blond hair was turning gray. Her fine-featured face had begun to wrinkle badly, but the fact that she had been a beauty in her youth was still evident—especially when she smiled. She did so now.

"Well, I'll be!" she said, walking into the yard. "I do declare, Jake. How come you waited so long to come back?"

"First time I've been in the area," he said, taking her hands in his own. "But I've been hungry for some of your good cooking for several years, now."

"That remark'll git you a big supper, young man. You and Ab jist ketch up on your man talk, I'll be gittin' the stove heated up." As Dory turned to go, a teenaged girl walked down the steps, stopping beside her mother.

"You remember Jody, I guess," Ab said, indicating his

daughter. "She's the only one of the children still livin' at home."

Indeed Jake remembered Jody, who had been no more than a towheaded tomboy when he last saw her. What he saw now was a beautiful young lady whose like he had until now only seen in pictures. She had green eyes as big as quarters, and her carefully combed hair was the color of honey.

Her lips parted on near-perfect teeth as she smiled and said, "Guess I've growed some since you left here, huh?" Not waiting for Jake to answer, she added, "I'll be sixteen tomorrow."

"Yeah," Jake said. "Yeah ... I guess you will."

Supper was followed by several glasses of home brew, and the men talked till late in the night. Jake learned that the "thousands" of sheep he had been told about were actually fifty head of Merinos that Ab was keeping on his northern section for experimental purposes.

"I keep a man and a dog up there all the time," Ab said. "I've deliberately kept the little critters on the same acreage for more than two years, jist checkin' to see how they do. They're all fat and sassy, and I'm convinced that a man can make twice as much money runnin' Merino sheep as he can with cattle."

"Or start a range war," Gannon offered.

"That is certainly a possibility," Ab said, pouring himself another glass of brew, "but I ain't the only man in Texas that knows about Merinos. I predict that when word gits around about how much money there is to be made, a whole lot of cattlemen are gonna be havin' second thoughts about sheep tearin' up the grass and foulin' the water."

"I've heard that they do both."

"Yeah, I know. But the truth is, they do neither. They do crop the grass closer, but it starts to grow out the minute you move the sheep to another pasture. As to the water holes, sheep drink their fill and leave, they don't stand around playin' in it the way cattle do."

Aside from keeping a weekly log on his sheep, and reading every book he could find on the subject, Ab had practical experience. Among the things he had learned were that sheep were much easier to herd than cattle—one man and a well-trained collie could handle several hundred head—and they needed far less care, less water and less grazing land. And they had a much higher tolerance of extreme weather.

"I believe," Ab said, "that Merino sheep are the safest and most profitable investment a rancher can make. I don't intend to start no range war, but when other cattlemen learn the things I know, I believe a lot of them will start runnin' woolies."

"Maybe so," Jake said, then retired to the bedroom he was shown.

He spent the following day in the saddle, riding over the same range he had worked on as a hired hand a few years earlier. Nothing had changed. Though not as pretty as his own place, the Lazy S was ten times as large, with some of the changes in vegetation just as abrupt. On the east side of the river were several dense stands of marketable hardwoods, while the west side turned to stunted mesquites and cedars. The ranch house was directly in the center of the county, and the plains gently rolled away to a higher elevation a few miles north. From a distance, Gannon watched the sheep grazing peacefully on a hilltop. The herdsman sat in the shade of a tree, his collie lying docilely at his side.

The ranch hands Jake met throughout the day were all cordial, and he exchanged names and handshakes with them. As he rode across the sprawling landscape, he saw no evidence that Ab had made any attempt to upgrade his herd from its original longhorn breed. Nor would he, Jake was thinking; Ab had already made up his mind to stock the ranch with sheep as soon as it seemed safe to do so. Jake also knew that Ab would save a lot of money by not having to fence, which was the coming thing all over. No need to fence in the sheep—the dogs would make sure they stayed where they were put.

Jake turned his horse into the corral at sunset and walked to the porch, where he seated himself. He was quickly joined by Jody, who pulled up a chair. The two sat in silence for quite some time.

Staring off toward the setting sun, the young girl finally spoke. "Do you think I'm pretty enough to ever git a man?"

"Why, sure," Jake said, making every effort to choose his words carefully. "I think you're pretty enough to get most any man you want."

"Well, there sure ain't nobody else ever said so," she said, pouting charmingly and avoiding Jake's amused expression. "Ain't no man ever asked to kiss me. Nor even talked, for that matter. Some of the hands sometimes nod their heads when they pass, but they sure don't say nothin'. I think Pa's told them all to stay away from me."

"I doubt that, Jody. Ranch hands just naturally keep their distance from the owner's family, especially the females. Nobody has to tell them, they just do it."

Jody seemed to accept Jake's explanation as gospel, and after a quick trip inside the house, she was back in her chair.

"Have you ever been to San Francisco?" she asked.

"Yes."

"I'd sure like to go there. Another town that's somewhere close to San Francisco is New Orleans. I'd like to go there, too."

"Uh-huh." Jake did not have the heart to tell her that

New Orleans was nowhere near San Francisco and was in fact in the opposite direction. He sat wishing someone else would join them on the porch, but no one did.

After a while, Jody got to her feet, saying, "There's somethin' I've been wantin' to do for a long time." Taking Jake's face in her hands, she lowered her head and kissed him hard on the mouth. "There!" she said, stepping away quickly. "That didn't hurt too much, did it?" Before Jake could speak, she was gone into the house.

Stunned by Jody's actions, Gannon jumped into the yard and began to walk around the premises. He had known her since she was a little girl, and had long carried that image of her. Nevertheless, he could not deny that he had enjoyed her kiss. And Jody was no longer a little girl. She was as much a woman right now as she would ever be, and the kiss had been wet and passionate.

She could be having children—maybe should be—meaning that she could be married, like a lot of other girls her age or near it. Jake was thinking these things as he sat on the top rail of the corral, his heart seeming to beat faster. Had the big, tough man fallen in love as the result of a single kiss? He did not know. He only knew that his insides had turned to jelly.

He slept fitfully throughout the night. Sometime before daybreak he dreamed that he was sleeping in the new house he would build at Cottonwood, the beautiful Jody Stewart lying in his arms.

"Why not?" he asked himself when he awoke in the morning. "Why not Jody?" Sitting on the side of the bed, he made a decision: he would ask Jody to marry him. If she agreed, they would postpone the wedding till he had enough time to accumulate more money and build a new home for his bride.

Jody squealed and kissed him again when Jake proposed, promising that no man would touch her in the meantime. Then Gannon was off to the house to talk to her father.

"I want to talk to you about something, Ab," he said, taking the chair he was offered, "but I really don't know how to start."

"I know it's tough," Stewart said, an understanding expression on his face. "You want to marry my little Jody. Right?"

"Well . . . uh . . . right," Jake stuttered. "Of course, we'll wait a year or two, till I get in better shape financially."

"Wait however long you like. I can't think of anybody I'd rather have for a son-in-law. You have my blessin'."

Jake and Jody sat on the porch for the next two hours, much of that time accompanied by Jody's mother. Though not exactly cool toward Jake, Dory was very quiet. Gannon supposed that she had already been told that he intended to take her baby. During the few minutes that they did have alone, Jody bluntly said that she was looking forward to sharing Jake's bed, and wanted to have as many children as she could. Unconcerned with the fact that it might not seem ladylike, she attempted to sit on Jake's lap. He got to his feet quickly and kissed her on the nose, saying that he must be getting back to the Brazos.

Jody stood close by as he saddled the gray, assuring him that she could cook just like her mother. She clung to him tightly as he kissed her good-bye, then he was on the trail to Cottonwood. He had thoroughly enjoyed his visit to the Lazy S, and the knowledge that Jody would join him on the Brazos in the not-too-distant future gave him a feeling of well-being.

He arrived in Waco long after dark, and decided to spend the night in town. After stabling his horse and registering at the hotel, he walked to the Texas Saloon for food and drink. Today was Saturday, and the saloon was crowded to its capacity.

He stood against the wall with a drink in his hand till a table became vacant, then seated himself and ordered his meal from a dark-haired waitress.

"Don't be shy about speaking up if you decide you want something else, now," she said, shuffling her hips in a wide swath toward the kitchen. Gannon was not interested.

Sitting at a table just inside the front door, he had just finished sopping the last bit of gravy from his plate with a tortilla when the door opened. He had not realized that it was raining outside till a man about his own age stepped inside, water dripping from his slicker.

Cradled in the crook of the man's arm was a Patterson revolving rifle, a devastating fifty-six-caliber weapon that could fire five shots in quick succession. Standing on unsteady legs and weaving slightly, the man had obviously had more than a social drink.

Taking a step toward Jake's table, he asked, "Yore name Russ Eagleton?"

"Nope," Gannon said quickly, looking directly into the man's bloodshot eyes.

He shrugged his shoulders and began to walk around the room, inspecting the patrons. A few minutes later, he was back at Gannon's table.

"I'm findin' it kinda hard to believe that you ain't Eagleton," he said.

"Look, fellow," Jake said sternly, getting to his feet and facing the man, "I don't give a damn what you believe. This is twice I've told you that I'm not Eagleton."

Shrugging his shoulders again, the man walked to the bar. He had a short conversation with the bartender, who was pointing to Jake's table and shaking his head. Seeming satisfied with whatever the bartender had told him, the man waved as he passed Jake's table and walked out onto the street.

Gannon was glad to see him go. He wanted no part of

the drunken man or the revolving Patterson. He paid for his supper and headed for the hotel.

Over a late breakfast in the saloon the following morning, Jake learned that the drunken man had eventually located Russ Eagleton and had shot off the top of his head with the Patterson. All over the affections of a saloon girl, Jake was told by the waitress who served his breakfast.

. "She's been bragging about it all morning," the waitress said. "Seems like nothing makes her feel quite as special as having men fighting over her."

The same old story, Gannon was thinking. He had never been able to understand how some men could convince themselves that they were the one true love of a woman who earned her livelihood entertaining men. Such love affairs usually lasted less than a week, or until some young, handsome cowboy came to town with enough built-up stamina for an all-night romp. Then the lady was in love again. The story remained the same; only the players changed.

Gannon had a short meeting with his banker, then rode to Cottonwood. He saw that Barnes was sitting under the Studying Tree. From somewhere, Mickey had come up with a small clay churn. He had made a lid from a circular block of wood, burning a hole in the center to accommodate the two-foot length of broomstick with a wooden cross nailed to one end. That was his dasher. He now sat churning his own buttermilk.

"I know you don't like the milk," Barnes said, as Jake returned from the barn, "but I've got some good butter here. I'll have hot biscuits in a few minutes."

"Sounds good, Mickey. Sounds very good."

Ten

Gannon's whole world changed at sunup two weeks later. He had just fed his horses and was returning to the cabin when he saw a rider on the opposite side of the river. Leading a pack horse, the man sat tall in the saddle astride a big Appaloosa. He rode south casually, obviously looking for a shallow area that would make fording easier. Jake stood beside the Studying Tree, listening to the horses splashing in the water around the bend. A short time later, the rider was in the yard. "You'll think you're looking into a damn mirror," the man in Jacksboro had said. Those words came to Jake's mind instantly, for the man facing him now was indeed a mirror image. Stopping his horse a few yards away, the man spoke in a deep tone of voice, identical to Jake's.

"You'd be Gannon," he said.

Jake nodded. "And you'd be Josh Reenow."

Reenow dismounted and dropped his horse's reins to the ground. Then, lifting his left pants leg up past the calf, he pointed to a bright red birthmark. The butterfly! "Onliest way yer ma could tell y'all apart wuz that birthmark on the calf o' yer twin's left laig," Aunt Rose had said. "Ever'body said it looked jist like a butterfly." Jake stared at the birthmark for some time. The two men were as alike as peas in a pod. Identical in age, size, appearance and movement. When they talked, it sounded as if they spoke with a single voice. Add all these things to the fact that Reenow wore the butterfly brand on the calf of his leg, and the signs were simply too overwhelming to be coincidental.

"Does this mean anything to you?" Reenow asked, continuing to point to the birthmark.

"It means that you're my brother." They crossed the few yards separating them quickly, embracing each other in a bear hug. Nothing was said for a full minute, as they stood looking at each other.

Then, shaking his head in disbelief, Jake walked to the porch and sat down. "There's just so much I don't know about this, Josh. Maybe you can fill me in. I didn't even know I had a twin till I was grown, then everybody said you died before your first birthday."

"I didn't know myself till last year," Josh said, taking a seat beside his brother. "Ma told me just before she died, said she couldn't go to her grave without me knowing the truth. Being unable to bear children of her own, she said she had Pa steal me from the Gannons because it just didn't seem right that they should have two babies while she had none. I traveled to Franklin, Tennessee, but I never could get any information on anyone named Gannon. I didn't have any way of knowing your first name till I kept running into people who had met you. None of them knew where to find you, but they all reminded me that you had quite a reputation. And they all agreed that you looked exactly like me. I knew then that you were my brother. I met some of your friends in Jacksboro a few days ago and they directed me here."

"Damn," Jake said, still shaking his head. He made a pot of coffee and fried bacon and eggs. Afterward, the twins sat on the porch talking until noon. Jake talked of his early years in Tennessee, and of their father's death during the Civil War. He talked of their beautiful mother, and of Uncle Jesse Ride and Aunt Rose.

Josh Reenow had been raised in New Mexico Territory, where he had been taken immediately after his abduction. Albert Reenow had been a jack-of-all-trades, seldom working at any one job for more than a few months at a time. The job he held the longest was his last. He was scalped by Indians while riding line for a large ranch north of Lordsburg. Ira Davis, the rancher, showed compassion for the widow and young Josh, giving them a small house to live in and supplying all their needs. Eventually, Maude Reenow began to cook for the ranch hands, and Josh did odd jobs around the barn or worked in the fields after school each day.

Josh left the ranch at the age of eighteen, traveling extensively throughout the West. He tried his hand at a variety of things over the years, but the only times he ever had any money to speak of were after his "winning streaks" at poker, a game at which he became particularly adept. It was after one of these streaks that he returned to the ranch to find his mother ailing badly. Just before her death, she told Josh of his abduction, and of his identical twin.

"I suppose you know what my original name was," Josh said to Jake.

"Your name was John. Aunt Rose said Ma picked our names out of the Bible: John and Jacob. She said the only way Ma could tell us apart was that birthmark on your leg, said we looked exactly alike."

"We still do," Josh said, putting his arm around Jake's shoulder. "I guess I won't change my name, though; it would create too many problems."

"I'm sure it would."

Josh's hat was the customary high-crowned Stetson, and his pants fit as if his two-hundred-pound body had been molded in them. He wore Levi's of blue denim, with the pockets held on by copper rivets. His flannel shirt was collarless. The blue denim jacket he had doffed shortly after his arrival was short and snug, with the same copper-riveted pockets. His boots were custom-made, with no fancy markings. And he wore the same flat walking heel that was preferred by Jake.

"First pants I ever saw with riveted pockets," Jake said, "and I'll bet that denim is cooler and more comfortable than canvas."

"It is, Jake. I found them in San Francisco two years ago and bought six pairs. I've got two pairs in my pack that I've worn only a few times. They're yours."

"I'd be happy to wear them, looks like we're the same size."

Josh began to open up his pack.

"Beats all in the hell I've ever seen," Mickey Barnes said when he arrived at the cabin later in the day. "I can't see a damn bit of difference in the two of you. Maybe you should think about wearing name tags."

Barnes baked a large pan of biscuits, then dished up the stew Jake had been simmering all afternoon. As had Jake on numerous occasions, Josh declined Mickey's offer of buttermilk, and drank water with his meal.

At bedtime, Josh hung his gunbelt on a nail and leaned his Winchester in the corner behind the stove. After refusing Mickey's offer to give up his own bed, Reenow placed his bedroll on the kitchen floor.

"No, Mister Barnes," he said, fluffing up the small pillow he carried in his pack. "This floor won't be anywhere near the hardest place I ever slept. I'll make out fine." His light snoring a few minutes later was convincing.

Jake lay on his bed for hours, waiting for the sleep that was slow to come. He could not stop the racing of his mind. Understanding life was an impossible task, he was thinking. A man could live for years with every single event falling predictably into place, going to bed each night knowing full well what was going to happen tomorrow. Then, in the twinkling of an eye his life could be changed forever. It was easy for a man to convince himself that he had control of his life. The fact of the matter was that a man had damn little control.

Jake could not remember ever feeling as happy as he did tonight, knowing that his twin, long thought to be dead, was sleeping only a few feet away. It was a link to his past, his family, his home. At last he drifted into fitful sleep, dreaming that he and Josh were kids again, living in Kentucky with their mother. When he awoke in the morning he felt as though he had spent the night hard at work.

Barnes was already up and gone to work when Jake roused himself from his bed. He found Josh seated on a large rock beside the river.

Josh asked, "Is the fishing good here?"

"Sometimes. I've got a fishtrap in that deep water across the river. Let's get in the boat and check it out." With both men paddling, they reached the deep water quickly. The trap was nothing more than a wire cage that rested on the bottom of the river, attached by a small rope to a tree limb that grew over the water. On one side of the cage was a wire funnel whose large mouth tapered steadily toward the inside, growing ever smaller. The trap could be baited with one thing or another, and once the fish were enticed inside the cage, very few ever found their way out. Pulling on the rope, Jake raised the trap from a depth of thirty feet, extracting two catfish and one bass.

"First bass I ever caught in a trap," he said. "They're usually not that stupid."

"Don't you suppose a crazy bass would taste the same as any other?" Josh asked, chuckling.

"I would imagine so."

After a late breakfast, the twins decided to ride around the ranch for a while. Jake wore the denims he had been given, and the fit was perfect.

"I sure like the feel of these pants," he said, moving his legs up and down. "And the riveted pockets are long over-due."

"The riveted pockets started in Virginia City," Josh said. "A man named Jacob Davis who ran a store there for Levi Strauss was the first to use them." Then Josh related the story of the rivets as it had been told to him many times.

It seemed that a man called Alkali Ike, who usually kept his pockets stuffed with ore samples, was forever com-plaining about the flimsy sewn pockets of his Levi's and demanding that Davis resew them. Davis, in a final at-tempt to please Ike, or perhaps even as a joke, carried the pants to a harnessmaker and had him rivet the corners of the pockets with square-cut nails. Within a matter of days, Davis was besieged by every miner in town, each demand-ing that the pockets of his own Levi's be riveted. A trade-mark had been born, and was very quickly patented.

"They switched to copper rivets a few years ago," Josh said, "to prevent rust, I suppose."

They stayed in the saddle most of the day, stopping once to talk with Barnes, who was busy chasing cattle from an area that was in danger of becoming overgrazed. They spent the noon hour on the north section, sitting be-

side the river. Each man talked of his childhood, and some
of the things that had happened to him since.

Jake listened well to the things his brother said, and
watched him closely. Josh's fluid movements and the general manner in which he carried himself suggested that he
would be a hard man to handle in a scrap, and more than
a little handy with the Peacemaker on his hip. Jake silently
wondered if his twin had enemies, for Josh was very
watchful of things around him, and at times seemed to be
trying to stretch his eyesight to greater distances.

Staring into the river as they ate their ham and biscuits,
Josh asked, "What were Ma and Pa like, Jake?"

"Pa was a big man; same size as us, the best I remember. He was a hard worker, kept half a dozen things going
all the time. He treated Ma like a queen, and he was easy
on me as long as I stuck to the rules."

"He died at Nashville, huh?"

"Yeah. He came through the Franklin fight without a
scratch, but they said he didn't live five minutes after the
Battle of Nashville started."

Josh wiped the sweatband of his hat with his necker-
chief, then reached into the sack for another biscuit. "And
Ma?" he asked.

"Ma was a beautiful woman, and the most kindhearted
soul I've ever known. She wasn't much bigger than a bar
of soap. She always canned enough food during the summer to feed a small army. We ate well, Josh.

"She stayed at home all the time. Even Uncle Jesse
couldn't get her to visit anybody. The man who ran the
sawmill preached on Sundays, and sometimes she'd go to
church for an hour or two. Then she'd spend the rest of the
afternoon telling me how little the preacher knew about
the Bible, saying she didn't even believe he could read.

"Looking back on those days, it seems that the only
goal she had in life was to see me fully grown. But she

didn't baby me, Josh; she was forever telling me to get out and test myself, and she wasn't bashful about giving me hell when I needed it." Jake sat quietly for a while, then added, "Her favorite food was boiled cabbage. I think she would have fixed it for breakfast if she'd thought I'd eat it."

Picking up a small, flat stone, Josh sent it skating across the water, a distasteful expression on his face. "Boiled cabbage, huh?"

Josh spent the next two weeks at Cottonwood, growing more noticeably restless with each passing day. Neither Jake nor Barnes was surprised when he said that he was craving some action, that he was going into Waco to hunt up a poker game.

"You won't have to do much hunting," Jake said. "There's at least one game in every saloon in town. Are you coming back here?"

"Sure, be back in a day or two."

Josh did not return in a day or two. It was six days later that Jake found him playing poker in the Texas Saloon. He was on one of his winning streaks, and had pocketed more than twenty-five hundred dollars from Waco's gamblers in five days of play. Sitting at a table at the back of the room, he was engaged in a four-handed game of stud when Jake appeared.

"Hello, Jake," Josh said, as he raked in another pot. "I was just thinking about getting on back to the river." He pushed his chair back, stood, and began to stuff his winnings into his pocket. "I guess now is as good a time as any."

A well-dressed, middle-aged man, who, judging from the huge stack of cash in front of him, was Josh's main opponent, sat directly across the table.

"Hate to see you quit this early, big feller," the man said. "You gonna be around to play some more tonight?"

"I sure don't intend to let you go back to Fort Worth with that," Josh said, laughing and pointing to the man's stack of currency. "I'll be back two days from now."

"Well, I'm sure I'll still be in town," the man said, baiting Josh by shuffling his currency back and forth, making sure that the large denominations of the bills could be seen, "and I just might take what you've got home with me."

The men at the poker table, as well as several others in the saloon, stared at the twins as if unable to believe their eyes. Jake motioned to Barnes, who had been at the bar nursing a beer, and the three walked around town for a while. Jake introduced his brother to several men, including the county sheriff.

At the general store, which many townspeople called the "Shebang," Jake bought a new shirt and an assortment of canned goods for the cabin. Next door to the Shebang was an ice-cream parlor, and each man had a large bowl. The parlor served three different flavors, and business was good year-round. During hot weather, the staff sometimes could not make the ice cream fast enough to accommodate the long line of customers, not all of them youngsters.

They were on the road to Cottonwood when Josh asked, "How old am I, Jake, and when is my birthday?"

"You were born in fifty-two, you'll be twenty-eight on September twentieth."

Josh was quiet for a while. After riding another mile, he spoke again.

"I always celebrated my birthday in October. I guess that's one of the changes I'll make."

At sunset, Barnes separated from the twins, saying he would take a different route home. He knew where a flock of turkeys was roosting in a tall oak, and would try to get one for supper.

It was almost dusk when the twins finished caring for

their horses, and the remaining light was fading fast. A short time later, they heard the report of a rifle across the river.

"You think that's Barnes?" Josh asked. "Hell, he can't see good enough to hit anything this late in the day."

"Mickey can see in the dark," Jake said, sounding as if he believed it. A few minutes later, Barnes rode in with a turkey.

Over coffee the following morning, Josh counted out two thousand dollars and pushed it across the table to Jake.

"I want you to keep this for me," he said. "Use it if you need to."

"No, no," Jake said, raising his hands defensively as if to refuse the money. "We rode right past the bank yesterday, why didn't you leave it there?"

"Because I don't trust banks, Jake." Josh walked to the stove and refilled his coffee cup. "And I've got good reason. Five years ago a banker in New Mexico Territory cleaned out his vault and skipped the country, taking eight thousand dollars of my money with him. I found the sonofabitch in Lincoln, Nebraska, a year later and put a bullet between his eyes, but I didn't get my money back. I hitched a ride out of Lincoln on a westbound Pacific Railroad freight train—only a few minutes ahead of a sheriff's posse, I learned later."

Jake tacitly folded the money and shoved it into his pocket. He refilled his coffee cup and stood in the doorway, his eyes glued to the river. "The money will be here when you need it," he said.

Josh left Cottonwood shortly after breakfast the following morning, saying he was going to Waco to play poker again. He said that the man from Fort Worth was a sucker with plenty of money, and that he intended to get it.

"He don't play poker worth a shit, Jake, and I can read him like a book."

"He's that bad, huh?"

"Hell, yes. All you have to do is watch him. He gets so excited that he damn near jumps out of his chair every time he pairs his hole card."

Eleven

Three days later, a rider galloped into the yard at Cottonwood.

"Your brother's been shot!" he shouted to Gannon, who was standing in the doorway. "Doc Crowe says he's dying."

Jake jumped into the yard, grabbing the bridle of the man's panting horse.

"What happened, Hank?" he asked.

"I don't know exactly. They say that Josh and Ike Meeks met in the middle of the street down by the livery stable. Josh shot Meeks right through the heart, but not before Meeks got lead into him. Meeks is dead, and your brother's in a bad way. He's been asking for you."

Gannon pushed his horse to its limit, making the ride to Waco in record time. A crowd of men had gathered outside Doctor Crowe's office, and Jake shouldered his way through. Just inside the door, he was intercepted by the doctor, who whispered into his ear.

"Right through the lungs, Mister Gannon; no chance." Doc returned to the bed and wiped the bloody froth from Josh's mouth. Handing the cloth to Jake, he said, "I'll leave you two alone, now. It won't be long."

Jake continued to wipe his brother's face, as blood began to trickle from Josh's nose. His shirt had been removed, baring the ugly wound in his chest.

"It's me, Josh," he whispered, "it's Jake. Can you hear me?"

Josh's eyelids fluttered and he nodded slightly. Then, as if using his last bit of strength, he slowly reached into his pocket and laid a large roll of bills in Jake's hand.

"Three ... three guns, Jake," he said, in a wheezing voice that was barely above a whisper. A coughing spasm sent a large clot of blood onto his chest, and started his nose bleeding again. Taking short, noisy breaths, he continued to speak in faint tones.

"Up against three guns ... the livery stable ... they—" He jerked once, then lay still. Josh Reenow was dead.

Jake looked around the room quickly to see if anyone else had heard Josh's last words. No one was there. Tears rolled down both cheeks as Jake stood beside his brother's corpse. Somehow, Josh looked much smaller with his arms lying peacefully at his sides, all color drained from his face. Only yesterday Mickey Barnes had said, "That twin of yours is a powerful-looking machine. I bet it would take half a dozen men to handle him." Not now, Mickey, Jake said to himself, as he stared at the ghostly figure. Not now.

After closing his brother's eyes and folding his arms across his chest, Jake pulled the sheet over Josh's head and left the room.

"Is he gone?" the doctor asked, as Jake emerged from the building.

Gannon nodded, and untied his horse from the hitching rail. Mounting, he said, "I'll be back for his body shortly." He rode directly to the livery stable.

"I'll be needing a team," he said to the aging hostler, who moved immediately to fill his order, "and put some hay and a blanket in the wagon." Jake intended to talk with the old man about the shooting, but decided to wait till later. As it turned out, he did not have to wait.

"I cain't be seen talkin' to you," the hostler said, his face hidden by the horses as he hitched them to the wagon, "but I saw that shootin' this mornin'."

"Figured you did," Jake said, walking around as if inspecting the wagon.

The old man continued to hide his face against the horses. "That yore cabin over at the bend of the river?"

"Yes."

"I'll be over there sometime after dark," the man said, bending over to hook a chain to a singletree.

Jake climbed into the wagon and drove away, confident that onlookers would never know that a conversation had passed between himself and the liveryman.

At the doctor's office, he hoisted Josh's body to his shoulder and carried it to the wagon, declining the offers of a few men who volunteered to help. He drove briskly out of town, his gray tethered to the rear of the wagon.

Jake chose a spot beside Big Red for Josh's final resting place. It was well past dark when he patted the last of the dirt into a mound atop the grave. Barnes stood nearby holding a coal-oil lantern.

"Hello the light!" a man shouted from a distance of a hundred yards. Recognizing the nasal twang of the hostler, Gannon called him in.

The old-timer soon dismounted and tied his horse to a small bush. After taking in the scene for a moment, he asked, "Who's in that grave beside him?"

"A thoroughbred saddle horse," Jake said.

The old man shuffled around a bit, a quizzical expression on his face. Taking a long pull from the cigarette in his hand, he coughed several times, then asked, "Why would you bury a human next to a horse?"

Leaning on his shovel, his eyes roving from one mound to the other, Jake appeared to be in deep thought. "Why not?" he finally asked. He received no answer.

A few minutes later, the old man sat at the kitchen table, relating the story of the shooting. "Yore brother outdrawed Meeks by a mile, Mister Gannon. Meeks never did even fire his gun."

"Never fired his gun? Why I was told—"

"I know what you wuz told," the hostler interrupted, "but that ain't the way she happened. Don't reckin nobody saw the whole thang 'cept me. Weren't nobody on the street at that hour of the mornin'. The marshal hisself is the man that shot yore brother down, done it with his Winchester." Barnes refilled the man's coffee cup while Jake listened attentively.

Blowing over the hot liquid, the old-timer took a sip and continued.

"The three of 'em come into the livery about seven o'clock—the marshal, Deputy Hallman and Meeks. They hung around for a while, not sayin' what they wanted. Then the marshal told me to git outta sight and stay there.

"I got outta sight, but then I clumb up the ladder to that winder in the loft so I could see ever'thang that went on. I saw yore brother come outta the hotel and start walkin' toward the stable. He might have slept at the hotel last night. I know it was mighty late when he quit playin' cards.

"Anyways, he wuz headed toward the stable, prob'ly fixin' to come back out here to yore place. The marshal and the deputy both hunkered down behind some hay

bales with their rifles cocked and ready. When yore
brother neared the stable, Meeks stepped out and challenged him to a gunfight. Meeks walked into the street at
a sorta kinda angle, so the rifles would have a clear shot
at yore brother.

"Meeks accused him of cheatin', and told him to draw
his gun. Yore brother done that awright, had that Peacemaker in his hand afore you could bat a eye. As I said,
Meeks never did fire, didn't live long enough. Jist barely
got his gun outta the holster. After the marshal fired, the
deputy took both rifles and run through the alley to the
back of the jail.

"Natcherly, the marshal reached the scene afore anybody else did. The first thang he done wuz pick up
Meeks's gun outta the dirt and stick it behind his own
waistband. No, sir, he didn't want nobody else handlin'
that gun, 'fraid somebody'd figger out that it hadn't been
fired. I betcha a million dollars that somebody fired it
later."

"I would think so," Jake said, staring at the wall. The
old man talked on and on, but could add nothing of signi-
ficance. Finally, after being assured that Jake had no whiskey on the premises, he mounted his horse and headed
back to Waco. The skinny old man had sworn on his
mother's grave that the shooting happened just the way he
described it. Gannon believed him.

It was past noon the following day when Jake arrived in
Waco. He rode in from the north, approaching the livery
stable at its rear door.

Leading his horse inside, he said to the hostler, "Just
leave the saddle on. I might be needing a horse in a
hurry." Jake backed the animal into an open stall, wrapping the reins around a post. "By the way, Wimpy," he
said, "I forgot to tell you last night. You and me are gonna

take a walk to the Texas Saloon. You've got a speech to make."

"No, no," the old man whined, "shore cain't do that. My ass wouldn't hold shucks, time the marshal got through with me."

"The marshal is already through with you, Wimpy," Jake said sternly. "He's not gonna be bothering anybody."

"You aim to kill him?"

Jake nodded.

"Well, you do that," Wimpy said, moving behind a stall as if trying to hide. "Then I'll tell the whole town—tell the whole county."

"That's not good enough," Gannon said, seating himself on an upended crate. "I'll protect you, Wimpy, but I've got to have some protection myself. I can't go after a lawman without the people of this town understanding why." Taking the hostler gently by the arm, Jake led him toward the doorway. "Come along, now, nobody's gonna hurt you. Just tell the men exactly what you told me."

"You gonna perteck me? You as good with that gun as yore brother wuz?"

"Yes," Jake said. Wimpy showed only slight resistance now.

Inside the saloon, Gannon banged his fist on the bar. "Listen up, everybody!" The room was quiet instantly. "Gather round and listen; Wimpy's got a story to tell you."

More than a dozen men formed a semicircle in front of the liveryman, their eyes curious.

"It's about that shootin' yesterday," Wimpy began, his high-pitched voice breaking. "I seen and heerd ever' bit of it, and she didn't happen nowhere near like the marshal said."

More men crowded in now. As Wimpy repeated the story verbatim, a few men nodded and whispered back and forth. Half way through the narration, a man slipped hurriedly through the back doorway, and Jake knew that word of the new development was now being carried to the marshal.

Wimpy concluded his description of the incident with a familiar oath: "... and that's the way she happened, I swear by ever'thang that's holy."

"There, Mort!" one man said to another. "You hear that? Didn't I tell you Meeks wasn't good enough to take Reenow?"

Gannon stood with his back to the bar, barely cognizant of the things being said around him. He was thinking of Josh Reenow and his devil-may-care attitude, of the volcanic laughter that lay just beneath the surface, always erupting at the slightest hint of humor. Josh had been of his own blood, and, from all indications, a decent human being. It was all clear to Jake now. Josh had known that he was facing three guns, but had been helpless against the hidden rifles. He had been forced to concentrate on the immediate threat in front of him: Meeks. Perhaps the marshal had also wanted Meeks out of the way, and had deliberately held his fire till Josh had done the job for him. Maybe he intended to get rid of the deputy later, leaving no witnesses.

Jake turned to the bartender. "Did Josh win any money from the house?" he asked.

The man shrugged his shoulders, wiping at a wet spot on the bar.

"I'll ask you one more time!" Gannon demanded in a threatening voice. "Did Josh win any money from the house?"

The bartender nodded.

"How much?"

"I heard it was a coupla thousand. The marshal said Reenow was a cardsharp."

A cardsharp? Perhaps, Jake was thinking, for Josh had

seemed to be a consistent winner. But if the marshal suspected Josh of cheating, why had he not called it at the table, as was usually done when a player's methods were questionable? Because the brave bastard preferred to shoot from ambush, Jake concluded.

"I'll be expecting you fellows to look out for Wimpy," he said to the men facing him. "Could be that some folks don't like what he's been saying." The men nodded, and quickly formed a circle around the old hostler. Gannon went out the back door.

The marshal's office sat cater-cornered across the street from the saloon, with a narrow alley on either side of the building. Gannon had no intention of crossing the street. He was well aware of the arsenal possessed by the marshal and his deputy, especially the sawed-off shotguns. He also knew now that either of them would shoot from ambush. He expected them to attempt the same game they had played with Josh, and was not surprised when he saw a slight movement in back of the jail. That would be Deputy Hallman, he decided, relieved that he now knew the lawman's whereabouts. The deputy could not get a shot at him without exposing himself to some degree, and maybe it would be enough.

The door to the marshal's office was closed, the shade drawn on its only window. Jake felt no immediate danger from there. With a keen eye focused down the alley to the back of the jail, he decided to see if the marshal had any sand in his craw.

"Hey, Marshal!" he shouted. "This is Gannon, and I'm calling you out!" Jake had moved a few steps in front of the saloon, so as to become a tempting target. A moment later, the deputy foolishly leaned around the corner at the back of the jail, a rifle pressed to his shoulder.

Whether Hallman had never been told of Gannon's prowess with firearms or whether he was just plain stupid would never be known, for with a draw that would be talked about for years Jake shot off the top of the deputy's head—a shot that when measured later would prove to be an unbelievable sixty yards.

Gannon continued to hold his position, waiting. That the marshal would fight, Jake had no doubt, for by now the man must be feeling like a cornered animal. Jake called again.

"Come on out, Bisco, your deputy's past helping you!"

After a moment of silence, the sound of a muffled shotgun blast came from the marshal's office.

"Why, he's committed suicide," a man said, stepping from the doorway of the saloon.

"Bullshit." Gannon did not buy the well-worn ruse. He walked backward into the saloon, then slipped out the back door again. He ran past half a dozen buildings, stopping when he was behind the livery stable. With ample room for traffic on either side, the stable stood at the end of the street. Peeking around the corner of the building, Jake knew that he could not be seen from the marshal's office. He dashed across a vacant lot, then moved from one building to another till he was behind the jail.

He doubted that the marshal would have locked the rear door when the deputy exited, for he would have been too busy watching the street. Hoping the hinges were well oiled, Jake twisted the knob and eased the door open. Removing his hat, he took a one-eyed look down the corridor, seeing no one. A few cells stood on one side of the hall, but they probably held no prisoners. It was the marshal's normal practice to pocket their money and send them on their way.

Gannon took off his boots and stepped inside in his stocking feet, gun in hand. Pausing to listen after each step, he made his way down the hall to the office. There, very much alive and peeking at the street around the window shade, stood the good marshal, a double-barreled ten-gauge shotgun in his hand. Gannon stomped his foot on the floor. When the marshal turned, Jake sent a bullet into his gut. The slot slammed the man against the wall, knocking him loose from the weapon. Gannon fired again, two inches lower.

"One for Josh," he said, as the wide-eyed marshal crumpled to the floor, "and one for me."

When Sheriff Dubar arrived on the scene twenty minutes later, he merely nodded to Gannon. He spent more than an hour questioning witnesses, among them Doctor Crowe.

"I don't remember his exact words, dammit!" the doctor exclaimed heatedly. "I was too damn busy trying to save his life. What I'm telling, Sheriff Dubar, is that just before he drew his last breath, the marshal told me he was the man who shot Josh Reenow. And there ain't no use in you filing no charges. Every single witness would come down on Gannon's side." The doctor spat a mouthful of tobacco juice in the general direction of a spittoon, then added, "Besides, I hear that Shannon Page is Gannon's lawyer. I don't have to tell you that Page would turn the trial into a three-act play."

Seeming satisfied, the sheriff crossed the room to Jake, saying, "I can't see that I have any reason to hold you. Unless the prosecutor decides to push it, I reckon it's over."

Half an hour later, Jake straddled his gray and headed home.

Twelve

After a month had passed with no word from Waco authorities, Jake felt that the shooting was history. With an emptiness in his heart that he could explain to no one, he spent most of his time alone. A week ago, he had begun to show signs of returning to normal.

He would not have to worry about money for a while, for Josh had left him with more than five thousand dollars. He bought another section of land from Henry Handy, then hired Handy's sons to help him move the cabin a hundred yards farther up the hill. Using three teams of horses, and placing small logs underneath the cabin, the men had simply rolled it to its new location. Gannon intended to build a ranch house in the shade of the towering Studying Tree and its smaller companion. When the new house was finished, the cabin would become a bunkhouse, complete with its own kitchen.

Handy and his sons would build the house with foot-thick logs, capping it off with a tin roof. Jake had spoken with a contractor in Hillsboro who would finish the inside. With the high cost of labor and materials, construction of the house would run more than seven hundred dollars, but for Jake it would be well-spent money.

With the additional land, Cottonwood would support more cattle. Speaking across the supper table, Jake said to Barnes, "We've got good grass and plenty of hay, Mickey, so I want you to take a trip to Jacksboro. Tell Cofield that I want a hundred head of breeders. I'll give you the cash to pay for them."

"You trust me with that much money?" Barnes asked, laughing.

Jake ignored the remark. "Get Bake Mellon and who-ever else you need to make the drive. I'll pay their wages." He ate in silence for a few minutes, then added, "Tell Bake to bring all his gear with him if he still wants to work at Cottonwood. Just make sure he understands that you're the foreman."

"I am?"

"You must be," Jake said, rising from the table. "I sure don't want the job."

The following morning, Mickey crossed the river and headed northwest, carrying with him a note from Gannon to Cofield. The note explained that Jake stayed home to oversee construction of the new ranch house.

When Barnes arrived at the McGill spread four days later, Cofield's greeting was chilly.

"I sure didn't expect to see you around here again," Bunt said, a granite expression on his face.

"Didn't have any reason of my own for coming," Mickey said, matching Bunt's flat tone of voice. "Here's a note from Jake." He headed for the bunkhouse to seek out Bake Mellon.

* * *

The cattle had been cut from the herd and bunched for the drive to Cottonwood, when Mellon informed Cofield that he would not be returning.

"Go ahead," Cofield said sardonically. "I hope by God you rot on that river."

Mellon said nothing more. Shaking his head in disbelief, he took his place beside the herd. Chambliss, who would be riding drag for the first leg of the drive, had overheard Cofield's comment.

"Pay him no mind, Bake," he said. "I don't think he's responsible for the things he says nowadays."

Last night, Cofield had asked Barnes about Jake's shooting incident in Waco. Mickey nipped the questions in the bud by saying that he had not been present when the marshal and his deputy were killed, and therefore felt unqualified to discuss it. Then, counting the money into Bunt's hand, Barnes had paid for the cattle in full.

Now, as the men prepared to move the cattle out, Bunt rode to the front of the line.

"We're not gonna be able to beat back all the calves, Mickey," he said, "even though most of them have already been weaned. Tell Jake that I expect to be paid for any that tag along with their mothers."

"I'll tell him."

"And tell him that I don't appreciate him hiring my best hand."

"I'll tell him that, too." Barnes knew that Jake would lose no sleep worrying about it. As Cofield mounted and turned toward the house, the men headed the cattle south. Perhaps thirty calves tucked themselves inside the herd, each sticking close to its mother. The riders made no effort to remove them.

The one-hundred-fifty-mile drive, made easier by the fact that most of the cattle had trailed before, took thirteen days, and was uneventful. The calves were no more than a minor problem, for as the cow goes, so goes the calf. It was close to sunset when they reached the Brazos. After being allowed to drink, the cattle were bunched on the west bank. Tomorrow, they would be pushed across the river, where, after being branded, they would scatter and begin to explore their new range. Deciding to sleep in his own bed tonight, Barnes left the five riders with the cattle and rode to the cabin.

As he often did in the early evening, Jake was sitting under the Studying Tree. "I've been watching for a while," he said. "They look mighty good from here."

"They're in top shape," Barnes said, handing Jake the bill of sale. "I'm sure you noticed the calves. Bunt says he expects to be paid for them. He also said he didn't appreciate you hiring Bake."

"Did you tell him that I'm ashamed of myself?"

"I figured he knew," Barnes said, heading for the cabin.

"There's a pot of stew on the stove," Jake called after Barnes. "As soon as we eat we can ride over and relieve the hands. I'm sure they're hungry, too."

Bake Mellon learned his way around the area quickly, and, just as Gannon expected, fitted in perfectly. Mellon was a hand, and his horse-handling ability was nothing less than amazing. Gannon himself had once seen Bake stand in the middle of a meadow and coax a half-wild bronc to him, even while holding a bridle in his hand.

"Them damn horses understand everything Mellon says," Cap McGill had once said. "He's just as firm with them as anybody else, but he does it so slow and easy. You can say the same words he does, but that horse will kick dirt in your face and light a shuck."

Jake knew that to be true. A few times he had attempted to copy Bake's methods, only to have the horse skedaddle to the far corner of the corral, making a rope necessary. On one such occasion, after Jake had spent a considerable amount of time trying to rope a mount, Bake had simply walked into the corral and called the animal to him.

Mellon had come to Texas from central New York. He had been raised by his grandparents, who owned a small dairy farm along the Mohawk River near the town of Utica. At the age of eighteen he had traveled to Jacksboro, where he soon gained employment on the McGill spread. As his skill with horses became obvious, he gained the respect of every man on the ranch, and the fact that he was a "Northerner" was soon forgotten.

Gannon had no way of knowing if Mellon possessed any fighting skills, for he had never been known to come to blows with any man. Nor did he carry a six-gun on his hip. The rifle he carried on his saddle was seldom fired, then only to obtain meat for the table. Jake, expecting to someday buy another "blooded" horse and turn the animal over to Mellon for training, was hoping Bake would be happy at Cottonwood.

Gannon had decided to enclose his holdings with barbed wire, figuring that in the long run he would save enough money on wages to pay for the wire. He would not be needed in the fencing process, so he decided that now would be a good time to visit the Stewarts. Especially Jody.

When he rode into the Stewart yard two days later, Jody, returning from the chickenhouse with a basket of eggs, was the first to see him. She set the basket down and ran toward him as he dismounted. But suddenly she stopped ten feet away and stood very still, as if not knowing what to do.

"Been hopin' you'd come 'fore cold weather," she said.

"Seems like when a fellow rides as far as I have he deserves a kiss," Jake said, removing his hat. "I don't think anybody's looking."

"Don't keer if they are." She rushed into his arms and kissed him several times, hanging on till he gently pushed her away. She stood beside him while he unsaddled his horse and turned it into the corral, then led him to the house. The Stewarts stood in the doorway, speaking words of welcome.

"Get a bottle of that blackberry wine I put up last summer, Dory," Ab said. Then, turning to Jake, he said, "Or maybe you'd rather have some peach brandy."

Following Ab into the house, Jake said, "The wine, I suppose."

The men talked till well past dark, conversation dominated by weather, grass and cattle. The now empty wine bottle had been replaced with peach brandy made from Ab's own recipe. Neither of the women had been seen for more than an hour, and Jake knew that a feast was in the making. He changed the subject.

"My house is already up, Ab, and the carpenters will be through with the inside pretty soon."

"Then I guess you'll be movin' in before long."

"I've been sleeping in it for two weeks, still cooking and eating in the cabin, though."

Ab poured himself another drink, and leaned back in his chair. "What you're gonna tell me next is that you're about ready to take Jody off my hands. Right?"

Jake nodded, not at all surprised that Ab had been able to see right through him. "I was gonna say it a little differently," he said, "but, yes, that's what I want to do. I haven't mentioned it to Jody yet, but I've been thinking about being married on Christmas Eve."

"That'll be all right with me, and I know it'll please Jody. That's all she talks about. Told her momma she'd been plannin' to marry you since she was nine years old."

Nine years old! Jake repeated to himself, as Dory appeared in the doorway to announce that supper was on the table.

Jody seated Jake at the end of the table, placing her own plate near his elbow. Ab thanked the Lord for the food, and Jake dug into a meal that was far superior to anything he could have bought in a restaurant—at any price. He had just finished a piece of custard that Jody herself had baked when Ab decided to make him squirm.

"I think Mister Gannon has an announcement to make." He looked down to Jake's end of the table. When Jake was slow to respond, Ab spoke again. "Go ahead, Jake, tell 'em what's on your mind."

Gannon, who sat staring into his plate, slowly turned his eyes toward Jody. "I was wondering if you might want to be married on Christmas Eve," he said.

Jody squealed, and was out of her chair instantly. She kissed Jake, jumped up and down a few times, then ran to her room.

As the door closed behind her, Ab helped himself to another piece of custard, saying, "She never did say what her answer was, did she?'

Jake stayed on the ranch for three days. During the afternoon of the third day, he saddled his gray and Jody's yellow mare, and the two began to ride around the ranch. Two hours before sunset, he picketed the horses on a hillside far beyond the sheep meadow. As they sat under the trees, Jody slithered into his arms and kissed him passionately, pressing her curvaceous body against him. Taking his hand in her own, she placed it on her breast, then began to unbutton his shirt. She kissed his chest wetly.

"I want to give you your weddin' present," she said softly, "right now." Jake had never intended that it should happen this way. But he was only human, and the nearness of her warm, luscious body was overwhelming. There, on a saddle blanket spread over a bed of leaves, Jody became, as she would say, a woman. Later, as she lay cuddled in his arms, she began to cry.

"Are you gonna be all right?" he asked.

"Yes," she said quickly. She was silent for a moment. "It felt jist like somebody was cuttin' me with a knife at first, but after a while it didn't hurt so bad."

"Are you sorry?"

"No, I'm glad. I wanted to do it for you."

"I love you, honey," Jake said, professing that affection for a woman for the first time in his life, "and I'm gonna take care of you." He kissed her eyes and patted her behind, then set about saddling the horses.

In the ranch house yard the following morning, Jake sat astride the gray as he said good-bye to the Stewarts. Jody stood at his stirrup, her small hands on his boot. Cupping his hand under her chin, he lifted her face.

"I'll be back two days before Christmas," he said. "We'll be married right here at the house, then I'll take you home."

"I'll be gittin' me a milch cow'n some chickens," she said, her eyes growing misty. "Ain't buyin' butter'n eggs from nobody." Smiling, Jake rode out of the yard, Jody's simple words ringing in his ears.

Arriving in Waco after the bank had closed for the day, he decided to spend the night in town, and conduct his business with the banker in the morning. He had not walked the streets of Waco since the day of the shootings, but he had no intention of retiring from society. Ordering a good feed of oats for his horse, he walked to the hotel, where he rented an upstairs room.

An hour later, he sat at a table in the Texas Saloon. He filled a glass from his pitcher of beer as he awaited the preparation of the meal he had ordered. No one spoke to him directly, though a few men nodded a greeting, then moved away. Whether they shunned him out of fear or because they disapproved of his actions a month ago, Jake could not tell. Nor did he care.

In a short while, he noticed that a huge mat had been placed over the dance floor, and men at the four corners were pulling it tight and straightening out the edges. He had seen it all before: a prize-fighting match was about to take place. Jake himself had participated in such things a few years ago when he was in dire need of funds.

He was just cleaning his plate when a man walked onto the mat. In a loud, commanding voice, he demanded everyone's attention.

"All right, gentlemen!" he yelled. "Coming up is the event we've all been waiting for!" He announced that a "grudge" match between two heavyweights was about to begin. A "winner-take-all" pot of money that had been established by the bar patrons over a period of several days would be awarded to the victor.

The bout would be a fight to the finish under London prize-ring rules. A knockdown would end a round, whether it took one second or half an hour. Even a slip was the end of a round if a man fell. Much was acceptable under bare-knuckle rules. One fighter might grab his opponent and bodily slam him to the mat, or hold him in a headlock while pounding him in the face with his free hand—all legal.

Such fights often lasted fifty rounds or more. The combatants were usually good actors as well as seasoned brawlers, and more often than not, the length of the fight would be determined by the size of the purse. Afterward, the fighters would split the money, then move on to the next town. There, another big "grudge" match would be staged.

As he watched the fighters step onto the mat, waiting to

be introduced, Jake had to smile. The same old format: the big, ugly brute versus the smaller, good-looking underdog. David and Goliath. Having no doubt as to the outcome of the "fierce" battle, Jake paid for his food and drink, and left.

He walked to the hotel and was soon sleeping soundly.

Thirteen

The carpenters had long since vacated the premises, and Jake was enjoying his new home. Fall usually brought much rain to central Texas, and this year was no exception. Jake would sometimes lie on his bed listening to the music of the rain splattering loudly on the tin roof, and daydream of the life he would soon be sharing with Jody Stewart. Both Barnes and Mellon applauded his decision to be married, eager to meet the young bride.

"You've got a lot of things going right for you these days, Jake," Mellon said. "it's time you started thinking about a family." Though Jake had been slow to mention it, at supper he brought up the subject of Jody's tender age.

"Sixteen's old enough," Barnes said. Then, smiling, he added, "Anyway, why should a man take an old bride when he can get a young one?"

"My mother was younger than that when she married,"

Bake said. Gannon allowed the conversation to die on its own, knowing that his own mother had given birth to twins at the age of fifteen.

The following afternoon, the men sat in the shade of the Studying Tree discussing where they might find a milch cow and some chickens, when a rider splashed across the river. As the man rode into the yard, Jake recognized him as one of Ab Stewart's hands who answered to the name of Joe.

"Coulda got here sooner if I'd knowed exactly where you live," the man said, dismounting the heaving animal. "Been followin' that crooked river for hours."

"What's the rush, Joe?" Jake asked, getting to his feet.

"Well ... it's Miss Jody, she ... she's bad off."

"What do you mean?" Jake yelled. "Come on, man, out with it!"

"The sheepherder found her up on the meadow, more dead than alive. Somebody'd beat her up real bad, and she didn't have on no clothes. She come to once and talked to her daddy a little bit, but then she lost her mind ag'in. The sheriff's out at the ranch now."

Gannon's expression turned to stone. He spoke to Barnes. "Pack up some food, Mickey, while I put a few things together." Then, turning to Mellon, he ordered, "Saddle my horse, Bake, and catch a fresh mount for Joe."

Twenty minutes later, accompanied by the messenger, Jake pointed his gray toward the town of Groesbeck. Little conversation passed between the men during the frantic ride. Pushing their horses to the limit, they arrived at Stewart's ranch shortly after noon the following day. Ab met them in the yard.

"It's mighty bad, Jake," he said, his eyes red and swollen. "She opened her eyes and asked for you yesterday, but she's been unconscious since then. The doctor spent the night with her. He left for town this mornin', sayin' he'd done all he could. Said we'd jist have to wait and see."

Jake was totally unprepared for the sight in Jody's bedroom. The swollen mass of black, red and purple that lay on the pillow bore no resemblance to the beautiful face he had kissed only a short time ago. Seating himself beside her bed, he took her hand.

"It's me, Jody," he whispered, "it's Jake. Can you hear me?" Jody slowly parted her lips in what appeared to be an effort to speak.

"She hears you, Jake," Dory Stewart said, her hand on his shoulder. "That's a good sign, ain't it?" A moment later, Jody opened her eyes. Offering a faint smile, she suddenly squeezed Jake's hand. Then, just as suddenly, her hand went limp, her smile faded and her eyes turned to glass.

Gannon had seen enough over the years to recognize death when he saw it. Nevertheless, he was on his feet quickly, checking for signs of breathing. He placed his ear on her chest in search of a heartbeat. Jody Stewart was dead.

"It's over," he said, turning to embrace her mother. He was quickly out into the yard, where he told Ab that Jody was gone. Ab followed to the porch, where Jake stood splashing water on his face from a pan.

"I didn't expect her to make it," Stewart said, "could tell by the way she looked."

Shaking water from his hair, Jake raised his eyes above the horizon. "She only asked for a milch cow and some damn chickens," he said softly.

"I've got to believe that the Lord'll provide that," Ab said, then walked into the house.

With the same minister she had chosen to handle her wedding ceremony officiating, Jody was laid to rest beside her grandmother the following afternoon. Though most of the area's residents attended the funeral, Tom Adderly, Ab's neighboring rancher to the south, was conspicuously absent. And with good reason: it had already been determined that some of Adderly's riders had been Jody's assailants. Immediately after being placed on her bed, Jody had regained consciousness long enough to speak a few words to her father.

"Curly ... never done nothin'," she had whispered, "tried to make 'em stop. He ... Curly never—" With those words, she once again lapsed into unconsciousness. Ab knew of only one person who answered to the nickname of Curly: Adderly's teenaged son. Ab passed that information to Sheriff Willow, who immediately headed for Adderly's ranch. Faced with the sheriff's piercing eyes and demanding questions, the boy broke down quickly.

"I didn't have nothin' to do with it," he said, "nothin' a-tall."

"The young lady talked some before she died," the sheriff said, "and she partially cleared you. But you ain't out of the woods yet, not till you do some talking. I want to hear the whole story. All of it!" The boy raised his eyes questioningly to his father, who stood beside the sheriff. Tom Adderly nodded, signaling his son to cooperate.

"We'd been ridin' around all day, drinkin'," Curly began, "me, Big Jim Cates, Lot Cameron an' Ben Taggard. Didn't drink much myself, 'cause I didn't have no whiskey of my own. They all had bottles, an' ever' one of 'em was drunk.

"Big Jim was the one jerked her outta the saddle. Then he took off her clothes an' held her down while Lot Cameron done it to her. Then Big Jim, then Taggard. All three of 'em done it.

"I begged 'em to leave her alone, but they jist laughed at me, told me to mind my own business. Ben Taggard was the last one done it. Then he started hittin' her in the head with a rock." The boy fidgeted and quickly wiped away a tear.

"I grabbed Ben's arm to try to make him quit, but Big Jim shoved me down. When I saw the blood on her face, I got sick to my stomach and lit outta there for home.

"They'd sobered up some by the time they come into the bunkhouse a few hours later. Ben said they was leavin' the country. Said if I knowed what was good for me I'd keep my mouth shet about what happened." Covering his face with his hands, the youngster lowered his head and began to weep.

Sheriff Willow laid his hand on the boy's shoulder. "You did the right thing by telling, son, and I believe your story. The girl said enough to convince me that you played no part in the attack. Just one more question: did any of them mention where they might be going?"

"No, sir. Didn't say no more'n I done said."

Tom Adderly followed the lawman to the yard and stood beside the horse as Willow mounted.

"Don't know how to tell you how bad I feel about all this, Sheriff, and I'm hoping you'll tell that to Ab and Dory."

"Sure will, Tom. Ab and me both have known you for more than twenty years. Nobody's gonna blame you."

Sheriff Willow related Curly Adderly's story to the Stewarts in Jake's presence, making no effort to hide the gruesome details. Afterward, he called Gannon aside.

"I know your reputation well enough to know that you're not gonna hold still for all this, Mister Gannon. All I ask is that you give me time to do my job, with no interference."

"How long?" Jake asked.

"A month," Willow answered.

"One month." Gannon walked away.

Knowing full well that the men had long since fled the

sheriff's jurisdiction, Jake rode by the Adderly ranch before heading to Cottonwood. The kid talked to him freely, adding a few minor details as Gannon continued the interrogation. Jake knew that most ranch hands did not own a horse, usually riding animals that belonged to their employer. He spoke with Tom Adderly. "Can you tell me something about their horses?"

"Cates has his own horse, a big roan with three stockings. Cameron and Taggard each took one of mine, both of them blacks with no particular markings. You shouldn't have any trouble spotting my Rocking TA brand on their hips, though."

"Can you give me a good description of the men?"

"Sure can, but my wife can do better than that. She's an exceptional artist, Mister Gannon. I'd say that she can draw pictures good enough for you to recognize any of them."

Jake waited. And waited. The lady took the entire afternoon with the drawings. When she laid them in his hand he was astounded at the quality—almost as clear as photographs. On separate sheets of paper she had created three characters that Gannon would recognize anywhere. He stared at the drawings, deciding that he had never seen any of the men.

"These are very good, Mrs. Adderly," he said, "the best drawings I've ever seen. I appreciate your hard work."

"Weren't no hard work to it," she said. "That's the way they look. I've had 'em all at my dinner table plenty of times."

Several times during the ride home, Jake took the lady's drawings from his pocket and studied them carefully. He had no doubt of their accuracy; he had known a few other artists in his time, and knew that they simply "saw" more than most people, and paid closer attention to detail. Mrs. Adderly had written the color of hair and eyes above each man's picture, and even mentioned the few freckles across Cameron's nose.

At Cottonwood, after being told of the ghastly event, Barnes and Mellon went about their ranch duties, correctly assuming that Jake should be left alone in his grief. Neither man spoke of the incident unless it was first mentioned by Gannon. Though Jake knew that nothing good could come of it, he found it impossible not to feel sorry for himself. He had known what seemed like more than his share of grief, most of it not of his own making. First, he had lost his father. Then only a few years later, his loving mother had been taken at a young age. Then when Josh came along, Jake had family again. But it was not to be. Josh was also dead. Now Jody. The woman who would have borne his children. This morning the thought crossed his mind that Jody might have been carrying his child when she died.

Gannon held no hope that Sheriff Willow would find her assailants; the lawman's jurisdiction was simply too limiting. A good horse could carry a man well out of a sheriff's reach within hours. And the U.S. marshals, who could cross county and state lines at will, were few in number, and already overloaded with cases. Policing the vast area of Texas was impossible. Even the U.S. Army was unsuccessful most of the time. Gannon had already accepted the fact that the task of tracking down Jody's killers would fall to him alone.

During the next three weeks he seldom left the house. When Mellon rode in before sundown and saw him sitting on the river bank with a fishing pole in his hand, he took it as a good sign. Perhaps Jake was coming around.

A few days later, Gannon delivered a "to-whom-it-may concern" letter to his attorney. He intended that the letter, written in his own hand on a single sheet of paper, should serve as his last will and testament. The document stated that in the event of Gannon's death, everything he owned should go to Mickey Barnes and Bake Mellon as equal partners.

"Is that good enough?" Jake asked, when Page had read the letter.

"I would have worded it differently," the attorney said, sealing the envelope and writing Jake's name on the outside, "but this letter will stand up in any court in the land. Do you expect to be living more dangerously than usual?"

"Maybe," Jake said. Then he walked out of the office and down the stairway.

Tomorrow would be one month since Jody's death, and today Gannon was back in Groesbeck. Stopping at the sheriff's office, he learned that the lawman had no leads as to the whereabouts of the killers. However, he did have a little more information on them.

Through Sheriff Bain, in Tarrant County, Willow had learned that both Cameron and Taggard were natives of Fort Worth, though there was no evidence that they had known each other prior to being employed by the Adderly ranch.

Lot Cameron was a twenty-four-year-old, blond-haired man of medium height and weight, who was said to be exceptionally fast with a six-gun. Sheriff Bain had described him as a conscienceless killer who in recent years had gunned down two men in Tarrant County, each time claiming self-defence. Cameron's crooked face, with a long chin that leaned toward the right side, would make him easy to recognize.

Less was known of Ben Taggard, though Sheriff Bain did ascertain that he was a six-foot, two-hundred-pound brawler who seemed never to lose a fight. That fact could be attested to by several men who walked around Fort Worth with faces that had been scarred by Taggard's knuckles and boot heels. One bartender stated that the man had picked fights in his place at least a dozen times. Taggard had green eyes, coal-black hair, and was missing one front tooth. Perhaps some man had gotten in a lucky punch.

Gannon spent the afternoon on the Adderly ranch, talking with the hands and asking them to relive any past conversations with the killers. He learned that Big Jim Cates was from somewhere in New Mexico Territory. A rider remembered that Cates had once received a letter from a brother in Santa Fe. Big Jim had said that his brother was a bootmaker.

A bootmaker named Cates! The prosperity of such a man would depend entirely upon the fact that he was well known and easy to find. Gannon quickly decided to begin his search in Santa Fe. After spending the night with the Stewarts, he headed west at daybreak, riding the gray and leading a small black pack horse.

It was nearing noon when Jake stepped from the train in Santa Fe a few days later. Wishing to attract as little attention as possible, he turned his horses over to a liveryman who solicited business at the depot. Then, turning up his coat collar against the cold wind, he headed down the street to a hotel, where he signed "Jake Payne" to the register. A short while later he found a small adobe building that sported a restaurant sign, where he seated himself at a table and ordered beefsteak.

Back on the street, he did not have to look far to find the bootmaker. Across the street and a few doors down, a wooden shingle proclaimed CATES' BOOT SHOP AND LEATHER GOODS—WILL CATES, PROPRIETOR. Gannon entered the building, where a large, middle-aged man sat behind an oaken bench, trimming leather. Laying his cutting tool aside, the man rose to his feet, offering a handshake across the counter.

"Howdy," he said, "I'm Will Cates. Is there something I can do for you?"

"My name's Jake Payne," Gannon said, grasping the callused hand. "I'm looking for Jim Cates, and I was told that you might be his brother."

"Yes, I am," Cates said, returning to his seat. "Sometimes regrettably so. What's he been into this time?"

"My business with him is a personal matter. I was hoping you might be able to tell me where to find him."

"Lord, no. Ain't' no love lost 'tween me and him, and I suppose I'd be the last person he'd contact. It's been more'n two years since he was here, talked me into signing a note for a horse he wanted to buy. He rode off on that roan, and of course I had to pay for it. Last I heard he was down in central Texas. I wrote him about a year ago but he didn't send any money, didn't even answer my letter. A few days after he left I learned that he'd tried to bed my wife while I was down here at the shop trying to make a living. No, sir, I don't want to ever see him again, 'cause I'd hate to have to shoot my own brother. I just might do it, too."

"Yes, sir," Jake said, turning to leave the building, "it sounds as if he'd do well to stay clear of you."

Moments later, Gannon took a seat on a bench in front of a dry goods store to reflect upon his verbal exchange with the bootmaker. A man who would participate in the rape and murder of a young girl would most certainly not be above making a play for his own brother's wife, but Jake found it odd that Will Cates would be so willing to discuss the matter with a complete stranger. Had he told the truth? Or was he merely a good liar? Jake decided to assume that the man had been lying, for he had simply been too open, and had volunteered too much information. The next time Cates left his shop he would have a shadow.

In the saloon, Jake bought a beer and took a seat at a

window, where he had a good view of Cates' establishment across the street. He had been watching for half an hour when the CLOSED sign appeared in the shop's window. Much too early in the day for a man to be closing his business, Jake thought. He would wait for Cates to leave the building, then follow. If the man took a horse from the livery, Jake would get his own mount and continue the surveillance.

Quite some time passed before it became obvious that Cates would not be coming through the front door. He had already gone out the back. "Damn," Jake muttered when the realization hit him. He hurried down the alley to the rear of the shop.

A stunted mesquite tree whose canopy provided some shade stood a few yards from the building. The scarred earth and animal droppings showed that the tree was being used as a hitching post. The fresh earth that had been kicked up meant that a horse had very recently left the tree in a hurry. "Damn," Gannon repeated.

The tracks led northeast, toward the Sangre De Christo Mountains. Jake headed for the stable and his own animal. During a short conversation with the liveryman, he learned that Cates lived in town, only a short distance from his shop, and seldom rode a horse.

"Ain't seen Will on a horse in God knows when," the hostler said, chuckling. "That little ol' mare he's got ain't nothin' a knowin' man would want to ride, nohow. I notice that he's been keepin' her up behind his shop lately, but I shore ain't seen 'im in the saddle. Jist leads her up there ever' mornin' with the stirrups danglin'.'"

Within minutes, Jake was headed east with his bedroll tied behind his saddle. Tracking the mare across the barren desert was easy, and Gannon moved along at a slow canter. As he neared the mountains, however, the terrain changed. Huge boulders and arroyos dotted the landscape and the earth supported more vegetation, making the tracking job more difficult.

Just before dark, he turned off the trail and rode a quarter mile into the trees. He unsaddled and picketed his horse on the sparse grass. Taking his bedroll, he returned to a spot near Cates' trail, where he was sure to hear any passing traffic. There he made his bed beside a fallen tree. Wherever Cates had gone, Jake felt sure that he would return by this same route. Moving his own horse well off the trail had been deliberate; he was taking no chances that a whinny by his animal might betray his presence if another horse came along.

The night was moonless, though the sea of stars overhead provided enough light for Jake to make out some of the objects around him. Several times he drifted off to sleep, only to have his own shivering wake him. Though he had two blankets, his bedding was inadequate for these mountains at this time of year. He vowed that tomorrow night he would have his pack horse, and the tarp the animal always carried.

It was past midnight when he heard the muffled sound of a horse moving at a fast walk. Lying still, he had only to turn his head slightly to watch the horse and rider pass within several yards of his bed. When the rider put his horse to a canter in the direction of town, Gannon was out of his bed immediately, scratching around for wood to build a fire. For the first time since sunset, he was soon warm and comfortable.

Though Jake had been unable to make a positive identification, he felt reasonably sure that the man who had just passed his hiding place was none other than Will Cates. He extinguished his fire and was soon headed for town at a fast clip. At the livery, he lighted a lantern and walked to the rear of the building, where Cates' mare stood munching hay. The animal had been ridden hard, and the hair on her back and sides was still damp. Gannon had his answer. After currying both the mare and his own mount, he headed for his hotel room and a warm bed.

Sunup found him back at the livery, where he saddled the gray and rigged his pack horse. The animal carried enough food and water to allow him to move almost continually, if the need should arise. And he would not sleep cold tonight; the pack horse carried a tarp and another blanket. Telling the hostler that he was headed for Texas, Jake rode south till he was out of sight, then turned northeast. He had lied to the man out of necessity, for hostlers were usually a ready source of information for anyone who would ask.

A two-hour ride brought him to the same log by which he had slept last night. Now, during daylight, he could read the tracks without dismounting. The small imprints in the sand had indeed been made by Cates' mare.

Will Cates had lied to him. The man had made a late-night ride, and according to the hostler, that would have been rare. Gannon was convinced that wherever the ride had taken Cates, its sole purpose was to pass word to his brother that questions were being asked. Jake had no quarrel with Will Cates—a man would naturally try to shield his brother.

How far had the bootmaker ridden last night? Jake had no way of knowing, for he could not even guess how long the man might have stayed out of the saddle once he reached his destination. Had he visited his brother personally? Passed the word to someone else? Was Big Jim Cates within seeing distance of Jake at this very moment? Or shooting distance? Gannon would have the answers in time, but he'd have given a pretty price to know just now.

Deciding that his present position might be precarious, Jake rode into the trees. He knew that few men would ride through the woods at night when they had a choice, and

Will Cates was no exception. The bootmaker's trail led in a northerly direction, parallel to the timber. As he rode through the trees, Jake could easily see the mare's tracks off to his left.

After an hour he stopped his horses. Up ahead he could see that the mare had taken an abrupt right turn into the woods. He quickly dismounted and stood listening for a long while. Hearing nothing, he tied his pack animal to a bush in a well-concealed area. Remounting, he rode east, deeper into the timber. He knew that Will Cates would not have ridden into the forest at night unless it had been absolutely necessary. So Jake might be near his quarry.

He rode east for several minutes, then made a wide circle to the north. When he turned back west after a time, he had made what amounted to a horseshoe maneuver. Though the gray moved through the woods as quietly as could be expected of a horse, after a while Jake began to feel like a sitting duck. He dismounted and tied the animal to a tree limb, then continued on foot.

Moving from tree to tree, much as he had stalked wild game, he had traveled only a short distance when his foot became entangled in some vines. As he bent to free his boot, something hissed past his shoulder. He was instantly flat on his stomach, aware that he was being fired upon, even before he heard the report of the heavy-caliber rifle.

He quickly hauled himself behind the large tree, where he quietly stood peering around for any sign of movement. He saw nothing stirring. The shot had come from some place directly ahead. He gauged the distance to be about three hundred yards. He must somehow circle his assailant and approach him from a different direction, for moving straight ahead was out of the question.

Back on his stomach, he crawled in the direction from which he had come, backtracking to a large stand of timber. He moved north for a while, then ran west for several hundred yards. When he was sure that he had passed the location from which the shot had come, he stopped behind a tree to regulate his breathing. Then he turned southeast and began to close the circle. With his reflexes attuned to the normal sounds of the forest, and his eyes alert for any kind of movement, he crept along at a snail's pace.

He moved as silently as a breeze, an action that was easier for him than for many men because he wore no spurs. Using the skillful stealth that had often brought him face to face with everything from bears to bobcats, he continued his stalk.

The rear of the cabin appeared abruptly. Had it not been for the straight line of vines clinging to the wall, Jake might have missed it. He eased himself along the west wall to the front of the small building.

There, lying in the yard behind a log, the barrel of his Spencer pointed east, was one Big Jim Cates.

Gannon stared at the man's back for a moment, then spoke. "Expecting company, Cates?"

The big man stiffened. Then, laying the rifle on the ground, he climbed to his feet and turned around to face the Peacemaker Jake held in his hand. Cates was big, all right, and much taller than Gannon had expected. He was dressed in overalls, flannel shirt and short jacket, with a six-gun strapped around his middle.

"I guess you'd be Gannon," he said.

Jake nodded curtly. "Where are Taggard and Cameron?"

"Texas, I guess, that's where I left them."

"What part of Texas?"

"I don't know, we separated in the desert. They went south and I went north."

Gannon stood motionless for a long time. Dancing before his eyes was a clear picture of Jody lying on her death bed—the red and purple face, swollen lips and blood-soaked eyebrows.

Then Cates was speaking again. "I didn't have nothin' to do with beatin' that girl up, now. That was all Taggard's idea, and I tried to make 'im stop. I've heard enough about you to know that I don't want to git in no gunfight with you." Cates unbuckled his gunbelt and let it fall to the ground. "Unless I'm wrong," he said, "you wouldn't shoot a man that wasn't tryin' to draw on you."

All of this from a man who only minutes ago had tried to kill Gannon from ambush. Jake was surprised at the big man's whimpering.

"You've been wrong about a lot of things lately, Cates," he said. "You were wrong when you jerked Jody Stewart from the saddle and raped her, and you were wrong when you stood by laughing while Ben Taggard beat her to death." His cocked Peacemaker was still trained on the space between Cates' eyes. The picture of Jody dying in front of her weeping mother passed through Jake's mind again. "And you're wrong about me." He squeezed the trigger.

Fourteen

An hour before sunset, Gannon stepped aboard the eastbound train, intending to ride as far as Rocky Flat. Only moments ago he had opened the door of Will Cates' boot shop and shouted to the man, "You'd better take another ride out to the cabin and see about your brother!"

Taking his seat in the passenger car, Jake was once again reminded that the Western movement was in full swing. The train that brought him to Santa Fe had been filled to its capacity. Now, headed east, only four passengers were aboard. A middle-aged couple sat in the rear of the car, sharing some reading material and laughing occasionally. About midway and on the opposite side, a man lay across both seats with his feet hanging into the aisle. Though one arm shaded his eyes and hid most of his face, he appeared to be about Gannon's own age, dressed expensively with a large leather briefcase in his lap. The man was no different from dozens of other whiskey drummers Jake had seen.

With few passengers, the conductor had little to do, and the train was underway quickly. Jake would ride the car all night, grabbing what sleep he could. Tomorrow, when the train stopped at Rocky Flat, he would unload his horses and begin the long ride south to western Texas. He had no specific destination in mind. He would simply wander along asking questions till he encountered a clue to the whereabouts of Taggard or Cameron.

Though he had never done it for personal gain, Gannon was an excellent manhunter. He had once tracked down a cattle thief that Cap McGill's hired range detectives had failed to find. And a few years ago he had rescued a lost six-year-old boy in the Big Ben country after other searchers had given up the hunt. A family had been camping near the Chisos Mountains when the youngest member disappeared. Gannon happened by four days later, and was dismayed that the searchers had already given up hope. Several men on horseback had scoured the mountains and desert landscape for three days before reaching the decision that a cat had gotten the boy and dragged him off to its den.

The West Texas heat was almost unbearable, and Jake knew that if the boy had braved the mountains or the desert, he was indeed dead. He concentrated his search along the Rio Grande, and the following day, he found the youngster sleeping in some bushes beside the river. He was tired, scared and hungry, but very much alive. When offered a reward by the boy's father, Jake declined, for the man appeared to be no better off than himself.

Gannon had no doubt that he would be successful on his current mission. Men such as Taggard and Cameron were seldom steady workers. They usually took the highroad, leaving a trail that could be followed with little difficulty. Inevitably, men on the run would eventually say or do something to attract attention, and people would remember, if the right questions were asked. Getting information out of almost anyone was a simple matter if a man went about it correctly, and Jake had long ago learned to think before speaking—a quiet man heard more.

The sun became a gigantic orange ball above the western horizon. Gannon stood on the platform at the rear of the car, watching the town of Santa Fe fade from view. He was soon joined by the young man who had been sleeping across the seats.

"My name's Dewey East," he said, offering a handshake, "originally from Fort Worth." They became engaged in conversation, and, as Jake had suspected, East was a whiskey salesman who represented a distillery in Frankfort, Kentucky.

"I must have tried everything in Fort Worth before I fell into this easy job," the drummer said. He had barely spoken of Fort Worth when Gannon handed him the drawings Mrs. Adderly had made. East studied the pictures in the fading light.

"That looks like Ben Taggard," he said, tapping one of the drawings with a forefinger. "I grew up with him."

"Have you seen him lately?"

"Nope. Last I heard he was in jail in San Antonio for killing somebody. I guess that's been four or five years."

They stood quietly for a while, listening to the wheels clacking over the joints of the rails. Declining the drink he was offered, Jake renewed the Taggard conversation.

"You growing up with Ben, and being friends, I was hoping you might be able to tell me where to find him."

"I didn't say I was a friend, mister. The fact is, I hated his guts, like most everybody else who knew him."

"Why didn't anybody like him?"

"Because he was a damn bully and a deadbeat, owed money to everybody around him. People were afraid to refuse when he asked for a loan. Then if somebody asked for the money that was owed, he'd beat the hell out of them." East took a drink from his bottle, then leaned over the rail and vomited. Obviously a man who consumed too much of his own product, he continued to heave long after he had purged the contents of his stomach. Then, just as suddenly as the siege had begun, it was gone. Wiping his mouth on his sleeve, he turned to face Gannon.

"Gets mighty hard to keep one down sometimes," he said, opening his bottle and replacing the lost drink with another. Jake nodded sympathetically, saying nothing. He wanted to hear more about Taggard as soon as East felt like talking. After hitting the bottle a third time, the drummer's face came to life, as if he might survive. A moment later, he spoke with a steady voice.

"I have no idea why you're hunting Taggard, but if you plan on doing something unpleasant to him, you're gonna have your hands full. That no-good bastard is tough. All the way through school and even after he was grown, I've never known anybody to go up against him that came out a winner. He's cold-blooded, and there's nothing he won't do to win a fight. He loves it!"

The salesman's description of Taggard matched with the one Sheriff Bain had provided. Taggard was undoubtedly a tough customer. Standing on the platform with one hand on the shaky guardrail, Gannon was hoping that soon he would have a chance to find out just how tough. East began talking again.

"There were four of them Taggard kids, two boys and two girls. Ben's brother got killed cleaning a loaded gun when he was about twelve. Their daddy said the accident happened to the wrong son, and most folks agreed with him.

"I reckon both of the girls turned out all right. They were pretty, but all the boys left them alone on account of Ben. Sally and Eunice were their names. Sally was the oldest and prettiest. She was courted by a man named Frank Duncan after Ben left home. I heard later that she married Frank.

"Anyway, Mister Gannon, you don't look to me like a man who'd be hunting Taggard just to say hello. If you get in a tussle with him don't let him get the upper hand, because he's an animal." Taking another sip from his bottle, East said good night and walked back inside the car.

Jake stayed on the platform for a while, staring into the blackness of the cold night, his mind on Ben Taggard. Now he had a starting place, and some names. The conversation with Dewey East had provided him with an excuse to avoid the grueling ride across western Texas. He would pay the additional fare and ride the train to Bald Rock Station, then head directly south to Fort Worth.

The winter's first snowstorm forced him to halt at a small community in North Texas called Coyote Springs. All morning he had ridden in the cold wind, and a few hours ago it had started to snow. Bent forward in the saddle with the brim of his hat down to his eyes, coaxing horses that showed no inclination to continue fighting wind-driven snowflakes, he had almost missed the tiny settlement. With visibility no more than ten yards, he was searching for any kind of shelter when he spotted a large, snow-covered pile of wood. A few more steps carried him past a small building that sheltered him from the wind. Now he could see that he had entered what might be called a town, a fact that did not go unnoticed by his horses. Both animals whinnied, sensing that they might soon be in dry stalls with plenty of grain to eat.

The snow let up enough to see that a few scattered

buildings stood along either side of the street, which was about as wide as it was long. Only one building showed light through its windows, and Jake correctly assumed that it was a saloon. He tied his horses to the hitching rail and stepped onto the plank sidewalk. A short wispy-haired man opened the door from the inside, attracted by the sound of Gannon stamping snow from his boots.

"Howdy," the man said, his peg leg striking the floor noisily as he stepped aside. "Welcome back to Ki-yoty Sprangs."

Back to Coyote Springs? Jake had never been anywhere near the town before, but assumed that the man had merely mistaken him for somebody else. Nodding, Gannon entered the establishment, which was much smaller than most saloons. A potbellied stove stood in the center, around which sat a handful of men.

Still standing near the doorway, he asked of no one in particular, "Is there someplace I can put up my horses?"

"Shore is," an old man said, making no effort to get to his feet. "Stable's at the end of the street. You'll find grain, hay and water easy enough."

The spacious livery stable appeared to be the best and newest building in town. A large corral encompassing at least half an acre stood at its rear, where several horses stood voluntarily braving the elements. Jake enclosed his own animals in stalls, and fed them generously.

Back in the saloon, he was served a bottle of whiskey by the peg-legged one.

"Guess you remember me," the man said, "ol' Pegleg Hines at your service."

Jake shook his head. "Nope." Hines moved to the opposite end of the bar when Gannon made no effort to continue the conversation.

As if on cue, talk had ceased throughout the room when Gannon took his seat. Gradually, the men began to communicate in muted tones, barely above a whisper. That Jake himself was the topic, he had no doubt. More than an hour passed, with Gannon sitting quietly at the bar, sipping his whiskey. At last the old man who had directed him to the stable appeared at his side.

"Gotta ask you to pay for your horses' keep in advance," he said, a hint of a smile parting his lips on uneven, badly stained teeth. "Be a dollar a day for two." Gannon pushed the money down the bar to the man, who immediately summoned the bartender.

"A little dram here, Peg," he said, holding up two fingers to signify a double. "Make it a good one." Holding the glass in both hands, the old-timer stared into the brown liquid for a while, then began to drink slowly, passing his tongue over his lips several times after each sip as if to savor the taste of the rotgut to its fullest. After a few minutes, he spoke to Gannon again.

"Don't reckon you'll do as good as you did the last time you wuz here, money's awful tight."

"Would you care to explain just what you're talking about?" Jake asked.

The liveryman took another sip from his glass. "You mean you don't remember riding off with half the money in this town two years ago? Ain't you a feller named Reenow, who just happens to always be holding the winning poker hand?" The old man drained his glass and sat with his mouth open, awaiting a response.

"No," Jake answered, pouring himself a drink and pushing the bottle toward the hostler. "My name is Gannon, and I don't play poker. Josh Reenow was my identical twin. He's dead, now."

"You hear that, fellers?" the old man asked loudly, jumping from his stool and facing the barroom patrons. "This man says he ain't Reenow a-tall. Says Reenow's dead. Claims he's a twin brother of the gambler." The noise level rose considerably throughout the room as the men began talking animatedly, each explaining to another why he did or did not believe Gannon's story. The old liveryman himself was skeptical.

"Why is it, then," he asked, turning to face Jake, "that you go by the name of Gannon and him by Reenow?"

"It's a long story," Jake said, "brought on by circumstances that neither of us could control. I don't intend to go into it."

"Nobody expects you to go into it!" a large man barked, pounding on the bar to gain everyone's attention. "I heerd about it more'n a month ago from a feller passing through. Josh Reenow was killed from ambush by a no-good lawman down in Waco. Less than forty-eight hours later that same marshal and his deputy wuz planted by Reenow's twin brother, a man that goes by the name of Gannon." Then, speaking to Jake, he asked, "Are you that same Gannon, mister?"

"I am."

"Then, bygod that settles it," Hines said. Opening a new bottle of whiskey, he yelled, "Belly up, fellers, dranks on the house!" The men rushed the bar, all of them reaching for the bottle at once.

"Take your time, men," Pegleg said. "The place ain't on fire. Jist one drank apiece, now." Catching Peg's eye, Gannon pushed money across the bar and pointed toward the cupboard, gesturing that the drinkers should be served an additional bottle. Hines was quick to comply.

"Older whiskey, fellers," he called, "Mister Gannon's bought you a bottle of the good stuff." To a man, the drinkers lifted their glasses into the air, saluting Jake's generosity. After a while, talk flowed freely around the room, no longer muted. Shortly, an old-timer who introduced himself as Ezell sidled up to Jake and thanked him for the bottle. Gannon poured the man another drink.

"That brother of yours was something else, Mister Gannon," Ezell said. "Stayed in town for three days. I watched that poker game myself, for the most part. Didn't have the money to take part, not for the kinda stakes they played. For two days they played right over there in that corner, didn't stop for nothing but to take a piss or maybe eat a bite.

"It was amazing how Reenow always lost the little pots and won the big ones. Ever'body in town thought he was cheating, and it was true that he had hands big enough to palm two decks of cards if he'd been of a mind to.

"The last hand told the story, and that story was that he wasn't cheating at all, he was just too damn good for folks around here. Yessir, that man knew exactly when to bet his money. On that last hand of draw he bluffed out two players who were holding better cards. Old Clint Haley threw in a pair of aces, and Harvey White folded two small pairs after Reenow bet 'em an arm and a leg."

"You mean Josh didn't have a good hand?"

"I mean Josh didn't have a damn thing, no pair at all. I turned his cards over and looked at 'em after the game broke up. Highest card in Reenow's hand was a damn jack. Talk about some embarrassed gamblers! Embarrassed and broke, too."

Jake was pleased to hear that his brother had not been a thief at all, but simply a good poker player. Relief swept over him. Josh had not been a cardsharp. A cardsharp would never put himself in a position to lose a large pot simply because someone had guts enough to call his bet, as Josh had done. A cardsharp would steal enough high-ranking cards to win the pot in a showdown. Smiling, pleased, Jake poured another drink for Ezell.

Gannon sat in the saloon throughout the afternoon, periodically checking the weather outside. By dark, the snowflakes had ceased to fall. But the wind had picked up—cold enough to chill a man to his bones in minutes. Strong enough to stop him in his tracks.

Holding his hat in his hand, the wind whipping at his clothes, Jake stood on the boardwalk listening to the gusts rattling loose boards on the shabby buildings. A large sheet of tin tumbled down the street end over end. There would be no traveling for him this night, he decided.

Close to midnight, after all of the drinkers had staggered to their places or residence, Gannon returned to the livery stable. The old hostler had given him permission to sleep there. Wrapping up in his blanket and covering himself with hay, he was soon comfortable. Even the sound made by the stable's resident rats was friendly. He listened to the howling wind outside. He had stumbled on to Coyote Springs through blind luck, and could just as easily have been stranded in a blizzard with two balky horses. Listening to the rats scampering around gnawing on the grain that was wasted by the horses, he soon relaxed completely, and slept soundly.

He was awakened after sunup by the hostler. The new day had brought a welcome change in the weather. The blizzard had blown itself out, and the ankle-deep snow was already beginning to melt in the morning sun.

"Don't go running off nowhere, now," the liveryman said from the small room that served as an office. "I'm gonna be cooking bacon and gravy purty soon."

Jake was hungry, and assured the man that he would remain close by. From the barnyard he had a view of the whole town, but could see no place of business that looked as if it might return a living wage for its owner. In fact, he could see no reason for the town's existence, and said so to the hostler at breakfast.

Chewing on a strip of bacon and sopping gravy with a biscuit, the old-timer answered, "Well, there really ain't no reason for the town being here, 'cept it gives us all someplace to be. Pegleg was the first one here. A trail boss left him to root hog or die pore after a horse fell on his leg and it set up gangrene. They cut the leg off, then gave him some supplies and left him here at the sprang. They took the herd on north, not giving a damn whether Hines made it or not.

"Well, he made it. Made hisself a peg leg and lived off of the land, which was mighty easy to do. That sprang puts out the best tasting water in Texas, and all the animals know it. All a feller had to do back then was sit down and wait on the game to come to him. Of course, it ain't all that easy now. People shot too many animals close to the sprang. 'Fore long all the game figgered out that it weren't no healthy place to drank."

"How many people are here?" Gannon asked. "What do they do for a living?"

"Usually about twenty, and they don't do nothing for a living. Several of 'em seemed to have a good deal of money put by, and I don't doubt that the law was looking for some of 'em. It could be that a few of 'em's got relatives that pay 'em not to come home." Pausing to chuckle at his own wit, the old man failed to mention which of the categories he himself fell into. "Anyway," he continued, "there's always a little money around, even though it's tightened up lately. Yore brother took a good-sized bundle out of town with him."

When they had finished breakfast, the old-timer pointed out a small can on the desk and informed Gannon that folks who ate usually contributed some money for food supplies. Jake gratefully dropped in a few coins, then bought a sack of shelled corn from the man. A short time later, he rode to the end of the street and turned south.

Fifteen

Fort Worth grew from a military camp established by General Winfield Scott at the close of the Mexican War, and was named for General William Jenkins Worth. Forty-two men of Company F, Second Dragoons, set up the camp on June 6, 1849. A year later, a stage line from Fort Worth to Yuma, Arizona, was introduced. The town was named seat of Tarrant County in 1860. Shortly after the Civil War it became a major shipping and supply depot for cattlemen, and its population grew rapidly.

It was past noon when Jake Gannon rode into Fort Worth and deposited his horses at the livery stable. He took a room at a shabby hotel well off the beaten path, where he was not even asked to sign the register. The beady-eyed clerk simply nodded and handed him a key when Jake paid the rent in advance.

He was back on the street at sunset, refreshed by an afternoon nap. He walked into a decent-looking restaurant and was quickly shown to a table by an aged Chinaman. The small man produced a menu, then began to scamper about the room, touching fire to the wicks of lamps. When Jake ordered the best beefsteak in the house, the Chinaman looked at him questioningly.

"Don't cook it too long," Jake said. The man nodded several times and was off to the kitchen. Half an hour later, Gannon was served the best meal he had eaten in months.

He spent the evening walking the streets, passing in and out of several saloons. He had conversations with many men, but never mentioned the names of the men he was after. He met no one who looked familiar, and at midnight he was back in his hotel room. Tomorrow, he would talk with Sheriff Bain, hoping that the lawman might have some new information. If the answer was no, Gannon would take the train to Hillsboro and ride back to Cottonwood. There his worn-out horses could rest for a while. Jake felt the urge to check on his holdings.

Talking with Bain the following morning, Gannon learned that Frank Duncan once owned a watering hole in Fort Worth, but had sold out a year ago and left the area, taking the former Sally Taggard and two small children with him. The sheriff did not know where the family had gone, but gave Jake directions to the saloon that had once been owned by Duncan, where the new owner was a man named Bill Lord.

As he walked through the batwing doors, Gannon realized that he had been in this same building last night, though he had spoken to no one. Two men stood behind the bar, and a few early drinkers were scattered around the room. He took a stool, ordered a beer, and sat quietly for some time.

Then, speaking to the bartender nearest him, he said, "I'm looking for a man named Bill Lord."

Wiping his red mustache away from his mouth with his hand, the tall, thin man moved down the bar and leaned forward. "Well, friend," he said in a deep voice, "I reckon you've found him. What can I do for you?"

At Gannon's request, the two men moved to a table, where Jake made known his interest in locating Frank Duncan. Gannon suspected that Duncan and Taggard had little in common, but if he located Frank Duncan he would have also found Taggard's sister Sally.

"I still owed Frank some money on this place when he left town," Lord said. "I done just like he told me to: sent it to the bank in Paris. That's Paris, Texas, not the French city."

"I know about where the town is," Jake said.

"Well, that's all I can tell you." Lord lifted his palms. "He surely must be living around Paris somewhere, else he wouldn't be banking there."

"Right," Gannon agreed.

Lord apologized for not being able to offer more information, then walked to his office and closed the door. Jake returned to his stool and pushed his mug across the bar to the remaining bartender, motioning for a refill. He would stay around for a while. He had a feeling that he might learn something more. He sipped the foamy brew slowly, occasionally making eye contact with the short, balding bartender, who appeared to be a little older than himself. Gannon finally broke the silence.

"Have a drink yourself," he said, pushing money across the bar. "It might help me get rid of this lonesome feeling."

The man's large red nose and heavy-lidded eyes suggested that he might be a regular drinker. He stood quietly for a while, staring at the whiskey bottles on the shelf behind him as if this might be his most important decision of the day. Then, reaching into the cupboard beneath the bar, he extracted a bottle and poured himself a hefty drink. Jake supposed that the man was drinking from his own private stock.

"Guess I could have a little eye opener," he said, taking Jake's money and inhaling the contents of the glass in one gulp. "I usually don't never take one durin' the day, but I ain't feelin' worth a shit this mornin'." He refilled his glass and returned the bottle to the cupboard.

Moments later, Bill Lord walked from his office. Bundled up against the cold morning, he informed the bartender that he would be gone for several hours. When he reached the doorway he stopped for a moment.

"Dammit, Harry," he said to the bartender, who was lifting his glass again, "be careful with that stuff. It's not even twelve o'clock, and you've already started." Then he was gone through the doorway and out onto the street.

"Bill jist don't know how it is," Harry said, pouring himself another drink. "He don't take more'n three drinks a week hisself, so he don't know what it's like to really need one."

"I know what you mean," Jake said, lifting his beer. "Some folks just don't understand fellows like you and me who need a few drinks every morning to get the day started."

"That's right," Harry said, lifting his glass. By early afternoon the bartender was well into his bottle. Though he maintained full control of his movements, his speech became accelerated and slightly slurred. The men had talked on many subjects throughout the morning, but Gannon had kept his own business to himself. Now, suggesting that Harry should have another drink, Jake steered the conversation in a new direction.

"You say you've been working here for three years,

Harry. I guess most of that time you were working for Frank Duncan, huh?"

"Yep. Frank was the best boss I ever had, knew how to leave a man alone and let him set his own pace. Never said nothin' about me havin' a drink now and then, neither. He knew I never got drunk enough to interfere with my work."

Jake watched as the man emptied his glass again. Then, deciding that now was the time to go hunting for information, he asked, "Do you know a fellow by the name of Ben Taggard?"

"As well as I want to," the barkeep said, taking another cigarette from a stack that he had rolled before starting work this morning. He touched the end with a sulphur match and blew a billow of smoke toward the ceiling. "He's Frank Duncan's brother-in-law, you know."

"Oh?"

"Yeah, and I can tell you this: Frank don't like him no better'n the rest of us do. Taggard even dislocated Frank's shoulder one night by slammin' him up against that post over yonder."

"Did Frank do any slamming of his own?"

"No. Ain't nobody gonna fight Ben Taggard. Leastways, not nobody that knows him. Best way I know to git beat to death would be takin' a poke at him. Feller'd be better off catchin' hisself a damn bear."

"A bear, huh?"

"Be about the same." Harry hustled off to the far end of the bar to serve two new customers, then delivered a bottle of whiskey to a table in the rear. When he returned, he continued the conversation.

"Frank ain't never liked Taggard," he said. "Told me once that Taggard was all the time gittin' money from Sally, who is of course Frank's wife. Now, Sally ain't got no way of makin' no money of her own, so when you git right down to it, it was all comin' right outta Frank's pocket."

"Large sums of money?"

"Depends on what you call large. Frank said he knew for sure that Sally bought two horses for Ben in jist a span of a few months. Folks say he ran the first one to death, and his good ol' sister jist bought him another one." Harry poured himself another drink, and Jake shoved payment across the bar.

"That Sally, now," Harry went on, "I tell you . . . that woman is sump'm else. I ain't never seen no man that didn't stand with his mouth open when she walked by. Ain't seen the like of her nowhere, 'cept maybe in a picture or two."

Jake had been told of Sally Taggard Duncan's beauty before and had no doubt that she was an exceptional woman, but right now his mind was on something else.

"I'd like to meet this Frank Duncan, Harry," he said. "I might have a business proposition for him."

"Lives up around Paris, as far as I know," Harry said. "That ain't near as long a ride as it used to be. A feller can take the train part of the way."

"Let's say I took that ride, Harry. You got any idea how I'd go about finding Duncan when I got there?"

"Nope. Don't know where he's livin' or what he's doin'. Somebody jist told me that he moved up there."

After receiving a detailed description of Frank Duncan, Jake said good-bye to Harry and walked out onto the street.

It was past noon the following day when he unloaded his horses from the train in Hillsboro. The train ride had been comfortable and scenic. He sat at a window, marveling at the speed with which a man could get from place to place in this modern age. Even when the great steam engine was fighting an uphill battle with the heavily loaded cars, the train moved at a greater speed than any other mode of transportation. On a downhill run it easily surpassed the top speed of a good saddle horse. The ingenuity and perseverance of the railroad builders had now made it possible for a man to sit in a warm car, sipping hot coffee, while effortlessly gliding over swollen streams and rivers that only a short time ago would have been considered impassable. Remarkable indeed.

He loaded the back of his pack animal and cinched the saddle down on the gray. He heard a familiar voice behind him.

"Hello, stranger."

Jake turned to see Bake Mellon standing thirty feet away, a big smile on his face. Gannon covered the distance quickly.

"Good to see you, Bake," he said, grasping Mellon's hand. "How are you? How are things at Cottonwood?"

"Great, Jake. That's the answer to both questions."

"Mickey with you?"

"No. He refuses to come to Hillsboro since he got into that shooting scrape over here. I just came in to get a few things, saw you get off the train from over at the feed store."

Gannon followed Mellon down and across the street, where the team was tied at the store's hitching rail. He tied his own horses to the rear of the wagon and climbed to its seat.

"You got everything you need, Bake?" he asked.

"I thought I did, but now I've got to go get a bottle of whiskey."

As they neared Cottonwood, Jake could see that the entire area had been fenced with barbed wire. At the road stood a gate made of peeled poles, and posts had been sunk into the ground in a fashion that allowed foot traffic to pass without opening the gate: a series of parallel posts a little less than two feet apart had been arranged to make a chutelike formation, with another post at the end. All a man on foot had to do was walk into the chute and make a quick turn around the post to the other side. The posts were too close together for a cow or a horse to make the turn. Gannon jumped to the ground and swung the gate open wide.

When he rejoined Mellon on the wagon, he said, "I guess you're gonna change the hinges on the gate."

"Uh-huh. The leather's just temporary. I've got metal hinges right here in the wagon. Ten gates on this property, Jake. The fence shouldn't be a problem for anyone passing through."

"I hope people read that sign asking them to keep the gate closed."

"Mickey might shoot somebody if they don't," Mellon said, whipping the horses to a trot. "That little fellow loves this place. I think he's given names to about half of the cattle."

Gannon chuckled.

"Mickey's the hardest worker I've ever known," Mellon continued. "He's not getting the proper rest, and it's gonna age him before his time. Maybe you could convince him that there occasionally comes a time when there simply isn't anything that needs doing. A man should take it easy and rest up for when he's got to hit it hard."

"I'll see," Gannon said.

Though he knew that Jake had been on a manhunt, Mellon did not mention the subject, perhaps knowing that Barnes would. Mickey would ask, and would want to hear all the details.

At the ranch house, Gannon filled the men in on the outcome of his trip to Santa Fe.

Barnes said, "Ab Stewart sent a man over last week to

check on you. We couldn't give him any news, 'cause we didn't even know where you went."

"Did the man mention any new information that Sheriff Willow might have on Taggard or Cameron?"

"No."

"Well, I've got another trip to make after I rest up a while, then I'll ride over and visit with the Stewarts."

Jake stayed on the ranch for nearly a month, then grew restless, unable to keep his mind on anything other than Taggard and Cameron. Even his fishing line was unproductive; the water was very cold, and the fish had gone deep.

Each night, he lay in his bed thinking of Jody, and how things might have been. She would have been lying beside him now, perhaps with a child on the way. The idea that Taggard and Cameron might be partying somewhere while Jody lay in the cold ground was almost more than he could bear. Tomorrow, he would begin the hunt again, and he would not stop until he found them.

Sixteen

On the tenth day of January, Gannon stepped from the T & NO train in Richardson, a settlement that had originally been called Breckenridge. When the railroad was built through the area in 1872, the town rapidly expanded around the station, and was renamed for a railroad official.

Jake intended to spend the night here, then tomorrow he would head for Paris on horseback. Coming off a month's rest, both he and his horses were in top shape for traveling. He stabled his animals, found a hotel room, then went looking. Hanging out in saloons was not one of Jake's favorite things to do. But evidently Ben Taggard spent a lot of time in such places. Throughout the afternoon and early evening Jake systematically visited the town's watering holes, subtly asking questions. He bought a beer at every stop, usually leaving it on the bar untouched.

He worked his way up one side of the street and down the other. He had come almost back to the hotel when he struck what might be pay dirt. At a small, run-down saloon with a sawdust floor that reeked of sour tobacco juice, he leaned against the bar and questioned the bartender.

"Sure, I know Taggard," the young man said, appearing to be no older than his late teens. "Haven't seen him in a couple weeks, though."

A couple weeks! Disregarding the foul odor, Jake ordered a beer. "You sure it hasn't been longer than two weeks since you saw him?"

"Well, yes, I'm sure," the barkeep said, playfully tossing his sponge into the air and catching it. Counting on his fingers, he added, "Come to think of it, it ain't been that long. I saw him a week ago last Monday." When Gannon offered to buy him a drink, the youngster declined, saying that he did not drink alcohol and never intended to. "That stuff is made to sell, not drink," he said.

The conversation lasted an hour, but Jake learned little more. The bartender remembered that when he asked Taggard where he was living, the man had answered, "Here and there." Taggard, the youngster said, was not the type of man you pressed for details.

At the hotel, Jake lay on his bed, contemplating his choices. Taggard had been seen right here in Richardson, so it was possible that he was living close by. If so, he would most likely get lonesome and thirsty before long, and the town's nightlife would become irresistible. When that happened Gannon expected to be on hand, for he had decided to stay in town for a few days. Gannon wondered whether Taggard was aware that Jake was on his trail. He supposed the answer was yes. It was likely that a description of Jake had been passed on to him.

It was also possible that Taggard this time had merely been passing through, and had stopped in Richardson for a few drinks. Perhaps he had been on his way to Paris. Lying in the cold room pondering the many possibilities was discouraging, so Jake gave his head a good shake to clear it, then slid under the covers. He slept soundly.

After breakfast the following morning, he conducted his vigil from his hotel room. Sitting at the window, he had an excellent view of the Elkhorn, the shabby saloon in which Taggard had been seen.

Gannon's search had largely been concentrated on the whereabouts of Ben Taggard, perhaps because young Curly Adderly had sworn that Taggard was the man who had actually beaten Jody Stewart to death. However, Lot Cameron had never been far from Jake's mind. He sat by the window now, studying the drawings Mrs. Adderly had made. Deciding that Cameron's lopsided face and long, leaning chin would stand out in any crowd, Jake folded the drawings and returned them to his coat pocket, continuing to keep one eye on the street below.

Sheriff Bain had said that although Taggard was a well-known brawler, Cameron was the more deadly of the two. Bain had been told, by men who would surely know, that the young gunman was extremely fast and held no more regard for human life than for that of a cockroach. Fancying himself the fastest draw in the world, he had been heard to say that no man alive could match his speed. He sometimes walked around in saloons, playfully drawing his gun and pointing it at people, saying "bang," then laughing gleefully at the others' discomfort. If a man expressed his displeasure at such antics, Cameron would attempt to goad him into a gunfight. His challenge had rarely been accepted.

Cameron was both childish and lucky, for most men simply would not tolerate silly games. A man had to be neither fast nor tough to put an end to such nonsense. Jake could quickly name several gunslingers who had drawn their last breath at the feet of ordinary family men who just happened to own sawed-off shotguns. Early-day Texans were a hardy breed, and it was impossible to tell by looking at a man whether he could be bullied or would fight to the death. Cameron had indeed been fortunate.

Today was Saturday. At noon, Gannon ate a bowl of red beans and rice at the restaurant downstairs, then returned to his room. He had just taken his seat at the window when he spied a familiar piebald walking down the street from the west. The rider looked even more familiar. Bundled up in heavy clothing, wearing a red scarf and a coat two sizes too large, Whitey Compton sat wearily in the saddle, his head bowed against the cold wind. Gannon raised the window quickly. Compton had dismounted and was tying his horse at the Elkhorn's hitching rail when Gannon yelled, "Hey, fellow! You lost?"

Turning to face the hotel, Compton could not readily identify the figure at the window because the room was dark, but the big, booming voice could not be mistaken.

"That you, Jake?"

"You've got me pegged. Come on up. Room two sixteen."

After entering the room and shedding his coat, Compton took a seat on the side of the bed and talked nonstop for several minutes. Recently, on three separate occasions, he had driven a wagon loaded with whiskey into Indian Territory, chores for which he had been paid handsomely. He now had as much money as he would need to get through the winter in style.

"It was the easiest money I ever made, Jake."

"Easy till you get caught," Gannon said. "They might not take you all the way to the courthouse, probably stop at the first tree with a stout limb."

"Nobody ever sees me, Jake, not on the route I take."

"Somebody will see you, 'cause they'll be there waiting for you. When half of the Indians on the reservation turn up drunk, folks are gonna start wondering where in the hell the whiskey's coming from. It's not like the old days, Whitey. This country's filling up with people, and a lot of them have got badges in their pocket. They'll stake out the whole north bank of the Red River if they have to." He handed Compton a tin can to use as an ashtray. Then, thumping his forefinger against the window pane to emphasize his words, he said, "Stop right now, Whitey, while you're ahead and alive."

Compton snuffed his cigarette in the can, then immediately rolled another, all the while in deep thought.

"I've gotta admit that you've never told me wrong, Jake. I guess my whiskey-hauling days are over." He would not mention the many other illegal activities in which he had been involved over the past two years. He knew that he had already created a witness against himself in a court of law, because Gannon would not lie under oath. He spoke again.

"You're the last man I would have expected to see today, Jake. What brings you to Richardson?"

Compton sat on the bed as Gannon talked of the events that had led to his manhunt. Whitey traveled far and wide, so Jake was not surprised to learn that the little man personally knew all three of the men involved in Jody's death. Then Jake showed him Mrs. Adderly's sketches.

"Must be a very talented lady," Whitey said, " 'cause she sure nailed them bastards. That's exactly how they look."

Gannon knew that to be true in the case of Big Jim Cates, at least, for when he faced the man he had been amazed at the likeness.

"I never have seen Cameron draw," Whitey said, "but from what I hear, he's anything but slow."

"That's the story I get," Jake said.

"Ben Taggard's a hard one to figure, though," Whitey said. "I called his hand four years ago over in Fort Worth. He refused to fight, Jake, just sat there on that barstool, staring at me. I learned later that he told somebody that I wouldn't make a pimple on a fighting man's ass." Compton took a long drag off his cigarette and blew a cloud of smoke toward the window. "He's damn lucky that I didn't hear him say it."

Gannon chuckled. Perhaps Whitey had caught the brawler on a day when the man felt charitable or didn't want to waste the energy. Jake doubted that Taggard feared the diminutive Compton.

Whitey said that he had known Frank Duncan for many years, but had neither seen nor heard of him since he sold the saloon in Fort Worth. He was surprised to learn that the man might now be living in Paris.

"What in the world would he be doing there, Jake? He's used to making lots of money, and there sure ain't much of it floating around that town."

"Don't know, Whitey. Maybe if he's rich he's just taking it easy."

"No, no, he ain't the type. He's always got a dozen things going. You can bet your saddle that he ain't taking it easy."

Two hours later, Whitey accompanied Jake on what of late had become Gannon's daily stroll around the town. Leaning against a post, Compton buttoned his coat across his throat and watched his own puffs of breath in the frosty air.

"I've got an idea, Jake," he said. "You go over and take a seat at the Elkhorn. Let me ramble around town by myself for a while and I'll find somebody who knows Duncan, knows where he lives and what he's doing."

Gannon considered the idea for a moment, then agreed. "Don't mention my name, Whitey. Not to anybody."

"Of course not, I don't even know you."

Selecting a table in the rear of the saloon, Gannon seated himself beneath a huge set of antlers mounted on the wall. A bartender with a well-trimmed beard served the pitcher of beer Jake ordered.

"Where's the kid who was working a few nights ago?" Jake asked.

"He only works Monday through Wednesday, never on weekends. He attends a school of higher learning somewhere close by, I believe." Scooping a coin from the table, the bartender dropped it on his tray.

"Who shot the elk?" Jake asked, indicating the antlers.

"Don't know. That's a Rocky Mountain rack; Colorado, I believe."

It was dark when Compton joined Gannon in the saloon. He bought a beer at the bar on his way to Jake's table. He had information on Frank Duncan.

"I talked with a fellow who's been working on a surveying crew up there, Jake. He said that Duncan owns a farm near Paris, and that his wife runs a general store that also serves as the post office. He said that Duncan could often be seen coming and going and appeared to be a busy man, but he had not been seen around the farm."

The surveyor had worked near the farm for several weeks, but had never seen anyone on the property. The land seemed to lie idle, he said, producing neither hay nor cattle. The farmhouse appeared to be vacant, for even during the coldest weather no smoke emitted from any of its three chimneys. He believed that the Duncans lived in back of the general store. All of that said, Whitey changed the subject.

"You've never seen Frank's wife, have you?" he asked.

"No."

Compton ground out his cigarette in the ashtray and began to roll another. "Looking at her will bring a fellow's reproductive instinct to life in a hurry." He licked the paper and gave the cigarette a final twist. "It's not that she ever does anything to attract attention, she always keeps herself covered and acts like a married woman. I reckon she was just born to be looked at, the type that a man simply can't help but notice."

"So I've been told." Jake put on his coat. "Let's get out of here."

Midnight was approaching when they returned to the hotel, and though Compton had rented his own room across the hall, he showed no inclination to go there. Once again seating himself on the side of Jake's bed, he began to talk.

"Old Frank Duncan might just offer you a reward if you do his brother-in-law in." Compton produced a small flask, tipped it to his lips, and returned it to his pocket.

"Why do you say that?" Jake asked.

"Well, it's a well-known fact that he hired Don Chew to give Taggard a beating. Chew's an ex–prize fighter from Houston. The story goes that Chew came all the way to Fort Worth and spent a week hunting Taggard. The problem was that when Chew found his man, he couldn't handle him."

"Taggard beat him, huh?"

"Bad, from what I hear. Folks that saw it said the fight lasted for half an hour, with Taggard getting the best of it right from the start. They say that Taggard was tired and bloody when it was over, but that he had beaten Chew to a pulp, breaking several ribs and dislocating a few other things. Chew spent a week in bed at the doctor's office, then left town with a brace on his neck."

Gannon sat in his chair, once again trying to figure out

what made Whitey Compton tick. "Did you know all this when you challenged Taggard to a fistfight?" he asked.

Whitey started for the door. "Sure, I knew it, but just 'cause he beat up Chew don't mean he could handle me. Right?"

Gannon stood staring at him with a crooked smile. "Right, Whitey," he said, closing the door after his friend.

Gannon awoke at sunup, washed the sleep from his eyes, and stood looking down at the street from the window. The morning was beautiful, the sun shone brightly, but it was cold, probably below freezing. Even as Jake watched, Whitey rode from the livery stable and tied his mount at the hotel's hitching rail. Compton had amazing recuperative powers. He could go to bed stumbling drunk, sleep two hours, and awaken looking like he had never had a drink in his life.

"Been up since daybreak," he said, as Jake opened the door for him a few minutes later. "Gonna be heading east, as soon as the saloon opens so I can get some whiskey. You want to have breakfast with me?"

"Sure do." Gannon reached for his hat. "Lead the way."

They soon joined the few customers in the dining room, and their food was served promptly. They relived a couple trail drives to Kansas as they put away a platter of ham and eggs, along with jelly and buttered biscuits.

"Better eat as much as you can if you're gonna drink all day," Jake said. "Whiskey rests a lot easier on top of a good meal. I read somewhere that a man can withstand cold weather better if he leaves alcohol alone."

"Maybe so," Compton said, draining his coffee cup and wiping his mouth on his sleeve, "but it feels different. I'll be getting a bottle, maybe two."

Twenty minutes later Whitey straddled the piebald and headed east, the twin humps of quart bottles inside his saddlebags plainly visible.

Seventeen

Gannon had spent five days in Richardson, and had a feeling that he should stay a little longer. On Monday morning he paid his rent for two additional days. He continued his surveillance from the window for the day, then walked to the Elkhorn shortly after dark. The young bartender was once again on duty. As Jake took a seat on a barstool, a mug full of beer came sliding down the bar and stopped directly in front of him, never spilling a drop.

Smiling like a target shooter who had just scored a bull's-eye, the kid joined Gannon. "I see you're still in town. Having any luck?"

"Nothing I could call good luck," Jake answered, taking a sip of the cold brew. "Just waiting for that cold north wind to settle, or change directions."

"Then you might be around for quite some time," the kid said, wiping his hands on his apron. "It's been blowing that way ever since I've been here, nearly a year, now." He pointed to a table in the rear of the room. "You might want to talk to that man over there. He just rode in, and it could be that he knows something you don't. I know for a fact that he knows Taggard."

Gannon's eyes followed the bartender's point. Seated against the wall and facing the doorway was a man of indeterminate age. His wide-brimmed hat and Henry rifle lay on an adjoining table. He busied himself by scratching at the label on his whiskey bottle with a thumbnail. His face was completely hidden by a forest of wild black beard and mustache, with small beady eyes and a long slim nose peeking out from the thicket.

Jake was soon standing beside the man's table. "Hello," he said, "my name's Gannon. May I sit?"

"My name's Eli Crump," the man said in a high-pitched, squeaky voice that sounded almost feminine, his mustache hiding any trace of the mouth from which the sound had come, "an' ya can set if ya want ta. I already knowed who ya wuz. Fact is, I wuz jist about ta come lookin' fer ya."

"Yeah? What's on your mind?"

"Well, it's like this." Crump lifted his mustache with one hand and poured whiskey into his mouth with the other. He coughed twice, wiped his mouth and continued. "I camped on th' trail with a feller that claimed his name wuz Whitey. Do ya know th' feller I'm talkin' about?"

Gannon nodded.

"Well, this Whitey says ya been huntin' Ben Taggard, an' that ya'd be willin' ta pay somebody fer puttin' ya on 'im. Is that so?"

"Maybe."

"Well, I can shore do it, but I ain't got nothin' else ta say till we git shed o' this maybe business."

"Do you mean that you know where Taggard is?" Jake asked.

Crump took another drink from his bottle then leaned across the table, speaking almost at a whisper. "Ya damn tootin' I know where he is, but it's gonna cost ya twenty dollars ta find out."

Jake sat quietly for a moment, then signaled the bartender to refill his beer mug. Leaning closer to the man, he spoke in the same low tones as Crump. "Are you saying you'll take me to Taggard for twenty dollars?"

"Didn't say that. I ain't goin' nowhere near 'im, but I'll tell ya where he is after ya put th' money in my han'."

Aware of the possibility that he was being taken, Jake handed over the money. What the heck, he had spent twenty dollars before with nothing to show for it. Crump folded the money and shoved it into his boot, then began to draw an invisible map on the table with his finger.

"Ya jist take th' trail north," he said, speaking even softer now, "an' stick with it till ya git within eight miles o' Paris. Ben's built a cabin on Frank Duncan's farm. When ya pass th' big house ya go about another mile, till ya come ta where th' old homestead used ta be. Ya cain't miss it, th' old wellcurb's still standin'. That's where ya leave th' trail. Turn inta th' woods an' go east fer about two miles, then ya'll be lookin' right at th' front door o' Taggard's shack."

"Is he alone?"

"He's always alone."

"How is it that you happen to know all this?" Jake asked.

"Don't make no never mind how I know. I jist know, an' I done tol' ya." Crump jammed his whiskey bottle into his coat pocket and was quickly out the front door.

Gannon sat at the table thinking for a while. He believed that Taggard was indeed living on the Duncan farm, but he did not trust Eli Crump. Jake had watched the man's mannerisms and body language closely, and decided early on that Crump was overplaying his hand. His shifty eyes had evaded Jake's own right from the start.

Two hours later Jake's suspicions were confirmed at the livery stable, where he learned that Crump had saddled his horse and headed north. Gannon thanked the liveryman and headed for the hotel. He knew now that Eli Crump and Taggard were birds of a feather, and had set a trap for him on the Duncan farm. The irony of Crump making him pay twenty dollars for information that was designed to bring about his own ambush brought a faint smile to Gannon's face.

At sunup, he put the gray to a slow canter and headed north. It was a frigid day, and he had tied an extra blanket behind his saddle. The hotel cook had provided him with a four-day supply of food and had filled both his canteens with fresh water. Intending to move fast, Jake had eliminated the bother of a second animal by leaving his pack horse at the livery stable.

Continuing the leisurely canter hour after hour presented no problem for the big gray, and Jake stayed with the well-marked northeasterly trail. He expected an ambush, but not this early in the game. Anyway, in this kind of terrain he could see for miles in every direction. All morning the gray continued to chew up the miles, and at noon Jake pulled off the trail.

He broke the ice on a small stream with his boot heel, allowing the horse to drink. Then, stripping the saddle, he picketed the animal on a patch of tall grass. His own meal consisted of tender roast beef and biscuits. The cook had even included a large red apple. Excellent fare, by trail standards. With his folding knife, Jake sliced the apple down the middle. Half for himself, half for the gray.

An hour later he was back on the trail, setting the same

pace. By day's end he had traveled more than fifty miles, and both he and his horse were weary. The sun was sinking toward the horizon when he took to the woods in search of a camping site. A few hundred yards off the trail, he came to a spring that flowed freely, and was frozen only farther down the ditch, where it became shallow. He built himself a bed of leaves and grass beside a fallen tree, and picketed his horse where it had access to both grass and water. He would build no fire tonight.

Awakening to a full moon a few hours past midnight, he was back in the saddle before daybreak. Another day of steady traveling brought him to the Duncan farm just before sunset. He halted his horse after topping a rise. A quarter mile ahead he could see the house that had been described by Eli Crump. "When ya pass th' big house ya go about another mile," Crump had said, "then ya turn east inta th' woods." Gannon had no intention of riding past the big house. He quickly guided the gray into the trees, and, after riding east for a mile, made camp for the night.

He did not saddle his horse the following morning. He merely moved the picket rope to new grass and broke the ice for the animal to drink. If Crump's directions were to be believed, Jake now calculated his own position to be a little more than a mile south and about that far west of Taggard's cabin. The tactic that Jake had used to bring down Big Jim Cates would be repeated today: he would make his final stalk on foot.

After washing down a cold breakfast with water from the spring, he jacked a shell into the chamber of his Winchester and added a sixth to the cylinder of his Colt. Then, moving silently, he began to negotiate his way through the dense thicket.

Reluctant to change a tactic that had worked at Santa Fe, he traveled east for more than a mile, then the same distance north. Now convinced that he was east of the cabin, he turned his footsteps west. He crept along very slowly, taking several seconds between steps. Standing behind a tree, his eyes roving over the landscape, he saw a sudden flick of movement. He remained motionless and stared at the same spot for some time. His vision slowly began to reveal a familiar sight: there, less than thirty yards away and directly in his path, a buck deer was bedded down in some tall grass.

Jake did not want the animal to run, for he knew—and was sure that Taggard would know—that deer never run through the woods unless frightened by something. Usually a man. Avoiding any sudden movement, Gannon stepped backward till he could no longer see the animal, then made a half-circle forward. If the deer decided to move now, it would slink off in the opposite direction.

Gannon was an excellent woodsman, having learned the craft while growing up in the hills of Kentucky, where having or not having meat for the table depended entirely upon the proper stalking of game.

Stalking a man was no different; the same rules applied. Jake had heard many people talk about the superior stalking ability of Indians. He had once mentioned this to an old Indian chief at Fort Sill. "Indian stalker no better than white man who know what he do," the old man had said. After thinking for a while, the chief added. "Best wood man I ever know was white man."

Jake continued to move slowly from tree to tree, and after a while came to a spring that had been boxed in with boards. The footprints around the water source—some of them made this morning—told him that he was close to his quarry. A thin coating of ice was beginning to re-form on the water after being broken—a sure sign that someone had visited the spring during the past hour. Staying near the spring would net him nothing, for it appeared that Taggard had already gotten his supply of water for the day.

Jake squatted on his haunches to peer through the dense underbrush.

Moving behind a tree, he unbuttoned his coat and stuffed the right side into his waistband, giving himself quick access to the Colt strapped to his thigh. Then he cocked the Winchester, keeping his thumb between the hammer and firing pin.

A faint trail led away from the spring. A few feet away it turned north into the trees. He was trying to figure out the lay of the land in that direction, when suddenly his body tensed. He had heard a horse stamping its foot, only a few yards away. He stood frozen in his position. Then, hearing no more sounds, he decided that the horse was probably tied to something and awaiting its rider— wherever he was.

Easing the hammer down on the Winchester, he palmed his Peacemaker. Any fighting now would be at close range. He backtracked a few steps, then turned north. He had traveled only a short distance through the brush when the cabin came into view. Two saddled horses stood at the rear of the small building, and Jake was not surprised that one of them was the small roan that the liveryman had described as Eli Crump's mount.

He waited only long enough for the horses to become acclimated to his presence, then crossed the small opening to the rear of the shack. Stealing along the north side to the front of the building, he could see that the hinged door stood halfway open, blocking him. Getting around that door and into the cabin would put him in a vulnerable position.

He quickly reversed his direction and circled to the south side. Then, his Colt cocked and at the ready, he eased along the cabin's windowless front wall to the open doorway. In one fluid movement he was inside the cabin with his back to the wall. He was alone. The cabin contained only a few bare necessities: a stove, two bunks piled high with blankets, one chair and a scattering of pots and pans.

A man with less experience might have decided to wait the men out, knowing that they would surely return to the cabin. But the flimsy shack could easily turn into a death trap if it came to a shootout. Gannon quickly retraced his footsteps to the spring. The men would be somewhere between the cabin and the main trail, which was two miles west. Recocking the Winchester and returning the Colt to its holster, he renewed his silent stalk.

He moved westward for an hour, pausing after each step to survey the area before him. Even the treetops did not escape his scrutiny, for he knew that more than one man had been ambushed from overhead.

Gannon saw the man. Twenty yards ahead and thirty feet above the ground, Eli Crump sat on a thick board that rested across two limbs of a large oak. He was facing west, the direction from which he expected Gannon's approach. Crump put a gloved hand to his mouth in a vain attempt to muffle a cough. Then he began to look around nervously. He scanned the area to his right. When he twisted for a look to the left, he was staring into the eyes of Gannon, sighting his Winchester. Crump whirled his rifle with a catlike motion, but took a bullet through the heart before he could bring his own weapon to bear. He coughed once, then tumbled from the tree and lay still.

"Yeeee-haaa!" Jake yelled, mimicking Crump's high-pitched twang. From a distance of a hundred yards, Taggard's response was immediate.

"Didja git 'im, Eli?"

"Yeeee-haaa!" Gannon repeated, then took up a position Taggard would have to pass before reaching Crump's body. Jake could hear Taggard lumbering through the forest. He passed within twenty feet of Jake, who stepped from behind a tree and sighted at the man's back.

"Drop the rifle, Taggard!" he commanded. "Drop it now, or die!" Taggard realized instantly that Crump was dead, and that it was Jake Gannon who now stood behind him. He held on to his rifle for a moment, as if calculating the odds in fighting a man who already had the drop on him. Then, he opened his hand and allowed the rifle to drop to the ground. Turning, he spat tobacco juice through the gap in his teeth.

"Guess yer callin' the shots, Gannon," he said.

"Take off your coat. Face down on the ground!"

Taggard complied. Jake searched him thoroughly, taking a knife from the man's pocket and flinging it into the brush.

"Where is Lot Cameron, Taggard?" Gannon demanded.

"Ain't got no way o' knowin'," Taggard said, speaking into the fallen leaves that muffled his voice. "I ain't been nowhere, ain't seen nobody."

Jake had expected just such an answer. Convinced that the knife and rifle had been Taggard's only weapons, Gannon ordered him to begin a slow march west, toward the main trail. When they crossed the trail and walked into a barren, sandy field, Jake came to a halt.

"Keep walking, Taggard. I'll tell you when to stop." Jake stood his ground as Taggard began to walk away. Ten yards ... twenty yards ... thirty yards. "That's it right there!"

Taggard stopped and slowly turned to face Gannon. All color drained from his face as he stood still, clearly expecting a fiery blast from the muzzle of Jake's Winchester.

Instead, Gannon laid his weapon on the ground. He unbuckled his gunbelt and laid it beside the rifle. He doffed his heavy coat and placed his hat on top of it. Then he walked toward Taggard. Confidence suddenly registered on Taggard's face as he realized that Jake intended to fight him man to man.

Neither man spoke. Both knew that it would be a fight to the death. They lunged for each other. Gannon's first punch landed on Taggard's throat, toppling him to the ground. "When a man goes down th' fight's half over," Uncle Jesse Ride had often said, "keep 'im on th' ground any way ya can." Jake delivered a hard kick at Taggard's head. Taggard evaded the kick by rolling away, regaining his feet. They came together in a flurry of hard punches in which each man scored several times, then moved apart. They circled each other now, each respectful of the other's punching power. A trickle of blood ran from the corner of Gannon's mouth, dripping off his chin. Moving in again, Taggard attempted to kick Jake in the groin, instead taking a left to the jaw and a short right to the mouth. Gannon had twisted the right-hand punch, splitting Taggard's lips.

Not wanting to trade punches with the muscular brawler, Jake continued to circle, using his longer reach to strike with viperous jabs, always feinting, moving in and out while searching for the opening that might end the fight. When Taggard lowered his head and made a mad rush, Gannon connected with a right uppercut inside Taggard's guard that lifted the man completely off his feet, sending him sprawling on his back.

Once again Taggard regained his feet quickly. This time he clutched in his right hand a rock half the size of a man's head. Continuing to circle, Jake scooped up a handful of sand and threw it into Taggard's face. Taggard blinked, and Jake sprang. A hard chop across Taggard's wrist sent the rock to the ground, then Jake waded in. He kicked Taggard's groin, and battered his head and face. Taggard was almost out on his feet. Jake measured a right to the chin that put the brawler down. This time, Jake was on top of him.

Pinning both of Taggard's arms to the ground with his knees, Jake pounded him in the face with both fists. Stopping to catch his breath, his eyes moved to the rock that Taggard had brought into the fight. Gannon stared at it while sitting atop the unconscious man. "Taggard jist kep' hittin' 'er in the head with that rock," young Curly Adderly had said. Gannon's right hand, seeming to have a mind of its own, slowly closed around the rock. Then, raising it high into the air, the hand brought the rock down on Taggard's head. Again . . . and again.

Eighteen

A short while later Gannon mounted the gray and rode south. He made no effort to bury either of the men, leaving the disposition of their bodies to Mother Nature. He rode slowly, because any jostling aggravated his ribs bruised from the twenty-minute battle with Taggard. He also thought that a bone in his left hand was broken.

In Richardson, he was advised to see Doctor Joe Cross, an aging ex-army medic who operated a dry goods store and ran a medical practice out of the same building.

"Shore it's broke," the old doctor said in a scolding voice. "What the hell didja expect? When a han' goes a-bangin' up ag'inst somebody's hard head sump'm's gonna give, an' it's most likely gonna be th' damn han'. A feller's s'posed ta use a little common sense."

"Yes, Doctor," Jake said, supposing that he must humor the old medic if he was to get his hand set properly.

"Does that hurt?" the old man asked as he held Jake's wrist and jerked hard on two fingers. A stab of pain shot up Gannon's arm and almost knocked him off his feet.

"Daaamn," he whispered weakly. "Is it gonna hurt worse when you set it?"

"It's done set," the old man said. He placed a splint on the hand and wrapped it tightly. "Keep this on fer three weeks, an' don't use th' han'. I mean don't use it a-tall." Then, looking up from his work expectantly, he added, "Ya do have th' three dollars on ya, don't ya?"

Jake produced the money and was out of the building quickly. He arranged passage for himself and his horses on tomorrow's train, then took a hotel room and slept the night away.

It was midafternoon two days later when he arrived at Cottonwood. Mickey Barnes spotted him riding through the gate, and stood in the yard waiting as Jake rode the last hundred yards. Never before had his foreman met him with a rifle in his hand.

"Something wrong, Mickey?" he asked, dismounting.

"Plenty wrong, Jake. I buried Bake two weeks ago down there beside your brother."

Shocked, Gannon dropped the horse's reins to the ground and sat on the edge of the porch, attempting to grasp the news. Bake Mellon! The picture of health. A man who had no enemies and no bad habits. Barnes stood by quietly as Jake stared off into space, swallowing hard as he realized that he would never see his friend again.

"What happened, Mickey?" he finally asked.

"Somebody shot him out of the saddle up on the north section, right there at that shallow place where the cattle go down to drink out of the river. His feet were lying in the water when I found him, so I guess he was letting his horse drink. The bullet hit him just below his left ear, so I doubt that he even heard the shot that killed him.

"Bake knew that I was fixing tenderloin steaks for supper, and that was his favorite food. When he still hadn't shown up by dark, I went looking for him. I couldn't find him or his horse. You can't really see anything with a lantern. Next morning the horse was standing beside the corral gate, and it didn't take me half an hour to find Bake."

"Have you seen anybody around the place that you didn't know?"

"Nope, but I know in my own mind who killed Bake. It was that crooked-faced sonofabitch you showed me the picture of, that Lot Cameron. I've been to Waco three times asking questions. I found four men who said that a fellow matching his description had been hanging around town talking about you just a few days before the shooting. One man admitted that he had given him directions to this place.

"Two days after I reported it, the sheriff came out and wandered around for a while, made a big thing out of riding up and down both sides of the river with his nose to the ground. He informed me that I had violated the law by burying Bake before someone in authority had had a chance to view the body. After I explained that I had kept the body out of the ground for twenty-four hours waiting for the law to get off its lazy ass and come out here, I told him to go to hell. He left here in a huff, and I haven't heard anything else from him."

Barnes went off to stable Gannon's horses. When he came back, he nodded toward Jake's bandaged hand. "Did you hit somebody?"

"Taggard."

"Good. Did you do him in?"

"Uh-huh."

Not asking for the details, Barnes headed for the

kitchen. "I'll have something to eat in a few minutes," he said.

After a meal of warmed-over beans and biscuits, the men sat close to the stove to drink their coffee.

"I'm gonna be needing a couple men to help me here," Barnes said, refilling their cups from the blackened pot. "It's almost calving time."

"I know," Jake said, burning his lips with the steaming liquid. "You're the boss, Mickey, hire anybody you need. Do you need some money?"

"Nope, still got more'n half of what you gave me before Christmas." Barnes paused a moment while they sipped their coffee. "I guess you realize that the man who shot Bake thought he was shooting you."

"Of course I do, nobody disliked Bake. At a distance, that mistake would be easy enough to make. He was long-waisted and sat about as high in the saddle as me."

"You gonna go hunting Cameron?"

"As soon as my hand and ribs heal, and the weather warms up."

Though Gannon had been raised in Tennessee and Kentucky, and had traveled extensively, he considered himself a Texan. He had long been disturbed at the inability of lawmen to curb the violent acts of riffraff who roamed far and wide across Texas, usually unmolested. Though many law enforcement officials were quick to blame their lack of success on insufficient funds and manpower, Jake believed that the problem was more often lack of will. He personally knew of instances in which lawmen had immediately headed for the back country after learning that a wanted man was in town.

During the weeks he spent waiting for his hand to heal, Gannon read stacks of newspapers, new and old. The papers reported that robberies and murders occurred throughout Texas every day, and that in ninety percent of the cases no one was ever held accountable. The *Fort Worth Democrat* published a long list of the fugitives' names. Along with each man's name was a list of the crimes he had committed, and the dollar amount of the reward that would be paid for his capture. Some had evaded lawmen for many months—even years. The amount of the reward closely related not only to the severity of the crime, but also to how long the name had been on the list.

A majority of the lawmen Jake had known were averse to risk taking, usually allowing crime to flourish all around them while being overpaid for a job that largely went undone. Of course, there was a different breed of lawman: the type who hounded criminals day and night, and would not hesitate to lay his life on the line in a showdown. Gannon believed that these few brave souls were woefully underpaid.

The weather did get warmer, and while his soul still ached as it ever would, the hand did heal. It was now the middle of March. Today Gannon was headed for Brady, a town in the center of Texas, less than two hundred miles from Cottonwood. During several days in Waco, he learned that Lot Cameron had been seen in many of the town's watering holes. Jake found several men who had actually talked with Cameron, the last one being the man who had directed him to Cottonwood.

"He said he was a-huntin' work," the old-timer said, pausing to pack his lip full of snuff. "He said he'd heerd you wuz in th' market fer a han', so I tol' 'im how ta git there. I jist had sold thirty gallon o' soggum surp ta them whiskey makers north o' town, so I had money. I bought 'im two or three dranks, an' that's th' last I saw uv 'im."

Two of the men who had talked with Cameron said he had mentioned the town of Brady. "Said his granddaddy on his momma's side had a spread out there," one of the men said. "Th' man's name is Adams."

With this information, Jake saddled the gray this morning and headed west. He left his pack horse in the pasture, deciding once again that the convenience of having the extra things the horse would carry was not worth the bother of an additional animal. Rolled up inside his blankets, he carried a change of clothing, and in his saddlebags, a four-day supply of food.

Gannon's cattle had come through the winter in excellent condition, and the cows were already beginning to calve. Barnes had hired two men from Waco, promising them work for two months. Decent and loyal, Mickey was a good cattleman who would not waste his employer's money, and Jake gave him free rein in such matters. Each of the hired hands had hit the ground working.

Even when Jake was home he was of no help to Barnes. He seldom saddled a horse. He spent much of his time walking along the river, with a mental load that was difficult to carry. He went to sleep every night thinking of Jody, and awoke with his mind on Lot Cameron. Gannon was certain that Cameron was the man who shot Bake Mellon out of the saddle, a man he did not even know. Cameron had no doubt ridden away believing he had just killed Jake Gannon.

According to the newspapers, men of Cameron's ilk abounded in Texas, sometimes shooting people at random for target practice. Jake wondered how many young children in Texas were fatherless because of such senseless killings. Instances of rowdies getting drunk and shooting the first man to come along were not unheard-of. All in the name of fun. And the sonsofbitches were getting away with it.

While sitting under the Studying Tree, Jake made a concrete decision: when he finished his business with

Cameron, he would begin his own private campaign against the criminal element of Texas. He would go after the crooks and killers himself. He had no desire to be a lawman; jurisdiction laws made the job too confining. As a private citizen, he could go anywhere he wished and use any means necessary to apprehend those who had been indicted by a grand jury. He would make the captures and accept the rewards.

The fact that he might be called a bounty hunter by some did not bother Jake. He had never concerned himself with other people's opinion of him. Now he cared even less. The bounty system had never been intended to make any man rich. It was just the citizens' way of paying the hunter for his time, and for the dangers.

The profession of bounty hunting was no less noble than that of a lawman. But while a lawman could sit in the shade and still draw a paycheck each month, the manhunter's pay was based entirely on production.

Cottonwood would support him even during his absence. Therefore, any money he might earn chasing criminals would be secondary to his burning desire to rid his adopted state of such characters as those who had sent Jody Stewart to an early grave. A reward had been posted in Groesbeck for Jody's killers. Jake expected to claim the reward—in her name, to build something nice around the home he had meant for her.

Located at the edge of the Hill Country on the Dodge Cattle Trail, Brady had become the seat of McCulloch County in 1876. A few miles southeast was the site where Tawakoni Indians had besieged James and Rezin Bowie and their small party. After a battle that raged for eight days, the fierce Bowie brothers had fought their way free. James, who would later die at the Alamo, erected a marker of sorts, proclaiming Calf Creek the location of the battle.

It was only two hours past noon when Gannon halted

for the day, ten miles out of Brady. Though he had been riding leisurely, he had been in the saddle since daybreak, and both he and his horse were tired. He picketed the gray along the creek, intending to move the rope every hour or so. Only a few tender green shoots had found their way through the older grass, and the animal would graze over each small area in short order.

Lying beside his fire and leaning on one elbow, Gannon was watching a small pot of beans that was about to boil when he saw a rider approaching from the north. The man in the saddle was very old. He stopped his horse no more than twenty feet from the fire, and sat very still. Although the brim of his hat was pulled low, completely covering one eye, the man appeared to be bald, for no hair showed above his ears. His weathered, leathery face was as withered as a prune. The one eye that was visible continued to shift back and forth between Gannon and his horse.

"Guess you just light any damn where you please," the man said in a voice surprisingly youthful.

"I suppose that's about it, sir," Jake said, getting to his feet. "Mighty big country, and I don't see that it's gonna hurt it any for a man to camp overnight."

"Nope. Not if that's all he's doing."

Gannon poked at his fire, moving the pot to a different position. He waved his arm over his belongings. "Seems like you should be able to tell by my gear that I'm on the move."

"Looks that way," the old man said, stepping down from his saddle with a grunt. "You got any coffee?"

Gannon nodded, then stepped to the creek to fill his coffeepot. Sprinkling in some grounds, he placed the pot on the fire beside the beans. "I usually don't make coffee except in the mornings," he said, "but I suppose a cup would go down pretty easy right now." He broke a dead limb across his knee and tossed the pieces on the fire. "Is this your property?"

"Yep," the old-timer said, stretching out beside the fire. "Been here most of my life, the name is Easterling. Me and my pappy came to Texas with Austin, back in the thirties."

"Well, sir, you certainly go back a long way," Gannon said, pulling the coffeepot off the fire just before it boiled over. "I guess you've seen it all."

"That, and more," Easterling said, taking off his hat to reveal a head that was indeed bald. "Me and my pappy fought Mexicans for every foot of this land, and they weren't all we fought. Pappy was killed and mutilated by Tawakonis on this same creek, not a quarter mile from this very spot."

Gannon offered no condolences, figuring the passage of time had probably dimmed the old man's memory of the incident, and perhaps dulled the pain. He poured two cups of coffee and handed one to Easterling.

"Would you happen to know a rancher in these parts named Adams?" he asked.

"Lord, yes," Easterling said, pursing his lips and blowing air into his cup. "I've been knowing Neely Adams since both of us were young men. His spread's about twenty miles north and west of here, on the other side of Brady."

"Thanks," Jake said nonchalantly, tossing his coffee grounds over his shoulder. "Somebody just mentioned his name back on the Brazos. I'd probably be wasting my time talking to him. He's probably already got all the help he needs."

"Oh, I wouldn't say that. Neely runs a lot more cattle than I do, and they're calving now. Spring roundup ain't far off, and if he ain't hiring right now he will be pretty soon. He'll be needing all the help he can get from now till the first of June."

The old man was a talker. He talked most of the afternoon, but asked few questions. He spoke mostly of Texas' War for Independence, and supplied a detailed description of how tough things had been in the old days. When Easterling finally halted to catch his breath, Jake changed the subject.

"Does this Neely Adams have a large family?" he asked.

"Oh, yeah. There's a bunch of them, boys and girls. Of course, they've all grown up and scattered to hell and gone. Lil was the oldest, and I believe she's moved back in. Neely brought her back after her husband was killed trying to bust a wild bronc. I think that damn boy of hers is driving her and Neely both crazy."

"Tell me about the boy."

"Fancies himself some kind of gunslinger, and some of the men who have seen him playing with it say he's plenty fast. More than anything else, though, he's just plain damn mean.

"Shot an old Indian squaw in the foot over at the trading post, then stood around laughing about it. People say the old gal wasn't doing anything but begging for food, but that damned Lot Cameron decided to make her do some kind of Indian dance."

Lot Cameron! The name Gannon had been waiting to hear.

"Even after he saw all the blood," Easterling continued, "Cameron kept shooting between her feet, making her hop up and down on one leg. People said he was still laughing when he rode off. When I heard about it, I paid old Doc Leonard to work on her foot, but I hear she's still a cripple. Lot Cameron is a no-good sonofabitch through and through, and it's a shame somebody ain't killed him a long time ago."

"Do you know where he is?"

"Not exactly. He's usually in and out over at Neely's place, but I haven't seen him in a year or two. Why?"

Gannon casually took the well-done beans off the fire. "I intend to kill him."

"Well, now, I believe the Lord'll bless you for that." Easterling was quiet for a long time. He declined the beans he was offered, watching as Jake filled a bowl and began to eat. When he had eaten the contents of the bowl, Gannon set it aside and began to eat from the pot.

"I thought there was something about you," Easterling said after several minutes. "Somehow you just didn't look like an ordinary fellow passing through. When you go talking about shooting Lot Cameron, you're sounding like my kind of man. You a bounty hunter or something?"

"He's got a price on his head, but that's not the reason I'm hunting him. Three men raped and killed the young woman I was about to marry. Lot Cameron was one of them. He's also been on my ranch lately, mistook one of my friends for me and shot him out of the saddle." Gannon did not know if he could trust the old man, but cared little if Cameron found out that he was in the area. If he truly was a man who enjoyed a gunfight, that would bring him out.

"That sounds exactly like something Cameron would do," Easterling said, rising to his feet. "I'll tell you what I can do, young man. I can find out if he's at Neely's place easy enough. If you'll stay put till tomorrow morning, I'll be back."

"I'll be in that grove of trees over there," Jake said, pointing.

Easterling nodded, then mounted his horse and rode over the hill.

Nineteen

True to his word, the old rancher returned to Jake's camp not long after sunrise. Late yesterday afternoon, Easterling had sent a rider to the Adams ranch on the pretext of discussing the upcoming spring roundup. The rider returned long after dark, saying that he had personally seen Cameron standing in the yard.

"I can't be getting involved in this no deeper," the old man said to Gannon. "Me and Neely's been friends for a long time."

"I understand," Gannon said, "and I appreciate your help."

"Well, I wouldn't be going on the ranch to call Cameron if I were you," Easterling said, remounting his buckskin. "I doubt that any of the hands like him, but I believe they'll all fight for the brand."

"I know. I have no intention of setting foot on Adams' property."

Easterling nodded, and kicked his horse in the ribs. He rode to the top of the hill, then turned sideways and gave Gannon a military salute. Jake took the gesture to mean that Easterling was wishing him luck. He answered with a wave of his own hand, then the old rancher was gone.

A short time later, Gannon rode out of the grove, his horse pointed toward Brady. Riding into town from the east, he first came to the livery barn. He made arrangements for the gray's lodging, then asked that he be allowed to feed the animal himself. The hostler quietly handed him a bucketful of grain. It was not that Jake distrusted the liveryman. He simply knew that all dumb animals acquired an affection for the hand that fed them, and repetition only strengthened the bond between man and animal. He curried the gray, then rehung the comb on a rusty nail.

"Which saloon has the most business?" he asked the sandy-haired hostler, who wore a patch over one eye.

"Texas Jack's," the man answered, his one brown eye sparkling. "Jack's got most of the girls, so that's where the men hang out." He pointed down the street. "About a block west, you can't miss it."

Gannon thanked the man and began to walk. A few minutes later he was seated at a table in the rear of the saloon, his back only a few inches from the wall. The establishment was large and luxuriously furnished. Jake thought that the room could easily accommodate two hundred people, and batwing doors led to a separate section that was obviously a kitchen.

A small hardwood dance floor lay directly in front of his table, along with a riser that held a piano with several of its ivory keys missing. A fiddle that was badly in need of varnish lay on top of the piano. Several signs plastered along the walls proclaimed Jack's roast beef the best Texas had to offer, thus simplifying Jake's choice for his noon meal. A small, dark-haired waitress took his order. When she returned with his food, Jake asked her name, gently shoving a dollar bill into the pocket of her apron.

"My name is Bonnie," she said, smiling cutely.

"I like company when I'm eating," Gannon said, in the most flirtatious manner he could muster, "even if I have to pay for it. Can you sit?" The girl eyed the money, still hanging halfway out of her pocket.

"Only if you buy me a drink," she said.

Gannon held up two fingers for the bartender to see, and Bonnie sat down. They talked for half an hour, and the girl opened up after Jake made it clear that he was not looking for romance. She spoke freely of her opinions about one thing or another, and dodged none of the questions asked by Gannon, who mentioned neither Lot Cameron nor the Adams ranch.

Bonnie said that the town did have a lawman, but that he was seldom seen. He spent most of his time at his own place, several miles south of town. When Jake left the saloon, Bonnie was three dollars richer. She stood by the bar, waving as he walked through the doorway.

He rented a hotel room across the street and settled in. He did not need to go anywhere else. He already knew where Cameron was. Nor did he want to talk to any man, especially the local badge-toter. He had all of the information he needed to carry out the plan that had formed in his mind during the past two hours.

It was shortly after dark the following night when the Adams ranch cowboys' nightly poker game was interrupted by a loud knock on the bunkhouse door. When the door was opened, a boy no more than twelve years old asked to speak with Lot Cameron. He presented Cameron with a letter sealed in a plain white envelope. When the boy was asked who gave him the letter, he replied that a woman in Brady had paid him to deliver it; he did not know her name. Then the kid remounted, and was quickly off the premises.

All eyes were on Cameron as he stood close to the lamp, reading the neatly written letter, obviously penned by a feminine hand:

Dear Lot:

    Although you don't know me and I've only seen you once, I can't get you out of my mind. I hope you won't think I'm too forward, but I desperately need to know if there could be something between us. Tomorrow afternoon at three o'clock would be the best time for us to meet, as I have a few hours of free time then. I think it best that we do not meet at my place of employment, so I will be at Bud's Place, a few doors down from Jack's. We can go for a ride, or do whatever you want.

                Signed: The new girl at Texas Jack's.

Cameron read the letter twice, then folded it. Smiling smugly, he waved it at the crowd, then stuck it in his coat pocket.

"Well, c'mon," one of the hands said, "what does it say?"

"Wouldn't you like to know?" Cameron said, laughing and jumping around the room in some kind of silly dance. "Wouldn't you like to know!"

Later, when he decided that he had teased them long enough, Cameron passed the letter around. All of the men congratulated him, most of them talking about what a lucky dog Cameron was to have fate smiling on him this way. Some new girl at Texas Jack's had a hankering for Lot's body, and had even paid to have that message delivered. Long after the light was out, some of the hands lay on their bunks enviously thinking of Cameron's letter.

While they were out slaving in the sun tomorrow, Lot would be lying up in the shade somewhere making love to some sweet little thing from Texas Jack's.

Shortly after two the following afternoon, Cameron approached Brady, riding at a slow canter. He slowed his lathered bay at the edge of town, then continued at a brisk walk. The street was deserted, for the day was unseasonably warm. Looking neither left nor right, he headed straight for Bud's Place. At the hitching rail, he jumped eagerly from the saddle, a look of wild anticipation on his face. He had made two steps toward the rough plank porch when a deep, booming voice stopped him in his tracks.

"That's far enough, Cameron!" Gannon yelled, stepping around the corner of the building. Cameron spun toward him, blinking his eyes several times. Jake had deliberately chosen the time and the place in order to put the sun in the eyes of his opponent. The man did not make a pretty picture. Pale and skinny, with dirty-blond hair and a head that was too big for his body, he had a long chin that jutted to one side of his lopsided face. Gannon could see anger in the man's eyes, but no fear. Cameron was obviously depending on his fast gun to get him out of the situation.

"Wha ... who are you?" he stammered. Then, not waiting for an answer, his hand moved toward the gun on his hip. He had barely cleared his holster when he felt the fire in his chest. He died instantly; Gannon had pumped two shots into his heart. Then, as Cameron slowly sank to the ground, Jake felt obliged to answer the man's question.

"I'm the new girl at Texas Jack's," he said softly.

Twenty

Gannon spent a week on his own ranch, then headed to Groesbeck and the Lazy S, where he spent a few days with the Stewarts. When informed that Jody's killers had come to a no-good end, Ab said that his prayers had been answered. His wife, not being vindictive, prayed for the souls of the killers, saying that they must be lying in a lonely grave somewhere with nobody to mourn them. That possibility did not bother her husband.

"They got what they deserved," he said, "and that's that."

Ab had been anxious to show Jake a Merino ram that he kept in a pen beside the barn. The animal was indeed beautiful, and the largest ram Jake had ever seen, with prime wool hanging from its body in large folds.

"Had 'im shipped in from back East," Ab said. "Cost me eight hundred dollars." Jake thought he had not heard correctly. Eight hundred dollars for one ram?

"I intend to buy some cheap ewes," Ab continued, "and breed the churro strain out of 'em with this ram. Merinos weigh ten percent more and produce twenty percent more wool; better wool, too. I won't turn 'im out with the ewes till breedin' time."

Ab had broadened his experiment with Merinos, and had even begun to let them mix and run with the cattle. He had decided once and for all to change his stock operation. He owned every foot of ground that he grazed, and would soon be stringing legal fences around his entire spread. He would hire men to dig irrigation ditches and wells, put up windmills to pump water, raise fodder crops for winter feed, and run a stock farm rather than a ranch. Each time a cowboy quit, he would be replaced with a farm hand.

Ab had learned that when sheep were sensibly handled they actually improved the grasslands. Left to themselves, they scattered, instead of clustering in the tight bunch that was so convenient for the herder but so destructive to the grass. If they were not overstocked and were afforded well-spaced water holes, no part of the range would suffer. Their hooves harrowed the soil rather than trampling it, and their droppings proved to be a valuable fertilizer.

He now knew that cattle and sheep could indeed share the same range land. Cattle showed no revulsion at the smell a scattered flock left on the grass and actually seemed to prefer the rich grass of the sheep's old bedgrounds.

"I don't graze no public land, Jake," Ab said, "so I don't think me puttin' up fences is nobody's business but my own. If the cattlemen don't see it that way, I'll hire as many men as I need to keep the fences up. I might have to send Dory off someplace if the goin' gits rough, but by God I intend to stand my ground."

"A man has a right to do whatever he wants on his own property, Ab, and I don't think any of your neighbors are gonna squawk about the fences. As for the sheep, the only times I've ever known of trouble occurring have been when somebody tried to run them on public land. I think you'll be all right with the woolies."

After eating a large supper prepared by Dory Stewart, Gannon retired for the night. Tomorrow, he would become a bounty hunter.

Just before Jake's visit to the Stewarts, Sheriff Willow had paid him the six-hundred-dollar reward that Limestone County had posted for Jody's killers. The sheriff had also provided Gannon with a stack of dodgers on several men who were wanted by the law for one crime or another. Jake's attention had immediately been drawn to the wanted poster of a man named Tag Renshaw.

Renshaw, a native of Anderson County, had been convicted of a double murder in that same county two years ago and was sentenced to hang. But Renshaw had overpowered a jailer and escaped, killing another man a few minutes later to gain a horse and a few dollars. The county had immediately posted a thousand-dollar reward for his capture, and last month the amount had been doubled, due to the clamoring of the area's residents.

Vernon and Willa Drake, a homesteading couple in their early sixties, had been murdered in their own cabin, and their bodies buried in shallow graves in the back yard. The evidence was overwhelming, and no doubt existed of the guilt of Tag Renshaw, who had even moved into the couple's cabin and made himself at home. He quickly began to sell off Vernon Drake's belongings: hogs, chickens and several head of cattle. To anyone who questioned his activities, Renshaw's answer was that the Drakes were on an extended visit to the East, and had hired him to dispose of a few things.

When the county sheriff continued to hear from concerned citizens, he sent a deputy out to the Drake place to check things out. The deputy arrived when Renshaw was off on one of his selling trips, and quickly found the bodies of the couple, which had been unearthed by animals. The following afternoon, Sheriff Jute and the deputy arrested Renshaw without incident behind the Drakes' chickenhouse. They had literally caught the man with his pants down, in the act of answering nature's call.

The trial was swift and direct. More than a dozen witnesses testified against Renshaw, the parade led by his own half brother, Louis Weems. With some animosity of his own, Weems stated that he had no doubt of Renshaw's guilt.

"He even tried to sell me that big red sow, an' I knowed damn well it belonged to Mister Drake," Weems told an attentive jury. The jury retired after several hours of heated testimony, and the verdict was not long in coming. Weems had been pleased, saying that Renshaw was a cold-blooded killer.

The town of Palestine, seat of Anderson County, lay nestled among the dogwood trees in northeast Texas, a three-day ride from Groesbeck. The county seat had originally been a tiny settlement called, like the big port city, Houston. In the 1840s it was discovered that Houston was two miles off center. Taking literally the legislature's guidelines that a county seat should be at the center of the county, the locals created the town of Palestine and named it the county seat. The small village of Houston quickly died.

Gannon rode into Palestine at midday, and immediately deposited his pack horse at the livery stable. Then, riding down the town's main street, he spoke to the first man he encountered.

"Know where I might find Sheriff Jute?"

"The sheriff lives about a quarter mile up the road

there," the man said, pointing. "Don't hardly never come down here unless somebody sends for him."

Jake thanked the man and rode up the hill.

Raymond Jute had come to Texas from Georgia twenty years ago, and was now serving his second term as sheriff of Anderson County. Though known by all to be a man who was conservative of his own physical energies, he was liked by most, and his job performance was considered at least adequate. Though he maintained a small office next to the courthouse, he conducted much of the county's business from his own home.

Jute was sitting on the porch of his small two-story house when Gannon dismounted and tied his horse to the hitching rail.

"I guess you'd be Sheriff Jute," Jake said, standing outside the short picket fence.

"You'd be guessing right," the sheriff answered, getting to his feet. Jute had a well-fed look, to say the least. Standing well over six feet tall, he weighed close to three hundred pounds. "Unlatch the gate and let yourself in." The men shook hands at the doorstep and Jake introduced himself, taking the chair he was offered.

"I won't be taking up much of your time, Sheriff. I just wanted to talk with you about a man named Renshaw."

"Tag Renshaw?" The sheriff chuckled. "Join the crowd. Everybody in the county wants to talk about Renshaw. If I don't get reelected next term, it'll be because of that sonofabitch."

"Well, I intend to take up his trail," Gannon said, smiling and chuckling along with the lawman, "and I'm looking for a starting place. Maybe if I'm lucky it'll put you in good stead with the voters."

Jute sat quietly in his chair, scratching his belly, then walked to the door and shouted to his wife to bring two glasses of tea to the porch. The woman complied quickly, and Jute returned to his chair.

"I ain't gonna pretend that I ain't heard the name of Gannon before," he said, "and if you're the one I've heard about there ain't no doubt in my mind that you could handle Renshaw if you found him." Jute walked to the edge of the porch to blow his nose, then reseated himself. Sipping at the tea, he continued.

"Finding Renshaw is the catch, Mister Gannon, and you ain't the first man that's tried it. Several men have gone hunting him before, and they've all come up empty. Jack Island trailed him for three months, before he ran out of money. Jack said he had a good lead on him in San Angelo, but just couldn't stand the expenses of the hunt. It costs money to travel, Miser Gannon; maybe you got it and maybe you ain't."

Jake assured the sheriff that he intended to stay with the hunt until he found his man.

"Well, you do that and you're gonna be a damn sight richer. The money's already in escrow. Two thousand smackers, and it won't take more'n an hour to transfer it from the bank to your saddlebags."

They talked for another hour, then Gannon bade the sheriff farewell.

Jake was soon following a narrow trail that snaked through the dense woodlands, closely paralleling a small stream. The beautiful blooming dogwoods seemed to dominate the forest. He had been told by Sheriff Jute that the trail would lead to the home of Nixon Weems, stepfather of Tag Renshaw. Weems' son, Louis, who had testified against Renshaw at the trial, also lived there. At the death of his mother, the younger Weems had moved back in with his father.

Gannon encountered both of the Weemses without ever seeing their cabin. As he rode from the forest, he could see the men hoeing corn at the far end of the field. He guided his horse between the knee-high stalks, stopping where the men stood.

"Hello," he said, wiping the sweatband of his hat with his hand. "My name's Gannon, and—"

"Hey! Git a holt o' that horse!" the elder Weems yelled. Jake jumped to the ground, grabbing his horse's bridle. The gray had helped himself to a stalk of the old man's tender corn, and was now crushing it between his teeth.

"Sorry," Jake said, hiding his amusement. "I'd be glad to pay for the corn."

"Don't need no pay, jist hang on to 'im."

Both men spoke freely concerning Tag Renshaw, and each expressed ill will. "He's gonna wind up at the end of a rope, jist like his daddy did," young Louis Weems said, an' it'll damn shore serve 'im right." The old man explained that the elder Renshaw had been hung for stealing horses.

"Tag's daddy weren't no small-time thief," Louis said. "He took whole herds at a time. And Tag hisself ain't eeb'm worth th' price of a rope. Somebody ought to beat 'im to death with a club, same way he kilt th' Drakes."

Nixon Weems said that he had married Tag Renshaw's mother when the boy was only four years old, and that Tag had been unable or unwilling to adjust to the change. When Louis was born, Tag's resentment of both the new baby and his stepfather became progressively worse. By the time Tag reached his teens he had become uncontrollable. At fifteen, after giving his younger half brother a beating and slapping his mother down, Tag moved out, taking one of his stepfather's plow horses with him.

He had stood trial for robbery in the town of Franklin three years ago, but had been acquitted. One of the jurors was heard to say after the trial that he knew in his heart that Renshaw was guilty, but the prosecutor had failed to present enough evidence.

Renshaw was known to be skilled with all kinds of weapons, and more than a little handy with his fists. Of medium height and a muscular two hundred pounds, he was described by the elder Weems as being "quick as a cat and strong as a ox." The younger Weems said that Tag had once strangled the family hound because it failed to chase a rabbit. "Choked 'im to death with his bare hands," Louis Weems said through clenched teeth. "That dog was tard, been huntin' all day, an' Tag jist kilt 'im 'cause he wanted to come to the house."

The men agreed that the San Angelo area might turn out to be a productive hunting ground for Gannon, for Renshaw had spoken of the town many times. Sheriff Jute had also talked as if the killer had been seen around San Angelo.

The twenty-four-year-old Renshaw had black, straight hair and green eyes, and was known to be a heavy drinker. A dozen empty whiskey bottles had been found in the cabin belonging to the Drakes, who were both teetotalers.

The sun was dropping into the treetops when Jake ended his conversation with the Weemses and took the trail back to town. He turned the gray over to the hostler at the livery stable.

"Guess you want 'im rubbed down an' fed good," the old man said. "Then I'll turn 'im in to the corral with your pack animal."

Jake nodded and headed for the office, where he had left his belongings earlier in the day. "Just need to get something out of my pack," he said over his shoulder. Gannon needed nothing from the pack, just wanted to check its contents, especially the sawed-off ten-gauge shotgun that he had rolled up in an extra blanket. Everything was just as he had left it, and the liveryman had said that the office would be under lock and key at night.

A short time later, after having registered at the hotel, Jake was seated in a small restaurant, enjoying a hot meal and a cold beer. The establishment looked exceptionally clean inside, and though more than twenty people were busy eating, the room was as quiet as a funeral parlor. Even the lady who took his order spoke almost at a whisper, and said nothing when she placed his food before him. Perhaps the people of this town were just not a talkative bunch, he thought. The hotel clerk had barely grunted when Gannon rented the room. And while the average liveryman would attempt to talk your ear off, the man at the local stable spoke only enough words to conduct business.

By the time Jake finished his meal, he realized that the real reason behind the people's silence was himself—Jake Gannon, *bounty hunter*. Sheriff Jute had probably told a few people of Gannon's business in town and the word had spread quickly. So this was how it was going to be. Very well, he thought, he liked his own company anyway. He paid for his food and headed for the hotel, not even looking at the clerk as he climbed the stairs to his room. He slept soundly, and awoke at sunup.

After washing himself as best he could from the pan of water provided by the hotel, he visited the same restaurant he had the night before. He was soon dining on pancakes, pork sausage laced with sage, and scrambled eggs. The coffee was excellent; the cook obviously used a little less water to make it than did most eating places. The silent treatment had not carried over from last night. His waitress this morning was talkative and friendly, and even flirted a little.

The trip to San Angelo would be a ten-day ride. Taking the pack horse's lead rope, Gannon stepped into the saddle and headed west.

Twenty-one

The community of San Angelo grew around Fort Concho, which had been established in 1867 at the junction of the north and middle branches of the Concho River. The frontier outpost had been created to replace Fort Chadbourne. The Fort Concho troops protected stagecoaches and wagon trains, escorted the U.S. Mail, explored and mapped new territory and occasionally clashed with Indians. Many well-known infantry and cavalry officers commanded the fort, including Colonel Ranald S. Mackenzie, Colonel William R. Shafter and Colonel Benjamin H. Grierson. Both black and white troops served there.

Across the river from the fort, Concho Street was the scene of most of the area's activity. Many businesses thrived along Concho, including the popular and prosperous saloon–parlor house known as "Miss Hattie's." The establishment, clean and fashionably furnished, was a home away from home for many a homesick soldier, and was openly tolerated by the fort's commanders. Lonesome cowboys of every description found comfort there, as did many of the town's most "upstanding" male citizens. The favorite activity of a few cowboys was to stand under the trees behind Miss Hattie's late at night watching the heads of outlying ranches, most of them respected family men, sneak down the back stairway.

Gannon camped ten miles out of town, and had breakfast the following morning in San Angelo. After stabling his pack horse, he began to ride up and down Concho Street. He quickly decided that locating any particular man in this town would be no easy task. Crowds of people jostled each other elbow-to-elbow along the sidewalks, and the street was filled to capacity with wagon traffic and saddle horses.

Jake guided the gray close to the sidewalk, then sat watching. He had never seen a street so busy. And though the ratio was sure to change when the sun went down, half of the people on the street were women and children, a proportion unheard-of in most towns.

He rode past Miss Hattie's a few times, then deposited the gray at the livery stable. The work he must do now could not be accomplished from the back of a horse. He traipsed around the town, hoping to spot a familiar face. Renshaw might have disguised his appearance, so Jake gave every man he met a good looking over. Half a dozen saloons lined either side of the street, and by late afternoon he had visited all of them.

He ate chicken and dumplings in a small restaurant at sunset, then headed for Miss Hattie's, where he walked to the far end of the bar and ordered a beer. The tall, skinny redhead who stood behind the bar made no attempt to start a conversation as he served the beer and took Jake's money.

Sitting at the back of the saloon, leaning against the wall, Gannon could see the entire room and the front door. For the next five hours he sat on the stool, but saw no man resembling Renshaw.

The drinks were expensive, and though the place was nothing less than a high-class whorehouse, Jake liked the quiet atmosphere. The girls moved around the room, but made no effort to hustle men at the bar. If a man wanted something other than a drink he had to speak up. Tonight, Gannon would pass up the opportunity. Each time he had succumbed to the urge over the past several months, he had walked away afterward with a clear picture of Jody Stewart in his mind, and a feeling of guilt that had lasted for several days. He knew that he must stop feeling that way if he was to live anything resembling a satisfying life, and the only way to do that was through repetition. Jody was dead, and he was alive. Placing his empty beer mug on the bar, he gave the smiling women a final look, then headed for the door. Maybe tomorrow night, he thought.

Eventually one of Miss Hattie's girls directed him to the settlement of San Marcos, saying that if he found a woman named Eve Jones he would probably find Tag Renshaw. "They wuz awful thick," the girl said, "and that's where Eve said she wuz goin'." Folding the wanted poster to reveal nothing but Renshaw's picture, Jake laid it on the bed before the dark-haired girl's eyes. "That feller in that pitcher hung aroun' Eve all th' time," she said, "an' I'm shore it pleased her. He never did say his name, an' I never asked. I know that they both disappeared on th' same night, so ya c'n add it up fer yaself." The following day, Jake was in the saddle again.

San Marcos, laid out for Anglo-American settlers in 1851, had once been the site of two Spanish missions re-

located from East Texas because of French and Indian dif-
ficulties. The town was established at the edge of the Hill
Country, and was the seat of Hays County. Springs within
the town gave rise to the cold San Marcos River.

A week later, sitting his saddle on its bank, Jake was
amazed at the clarity of the river, which was said to be fed
by more than two hundred springs. He rode till he found
a shallow place to ford.

Leaving his pack horse with the liveryman, he rode into
town by way of a residential street. Homes that were su-
perbly built and shaded by live oaks lined both sides of the
street. He reached a small commercial area, where he registered at a one-story dilapidated hotel. Then he rode his
horse back to the livery stable and returned to the hotel on
foot.

He was not long in learning the whereabouts of the
woman named Eve Jones. The desk clerk answered
quickly when asked if he knew the lady.

"Uh-huh," he said, a slight grin appearing on one side
of his mouth, "room sixteen, down the hall there."

Jake stood silently for a moment. He had not expected
it to be so easy. The woman was right here in the hotel.

"Is she alone?" he asked.

"She ain't never alone for long, mister. You want to see
her?"

"No, no," Jake said quickly. "In fact, she wouldn't even
know me." Gannon fished around in his pocket for a
while. "I don't want her to know that I even exist." He
pushed a ten dollar bill into the man's hand. "Would this
make you forget that I asked about her?"

"Mister, for this kind of money I could forget my own
name."

Gannon walked down the hall. The hotel had eighteen
rooms, with a back door that had been left open for a
breezeway. Jake's own room, number seventeen, was one

door down and across the hall from the one occupied by
Eve Jones. He left his door ajar so he could hear the footfalls of anyone moving around in the hall, and anyone approaching number sixteen through the back door would
have to walk past him.

Raising the room's window, he welcomed the cool
breeze from the river. He kicked off his boots and lay on
his bed for most of the afternoon, occasionally peeking
through the doorway to investigate some small sound.
There was no traffic at Eve Jones' door, though he had no
doubt that she was inside.

The view from his window was a parking lot, and several wagon teams and saddle horses were tied to hitching
rails. Tomorrow his gray would be there, saddled and
ready. An hour before sunset, he opened the door to his
room and stood in the doorway till dark. Jake was a pa-
tient man. A successful hunter never got in a hurry, and always moved against the wind.

It was hunger that finally moved him from the hotel. He
was just about to enter a small restaurant across the street
when a painted woman stepped from the establishment, almost running into him. Maybe thirty years old, she had
thick auburn hair that was twisted into a swirl, piled atop
her head and held there by several large combs.

"Oh, excuse me," she said.

Tipping his hat, Jake watched as she scampered across
the street and disappeared inside the hotel. He was sure
that he had just come face to face with Eve Jones, and believed that keeping her under close surveillance would
lead him to Tag Renshaw. Had she been outside the hotel
all afternoon? Had she walked down the hall without his
straining ears detecting her footfalls? He assumed the latter, for she wore shoes that were made from a soft material
and resembled moccasins. It was unlikely that she had
been moving around town in such flimsy footwear.

After a supper of roast pork and sweet potatoes, he walked past the parking lot and to the rear of the hotel. He wanted a look at the back door from the outside.

Walking forty yards into the shadows, he sat on a tree stump beneath the canopy of a large live oak, where he had a clear view of the hotel's rear door. He held his position till long past midnight, but saw no action.

Gannon lay on his bed with his boots on for several hours, listening. With his door ajar, he kept his Peacemaker in his hand. There was little doubt what Renshaw would do when finally cornered. Already sentenced to hang, the man would fight to the death. Anderson County authorities had assumed as much when they issued the poster reading "dead or alive."

Two hours before daybreak, Jake locked the door and closed the window. Then, slipping out of his clothing and beneath the covers, he was sound asleep in minutes.

After breakfast the following morning, he spent some time walking around the area, always keeping an eye on the hotel. The town marshal, a six-footer who was getting on in years, approached Jake, who was leaning against a vacant building.

"Howdy," he said, offering a handshake. "My name's Jim Biggers."

Gannon took the outstretched hand. "Good to meet you," he said. If the fact that Jake had not give his own name mattered to the marshal, it did not register on his face.

"Ain't seen you before," the lawman said. "In town for the fishing?"

"I guess you could say that," Gannon said. "Mostly I'm just taking it easy, enjoying your little town's hospitality."

"Well, come one, come all. The more the merrier, I always say." The marshal chuckled, and sauntered up the street.

An hour later, Gannon rode the gray into the parking lot, which was filled to its capacity. Today being Saturday, all of the hitching rails had already been taken, lined on both sides by wagon teams and saddle horses. After pausing at the watering trough and allowing the gray to drink, he rode to the far edge of the lot and tied the animal to a sapling.

A short time later he entered a small saloon, located three doors down and on the same side of the street as the restaurant. Ordering a beer as he passed the bartender, he moved to the far end of the bar, taking a stool. As usual, he had taken a seat that offered a good view of the front door. For the next two hours he sat watching, fruitlessly.

The bartender served Jake's third beer. A giant of a man, with a graying mustache and wrists the size of two-by-fours, the man likely served double duty as a bouncer. Pointing to the several poker games in progress across the room, the man said, "There's some big money in that game over by the wall. Do you intend to take 'em on?"

Jake took a sip of his beer.

"Nope," he said, shaking his head. "I don't play poker."

The bartender looked surprised. He shrugged, saying, "Well, I guess it ain't the first mistake I ever made, but I'd have sworn that you used to play poker in here. Just some fellow that looked like you, I suppose."

Jake had once again been mistaken for Josh Reenow. "I suppose," he said.

Jake was sitting inside the restaurant when the thunderstorm came. He sat beside the window, watching the deep puddles form in the street. Water that would quickly be transformed into mud, once traffic resumed. He ate an early supper, then, between downpours, rushed across the street to the hotel. He was halfway down the hall when he noticed that the door to room sixteen was opening—just wide enough for a man to squeeze through. Gannon

stopped, bracing himself. The man who squeezed through
was none other than the desk clerk. As the two passed
each other in the hall, the clerk grinned sheepishly, and
hurried toward the front desk.

Gannon sat on his bed thinking, watching the steady
rain through the window. The clerk obviously knew Eve
Jones better than Jake had realized. Which, of course, was
no indictment against the little man. It was by no means
uncommon for hotel help to assist whores. Jake supposed
that the clerk was handsomely rewarded for steering customers down the hallway. Perhaps one of the those rewards was his own free passage to room sixteen. Jake
decided to have another talk with him. He was soon at the
front desk, leaning over the small man.

"Can I help you?" the clerk asked, smiling.

"I just wanted to remind you," Gannon said sternly but
softly, "that when I pay for something, I expect to get it."

"Look, big fellow," the little man said indignantly, his
face turning red, "I do what I'm paid to do. I told you I
could forget my name for ten dollars. Ask me what it is
and see if I ain't forgot." Gannon nodded, and returned to
his room.

The rain continued most of the night. When Gannon
stepped into the hall the following morning, he saw muddy
footprints leading from the back door to room sixteen. But
there were no tracks leading from the room to the back
door. He was out the front door quickly, then circled to the
rear of the hotel.

There were indeed two sets of tracks—one coming, one
going. The footprints were large, and matched perfectly
with those in the hallway. The man had simply stayed in
the room long enough for his boots to dry. Or perhaps
they'd been cleaned by himself or the woman. Jake headed
across the street for breakfast.

Gannon learned the name of the hotel clerk from a man

in the restaurant, and decided to have yet another talk with him. The little man turned on his commercial smile when Jake approached the desk.

"Good morning, can I help you?"

"I need to talk to you, Shorty, someplace away from here." The man eyed Gannon questioningly. "I'll make it worth your while. The parking lot at noon?"

Shorty nodded, the smile returning.

When Shorty arrived at the parking lot, Gannon stood beside his horse at the watering trough. He produced the picture of the wanted man, carefully folded so that none of the lettering showed.

"I need some information on this man," he said. Shorty gave the picture no more than a casual glance, and said nothing until Jake dropped ten dollars in his hand.

"Ain't got nothing to say," Shorty said, looking around the parking lot. "Not for no ten dollars, I ain't."

Gannon thought for a moment. "I'll be honest with you, Shorty. That man is a cold-blooded killer, and he would wring your neck if he caught you coming out of Eve Jones' room."

The little man shot back immediately. "It's obvious there's a whole hell of a lot you don't know about the way things work. I get all I want with or without her, because there's always at least one whore working out of that hotel." He thumped the picture. "And that man ain't gonna do nothing to me. He don't give a damn who humps Eve Jones, as long as she keeps some money coming in. I can jump in the saddle and get a free ride any old time I want to, that's part of the deal. I don't give a damn about him or her either one, but I don't sell information cheap."

Gannon stood quietly for a moment. The little squirt had bested him. Reaching into his pocket, he came forth with another ten.

"Fifty dollars," Shorty said, a note of finality in his voice. With no hesitation, Gannon sweetened the pot.

"The man's name is Bill Clyde," Shorty said, his voice now businesslike, "and he lives in a cabin out on Cedar Creek. Same place Eve Jones' folks used to live. Eve stayed out there with Clyde for a while, then moved into the hotel."

"Do you think he would be at the cabin now?"

"Yeah, he stays there all the time. Only comes into town about twice a week to pick up money from Eve, and buy a new supply of whiskey. He was in town last night, so he won't be back for a few days."

So the muddy footprints in the hallway had been made by Tag Renshaw, while Gannon slept like a baby only a few feet away. Jake bristled with irritation at the thought.

Shorty's directions to the cabin were simple: ride east for a mile to Cedar Creek, then follow the stream north for two miles. The cabin could be seen without ever leaving the woods, Shorty said, for it rested in a small clearing, accompanied by a shed and horse corral. Gannon thanked the little man and mounted his horse.

"No thanks necessary," Shorty said. "You paid."

Riding north on Cedar Creek, Gannon was just approaching the clearing when he heard a dog bark, the sound quickly echoed by the yapping of several others. Peering through the brush, he could see three hounds in the yard, their noses pointed in his direction. Reining the gray, he made a hasty retreat down the creek, stopping half a mile away.

Off the trail and hidden behind some cedars, he sat his saddle, thinking. There was no way, day or night, that he was going to approach that cabin without the hounds announcing his arrival beforehand. It had not occurred to Jake that Renshaw might have dogs. Their noise had no doubt alerted the man, and the fact that no one had appeared after their warning was likely to make him even more cautious. Gannon turned the gray toward town. There was nothing to do but continue his surveillance of the hotel. Renshaw would eventually show.

Returning to the hotel, he slept all afternoon. He must stay awake and outside the building all night—every night. He would station himself behind the hotel near the back door.

Two nights later, Gannon's vigilance paid off. The full moon lighted the rear and west side of the hotel. Jake stood on the building's east side, just around the corner from the back door.

Before daybreak, he was alerted by the same sound that had been his undoing on Cedar Creek: a couple blocks away some of the town's dogs had started to bark. Someone was stirring. Plastering himself to the wall, Gannon watched a rider come into view at the end of the street and turn toward the hotel.

Riding up the hill cautiously, the man stopped several times to look over the area. Then, heading straight for the live oak, he disappeared in the darkness beneath its canopy. Several minutes passed. Jake continued to stand motionlessly. He had played the game before, and he knew that although he could not see the man, neither could he be seen, for the moonlight was almost as bright as day between them. Besides, he had more time than Renshaw; daylight would be coming soon.

The man stepped from the darkness ten minutes later, a Peacemaker in his hand. Even at this distance, Gannon had no problem identifying him as Tag Renshaw. Renshaw walked toward the rear door. Palming his own weapon and pointing it at Renshaw's heart, Gannon stepped around the corner of the building.

"The game's over, Renshaw!" he shouted. Gannon fired almost as he spoke, for Renshaw had raised his shooting arm. The early morning stillness was shattered by two shots that rang out almost in unison. The wanted man had indeed gotten off a wild shot of his own as he was going down. Renshaw dropped his gun and fell forward on his face, never to move again.

Daybreak was coming on fast, and Marshal Biggers was soon on the scene, rubbing sleep from his eyes.

"What happened here?" he asked, glancing at the corpse, then picking up Renshaw's gun and sniffing the barrel.

"Well, what you can see right off," Jake answered, "is that he tried to kill me. What you can't see is that he escaped from the Anderson County jail after being sentenced to hang for a double murder. That's Tag Renshaw."

"Tag Renshaw," the marshal repeated. "I've heard that name." Biggers ordered two men who were standing by to carry the body to his office, a block and a half away. Gannon handed the wanted poster to the marshal.

"It says Tag Renshaw's wanted dead or alive," the lawman said. "Well, that's Renshaw, an' he's damn shore dead or alive."

An hour later Gannon was headed east. He had paid the local undertaker to bury the body. In his pocket he carried a letter stating that Tag Renshaw had been killed in a gunfight at San Marcos, and would be buried there on this date. The letter further stated that Renshaw had fallen to the gun of Jake Gannon, and was signed by both Marshal Biggers and his deputy, each man saying that he had personally witnessed Renshaw's dead body. The letter, addressed to Sheriff Jute, was all Jake would need to collect his reward.

Twenty-two

As he rode through the gate at Cottonwood, Gannon could see several riders gathered at the Studying Tree. Putting his horse to a gallop, he was quickly on the scene. Sitting his horse, with his wrists tied behind him, was a blond-haired man who appeared to be in his early twenties. An expertly knotted hangman's noose dangled at the end of a rope that had been thrown over a limb of the huge cottonwood. A red-haired woman of about the same age sat her own saddle a few feet away. Her wrists were also tied.

Stepping from the saddle and wrapping the reins around the hitching rail, Gannon asked, "What's going on here, Mickey?"

"Caught 'em right in the act, Jake," Mickey Barnes said, with both of the new Cottonwood riders nodding their heads in agreement. "They cut the fence up on that northwest corner and made off with eighteen head. We got the cows back, though."

Gannon sat on the doorstep, looking the young couple over. They did not look poor. Both wore good clothing and rode good horses. The young man was clean shaven, and the woman, though homely, wore men's clothing that had recently been pressed with an iron.

"Was the woman in on it?" he asked.

"Hell, yes," Mickey said, his voice rising in anger. "In fact, it looked to me like she was the ramrod. He didn't show any fight, but she took two shots at us before I could get a rope on her."

Gannon sat on the step for quite some time. Then, getting to his feet to lead his horses to the barn, he said, "Find another tree, Mickey. I don't want anybody hanging on the Studying Tree."

"All right," Barnes said, taking hold of the condemned man's horse. "You don't object to the hanging, then?"

"Not if you're gonna hang 'em both." Gannon led the horses to the barn. When he returned to the yard five minutes later, the men were standing just as he had left them. Barnes had an odd look on his face.

"I don't know that I could hang a woman, Jake," he said. "We intended to take care of him, then take her to Sheriff Dubar."

Gannon shook his head emphatically. "Then take both of 'em to the sheriff," he said. "She knows the rules of the West as well as any man, and you said yourself that she's at least as guilty as he is. She gets no special treatment just because she's a woman. Tell Sheriff Dubar what happened here, and I want all three of you to sign the complaint."

The three men left for Waco with the prisoners.

Jake roped and saddled a small bay that he had never ridden before and headed for the northwest corner. He found the place where the fence had been cut easily enough, and noted that it had been mended with new strands of wire. He supposed that Barnes had forced the rustlers to drive the cattle back into the pasture, perhaps even making them repair the fence.

He rode about the area for more than two hours, pleased that Barnes and his men had the place in top shape. More than half of the cows had calves close by, and all were fat and frisky. More than enough hay grew in the upper meadow to get the cattle through even a hard winter. Barnes had chosen well when he hired the new hands.

Returning to the house, he walked to the graves of Josh Reenow, Bake Mellon and Big Red, where he stood for several minutes paying his respects. The graves had recently been cared for, and even a small bouquet had been placed at the head of the big thoroughbred. Jake had to smile. Little Mickey Barnes thought of everything.

He had just put on a pot of vegetable soup and dragged a chair into the shade of the Studying Tree, when Henry Handy Junior rode into the yard.

"Pa thought you might ought to be told," he said, keeping his seat on the barebacked mare, "Pop died in his sleep last night."

Jake was on his feet, removing his hat. "I can't tell you how sorry I am to hear that," he said.

"Well, we all knowed you an' him was all the time visitin' back an' forth, figgered you'd wanna know. Pop lived a good life an' died without sufferin'. Ain't gonna be no cryin' an' carryin' on. We'll bury him up there on the hill with the rest of the Handys about noon tomorrow. If you wanna come, you're welcome."

"I'll be there, Junior, and tell your folks that I'm sorry."

The boy turned the mare and rode off in the direction from which he had come.

Gannon sat under the tree for a long time, digesting the unwelcome news. Pop Handy had indeed been a friend, and Jake would miss him sorely. At this very moment there was a bottle of whiskey in Gannon's saddlebag that had been bought as a gift for the old man. But, as the youngster had said, Pop had lived a good life, much longer than any man could reasonably expect, and his death must be accepted. Time waited for nothing, and the old must expire to make room for the new. Returning the chair to the porch, he walked into the kitchen to check on his soup.

It was past sundown, and Jake had already fed the animals when Barnes and the new hands rode into the yard.

"We signed the complaint," Mickey said, "and the sheriff put both of them in jail. He said he wants to talk to you about another matter as soon as you have the time. I told him I didn't know when you'd be in Waco again."

"I'll see what he wants in a few days," Jake said. "I guess you fellows didn't know that Pop Handy died last night."

"Damn!" Rusty Fields said. "I sure did like him. Ain't been but a few days since he offered me a drink of whiskey."

"What happened to him?" Barnes asked. "I mean . . . did he just up and die all at once?"

"One of his grandsons rode over," Jake said. "He said the old man just died in his sleep."

"Well, it's bad about him dying," Nate Farlow said, rolling a cigarette, "but if a man's got to go, that sure sounds like the easiest way of doing it."

"They'll be burying the old man up at the Handy graveyard at noon tomorrow," Jake said. "I guess we should all go up and show our concern."

The men nodded in agreement, then headed for the bunkhouse.

The new hand named Rusty Fields, a young man of about twenty, cried like a baby as Pop Handy was laid to rest. He apologized later, saying that he did not know what had come over him.

"There ain't a damn thing wrong with what you did, Rusty," Gannon said, his hand resting on the sandy-haired Fields' shoulder. "Don't give it another thought."

The new hands were both native Texans. Nate Farlow had grown up in the Fort Worth area. Thirty years old and on the skinny side, he was almost as tall as Gannon. He had brown eyes that seemed to have a permanent squint, and dark wavy hair. Farlow had a good horse of his own, and had voluntarily thrown it in with the ranch's string.

Rusty Fields owned no horse. He had grown up on a farm a few miles south of Hillsboro, and had been on his own for only two years. He had no formal schooling, and was totally unwise to the ways of the world. But he was hard as nails and had plenty of sand.

Mickey had expressed his desire to keep both of the men year-round.

"You're the boss, Mickey," Jake had said. "Can we afford to keep them through the winter?"

"Could be that we can't afford not to. Men like them are hard to find, and they both understand our operation. Neither one of them is as good as Bake was, but who in the hell is?"

When told by Barnes that Jake had agreed to extend their two-month arrangement to a year-round job, both Farlow and Fields expressed their gratitude.

"Not many ranch hands that I know have year-round work, Mister Gannon," Farlow said, "and we certainly appreciate it."

"Don't thank me," Gannon said, "thank Mickey. He calls the shots around here. And by the way, my name is Jake. Just Jake."

* * *

The following morning Gannon ate breakfast in Waco, then climbed the stairs to Shannon Page's office. His main purpose was to remove Bake Mellon's name from the will Jake had written some time ago. Mickey Barnes now stood to inherit the entire Cottonwood spread, should Jake expire prematurely.

A few minutes later, he tied the gray to the hitching rail in front of the sheriff's office. Walking through the open doorway, he received a smile and a nod from Sheriff Dave Dubar, who was standing beside his desk with a flyswatter in his hand.

"I got your message, sheriff," Jake said, pulling up a chair with the toe of his boot. "Barnes says you want to talk."

With slightly stooped shoulders, Sheriff Dubar was not a big man, probably weighing no more than a hundred fifty pounds. Though he wore a high-crowned Stetson on the street, here in the office he was hatless, his dark hair badly in need of a comb. The lawman took a swing at a quick-moving fly, then seated himself at his desk. Speaking with unexpected familiarity, he said, "Good to see you, Jake. I never did get a chance to thank you for ridding this town of Marshal Bisco and his deputy. I'm thanking you now."

Gannon nodded, and remained silent.

"Coupla things I wanted to talk to you about," Dubar said. "I guess you knew that your old buddy Whitey Compton was doing time."

"No."

"Well, he is. They nailed him up on the Red, hauling whiskey into Indian Territory. They said he had two wagons coupled together and pulled by a four-horse team. Loaded to the hilt with rotgut. He won't be having to make none of his own decisions for the next eight years."

"Well, I'll be damned." Jake was disgusted. Whitey had

promised him faithfully that his whiskey-hauling days were over. The little man's devil-may-care attitude had finally gotten him into trouble. And the chances that Whitey would learn anything from the long years of incarceration were slim. Jake had long since given up on trying to understand the workings of Compton's mind.

Sheriff Dubar spoke again. "Sheriff Willow, over at Groesbeck, told me about your recent successful manhunt, and I hear that you brought Tag Renshaw to justice since then. The state of Texas needs a hundred men like you, Jake." Rising from his chair, Dubar began to walk around the room.

"Coleman County Sheriff Grady Lee is a friend of mine, and he's asked me to get in touch with you. There's a fellow down at Calvert named Sam Curtin who does a little manhunting, and Grady tried to get hold of him. Do you know Curtin?"

"No." Gannon had heard the name, for Curtin was known all over Texas as a man who was extremely fast with a six-gun, and deadly accurate as well. Some folks called Curtin "The Judge." Why, Gannon did not know.

"Well, Coleman County wants these men real bad," Dubar said, dumping two wanted posters into Gannon's lap, "and Grady's got an election coming up in the fall. As I said, he tried to get Curtin on their trail but the man was either too busy or not interested. Didn't even answer Grady's letter."

Gannon sat looking over the posters. He had never seen either of the men pictured. However, he did see one possible reason for Curtin's lack of interest: the reward for each man was only five hundred dollars.

"I don't suppose Coleman County wants these men too bad," Jake said, handing the posters back to the sheriff.

"I know it's not the heftiest reward I ever saw," Dubar

said, "but old Grady's the nicest fellow you ever met, and he needs them bastards bad."

"I'm sure the sheriff is a nice man," Gannon said, "but the reward ain't coming out of his pocket. Tell him to see if the county is as nice as he is. If they quadruple the reward, I'll get on the job. You can send somebody out to the ranch if they up the ante."

As Jake mounted and turned the gray toward Cottonwood, Sheriff Dubar was standing in the doorway. Gannon yelled over his shoulder, "And tell Sheriff Lee to put it in writing!"

Traveling on the river road, Jake was two miles from home when a young buck deer stepped from the woods and into a small clearing, offering a broadside shot. Jake unsheathed his Winchester and fired. The animal dropped in its tracks.

Though the carcass weighed less than a hundred pounds, Jake spent half an hour trying to get it aboard the gray. The horse was having nothing to do with the dead deer. Once, the gray even lay down on his side when Jake attempted to load the kill on his back. When Gannon tied the reins to a limb high enough that the horse could not lie down, the gray simply sat back on his haunches, allowing the deer to slide over his rump. All the while, the gray was making sounds that Jake had never heard before, sounds between the bawling of a calf and the howling of a hound.

Finally, Jake began to laugh and pat the horse's neck. He placed the carcass in the fork of a sapling, then mounted and rode to the barn. He roped his pack horse and went back for the deer.

Mickey Barnes took charge of the venison when Gannon reached the bunkhouse. He had been busy in the kitchen preparing the evening meal. Within minutes, he was expertly butchering the carcass.

"This is gonna be some good eating, Jake," he said.

"I'll smoke some of it, so it'll last a little longer. I guess you should consider yourself lucky to get it. They're getting damn scarce around here. The last three times I've gone hunting, I've come home empty-handed."

"People, Mickey. Too many people moving in. Five years from now you won't be able to buy a deer in this part of Texas."

Later, the two sat in the kitchen talking, as Mickey fried venison steaks. When told that Whitey Compton was now in prison, Barnes just grunted. Watching the little man sweating over the hot stove, Jake came to a decision.

"We need a cook around here, Mickey," he said. "I mean somebody that does nothing but cook and worry about supplies."

Barnes faced Gannon with a big smile. Wiping the sweat from his brow with his sleeve, he said with a soft chuckle, "Do you want to hire a cook? Or do you want me to do it?"

"You do it. You're the one that's gonna have to live with him. Go into Waco tomorrow and look around. An awful lot of men are out of work over there. See if you can find somebody who knows how to make pies and cakes. We could wind up eating like Cofield's bunch does."

"I don't think I'm gonna find a cook like Marie, but I'll go looking tomorrow."

When Barnes returned from Waco the following day he was not alone. Sitting beside him on the wagon seat was a man who appeared to have been eating very well. Claiming to have worked as a cook in some of the better hotels around Dallas and Fort Worth, the fifty-year-old balding man answered to the name of Fats Diamond. The man jumped from the wagon to the ground with surprising agility. He laughingly walked among the men of Cottonwood introducing himself, his huge belly shaking with each chuckle.

"Howdy," he said, grasping the hand of Nate Farlow. "My name is Fats, and I'm gonna be your next stomach problem." Then he moved on to the next man. When he reached Gannon, he turned serious.

"I certainly hope I can please you, sir," he said. "Just tell me what you want to eat, and I'll take a stab at it."

"Surprise me," Jake said.

Fats Diamond's first supper, though late in coming, was the best meal that had ever been cooked at Cottonwood. The small dining table was covered with plates and platters of scrumptious cooking, and biscuits as light as any Gannon could remember.

"I could have had everything hot at the same time," Fats said as he poured more coffee for each man, "if I'd had a better stove."

"Take Fats to Waco tomorrow, Mickey," Gannon said, helping himself to another wedge of apple pie. "Let him pick out the stove he wants. I'll build an extension on this table while you're gone."

Twenty-three

Two weeks later, Jake was sitting with a fishing pole in his hand when Dubar's deputy halted his horse on the bank of the river.

"The sheriff says to tell you that he's heard from Coleman County," the deputy said. "Says he'll be around the office all day tomorrow."

Jake said he would be in Waco before noon.

Sheriff Dubar was sitting on the porch just outside his office door when Jake arrived the following morning.

"Been expecting you," he said. "Glad you could make it." Jake followed the lawman into his office, where Dubar produced a letter written by Sheriff Grady Lee.

"The county fathers refused to raise the amount of the reward, but as far as you're concerned, this amounts to the same thing."

Jake read the letter, which stated that Coleman County

would pay two thousand dollars each for the wanted men, dead or alive, providing Jake Gannon was the man who brought them down. The letter was signed by Sheriff Lee and two of the county fathers. Gannon shoved the letter into his pocket.

"I'll take this along just in case I need it," he said, laughing. "Why are these jokers worth more if I find them than they are if somebody else does?"

"Grady just thought you were the right man for the job. He ain't physically able to go off hunting them himself."

Gannon smiled again. Why in the hell people continued to reelect men to a county's top office who were incapable of handling the job was a mystery to him. However, it was a fact of life. Jake had known many elected lawmen who were well past middle age, and he knew one sheriff who actually needed help getting in and out of the saddle. Ability and agility were rarely prerequisites. Getting a county's top job often required no more than that a man be skilled in oratory, and that he know the right people and have the right connections. Having little knowledge of and no time for politics, most residents of a given county voted as they were told.

Assuring Dubar that he would take up the hunt very soon, Jake returned to the hitching rail and mounted the gray. The sheriff followed, and stood beside Jake's stirrup.

"Them bastards didn't get their pictures on them posters for singing too loud in church," Dubar said. "They're both as mean as rattlers, and you better not give 'em no quarter."

Jake clucked to the gray and turned it toward home, the sheriff's words ringing in his ears. Gannon had a mean streak of his own that could be called up at a moment's notice. In fact, he had been taught by the meanest man in Kentucky.

"Ain't no sitchy thang as a dirty fight, Jake," Uncle

Jesse Ride had said. "Th' onliest thang that matters is that ya win, an' it don't matter a damn hill o' beans how ya do it. When ya fightin' a man, always kick 'im in th' nuts th' first chance ya git. If ya thank it's gonna turn inta a gunfight, blast 'im right between th' horns. That'll end th' argument ever' time. An' don't go atellin' 'im about it afore ya do it." Even as a teenager, Jake had more than once had to fight full-grown men when he was off someplace with Uncle Jesse. He believed to this day that Uncle Jesse had set the fights up deliberately, so that his nephew could gain the experience. "There's a thousand ways ta whup a man's ass, Jake," Ride had said, "an' that's most times whatcha gonna have ta do if ya git ta arguin' with a feller. I mean, ya can talk yaself blue in th' face, but I ain't never seen nobody that didn't understand a good ass whuppin'." Uncle Jesse had then proceeded to teach Jake many of the "ways."

Having no idea how long he would be gone, Jake decided to be as comfortable on this trip as the trail allowed, and to be in no hurry. He led the largest mare he owned to town and had her fitted with a new packsaddle.

The following morning, after having the cook prepare a four-day supply of food, he headed west. He rode at a steady pace throughout the morning and much of the afternoon, camping beside the Leon River at sunset. He picketed his horses, then placed his tarp and bedroll under some scrub oaks. He ate a pound of beef and six biscuits for his supper, washing it down with water from his canteen. Then he built a small fire for coffee. A short while later he sat sipping the hot liquid while reading a short life history of the wanted men, provided by Sheriff Dubar on a separate sheet of paper.

Doby Wills had been a scoundrel all of his life. A tall man who weighed more than two hundred pounds, the red-haired, freckle-faced thirty-year-old answered to the nickname of "Red." Even as a teenager he had been in trouble with the law, serving lengthy jail sentences in both Tarrant and Dallas Counties. At age twenty-one, he had been sentenced to ten years in the Huntsville penitentiary for cattle rustling, a sentence that had later been reduced because someone knew the right strings to pull. While in prison, he had been charged with the attempted murder of another inmate, but the case had never come to trial. The charge had somehow mysteriously disappeared from the court docket.

Doby Wills was now charged with torturing and murdering the very man who had freed him from prison—his wealthy uncle, John Wills. The aging rancher had been found by a neighbor, more dead than alive. Doby Wills, along with an accomplice, had locked the old man in the bedroom of his own home, withholding both food and water in an attempt to extort money from him. After several days, Red had carried a bucket of water to his uncle's room, but no food. John Wills' claim that he kept only a few dollars around the ranch, and his plea that he should be set free to raise the money, went unheard, for the duo believed that the old man had a hidden fortune. Though the rancher was known to be well-off, no large accumulation of money was ever accounted for after his death.

Though they had starved the rancher for three weeks, neither of the men had beaten him—until the last day. Finally convinced that they were not going to break him, they visited the old man's bedroom one last time. With sticks of firewood, they beat him into unconsciousness, leaving him for dead. Then, taking everything they could carry, along with two of the rancher's best horses, they were gone.

But the old man was not dead. A mere skeleton of his former self, he was found a few hours later by his closest neighbor. He lived for more than twenty-four hours, long enough to tell the entire story to the sheriff. He named both of his assailants, and went to his death trying to understand how his own nephew could turn on him.

Mack Todd had been Red Wills' accomplice in the heinous crime. A dim-witted, dark-haired man who was said to idolize and emulate Wills, he was a year younger. Most folks believed that the simple-minded Todd might be the deadlier of the two, for though Wills was known to be a fast gun, Todd was probably faster. He had had little to do except practice the fast draw while Wills was in prison. The two men were distant cousins, and Todd had been a frequent visitor at the state pen during Red's incarceration.

Coleman County encompassed a huge area of large-scale cattle ranching. The town of the same name was barely five years old, having been founded on Hords Creek in 1876. A typical frontier settlement, its first store was hardly completed before a cemetery was laid out to accommodate the loser in a gunfight between two cowboys. The town quickly became a supply point for the outlying ranchers, who had profited handsomely from the rolling, grassy plains and wide bottom lands. Sheriff Lee had been one of the county's first white inhabitants, and laid out some of the town's first buildings, including his own office. Though now past the age of sixty, and not in the best of health, the sheriff still clung to the reins as the county's top law official, refusing to step down so that his younger deputy, Kick Hobson, might become a candidate.

Gannon rode into Coleman at midmorning, and had no problem finding the sheriff's office. The bars on the windows of the second-story jail could be seen from anyplace in town. He was in the act of tying his horse at the hitching rail when the sheriff walked from his office, stepping off the plank sidewalk and into the street.

"Howdy," he said excitedly, his right hand outstretched, "I'm betting you'd be Jake Gannon."

Gannon nodded, taking the man's hand.

"Sheriff Dubar said you were a tough-looking customer," the sheriff continued, stepping backward so as to get a better look, "and bygod he was right. I mean, just one look is all it takes to know that you ain't nobody to be messing around with."

A man in his thirties stepped from the office, a badge pinned to the front of his shirt.

"This is my deputy," the sheriff said. "His name is Kick Hobson, and I've known him all of his life. Me and his daddy's been friends since boyhood, played together all over this country. Me and his daddy—"

"Have you got a cup of coffee, Sheriff?" Jake interrupted. Gannon enjoyed conversation as well as any man, but hated pointless prattle. Sheriff Lee took the hint, and did not speak again until spoken to.

Taking the letter from the pocket of his vest, Gannon said, "Sheriff Dubar gave me this." He passed it to Lee. "Are the facts correct? Two thousand dollars for each man?"

Lee looked at the letter, then handed it back. "Two thousand dollars for each man," the sheriff repeated, "and the money's waiting. You bring them or acceptable proof that they're dead to this office, and you get four thousand dollars."

Gannon wanted to see the house in which John Wills had been tortured, and the deputy agreed to meet him at the livery stable at one o'clock.

The deputy was on time.

They rode north-by-northeast for almost an hour, then stopped at a small stream to water the horses. Jake could see the unstately building a hundred yards up the grassy slope. Made of rough-cut lumber, the single-story house appeared to have eight or ten rooms. They rode up, dismounted, and stepped onto the porch. They walked through unlocked doors, visiting every room in the house.

The last place they visited was the bedroom in which the old rancher had been held hostage. Gannon stood beside the bed for a long time, staring at what appeared to be bloodstains on the covers. Perhaps in the last stage, the old man had been too weak to walk to the door. Or to beg. Jake thought that the perpetrators were less than human, and he would treat them accordingly when he caught up to them. The wanted posters read dead or alive, and Jake would consider nothing less than the former. Turning them over to the law so that a compassionate jury might let them off with a few years in prison was out of the question. With his dying words, John Wills had convicted his killers; Jake Gannon would be judge, jury and executioner.

Turning to the deputy, he said, "I need a starting place, Kick. Do you have any idea which way they might have headed?"

The deputy thought for a long time. "I've known both of them for a lot of years, Mister Gannon. Ain't neither one of them worth the damn salt on his last meal. But I don't believe you're gonna find them together."

"No?"

"Hell, no. They never did go around together much, just when Red needed Mack for something. Mack Todd ain't got sense enough to pour piss out of a boot, and Red just used him. The men are direct opposites. Red likes to drink whiskey, shoot pool and chase women. Mack hates towns. You're gonna find Mack holing up somewhere, but Red'll be right on Main Street. He talked about San Antonio a lot; you might start there. I'll tell you something else: either one of them can shoot the eye out of a squirrel, and do it damn quick. Especially Mack Todd."

"Thank you, Deputy, I'll keep that in mind."

* * *

San Antonio was the most colorful town Gannon had ever seen. Located on the San Antonio River, at the southern edge of the Texas Hill Country, the town had sprung from an Indian village in 1718. Mission San Antonio de Valero, later called the Alamo, had been established by Spain, and an accompanying fort, San Antonio de Bexar, protected mission endeavors. San Antonio remained the chief Spanish, then Mexican, stronghold in Texas until after the Texas Revolution.

By the time Gannon had stabled his horses, darkness had settled in. Throwing his saddlebag across his shoulder, he walked to an area where the saloons adjoined each other and painted women stood in lighted doorways. He rented a room at a run-down hotel. He washed and shaved. A few minutes later he was out on the street, acquainting himself with the noisy two-block area. Piano or fiddle music blared from almost every doorway, and Mexican troubadours strolled along the street playing and singing.

A man leaned against a building, holding a guitar that must have been two feet thick. When Gannon dropped a coin into his bucket, the troubadour broke into a Mexican love song. Though Jake understood few of the words, he enjoyed the beautiful melody, and the man made his guitar sound like a miniature orchestra. Jake asked him if he spoke English, and he did not. Gannon soon walked away in search of a restaurant. He also needed to make friends with someone who spoke both English and Spanish.

The beautiful blue-eyed waitress who served his food initiated a friendly conversation. She was twenty years old, and had been in the area all of her life.

"Do you speak Spanish?"

She fluttered her eyelashes. "Of course I do. I grew up playing with Mexican children, sir."

"Jake."

"Jake," she repeated. "My name is Julie." She seated herself at his table, for there were no other customers.

"You're a beautiful woman, Julie," Gannon said, "and I'd like to know you better."

"I think I'd like that." She fluttered her eyes again. "I get off work in two hours."

"I'll be here."

A week had passed since their first meeting, and this morning the sun was already shining on Gannon's bed when he opened his eyes. He kissed the young woman lying beside him, then slipped on his pants and reached for his saddlebag.

"I'm looking for these men," he said, handing over the wanted posters, "and I thought you might have seen them." He watched her eyes closely, and thought he saw a sign of recognition as she glanced at the pictures.

"You didn't tell me you were a lawman."

"I'm not. I'm just an ordinary citizen trying to help stamp out their breed." Jake told her the whole story. He left out none of the ghastly details.

Sitting up in bed, she continued to stare at the posters.

"I've seen them, Jake," she said sternly. "I've seen both of them many times, but not lately. They ate breakfast in the restaurant almost every morning last spring. They always looked dirty and wrinkled, like they lived outdoors somewhere." She pointed to the picture of Red Wills. "This one said his name was Tom, and always tried to flirt with me. I didn't want anything to do with them, Jake. I could smell them before I got to their table."

The girl had made no effort to get out of bed. With both arms around his neck, she kissed him passionately, pulling him toward her. He fumbled with his belt buckle, then kicked his way out of his jeans.

Later, as they walked the streets, she held tightly to his arm. This pleased him, for it made him appear to be just another cowboy in town.

At Jake's suggestion, Julie informed her boss that she intended to take a few days off, then the two had supper at a fancy restaurant.

Twenty-four

Julie lived in a small cottage at the edge of town with her mother and her stepfather, whom she introduced as Joe and Eula Mackey. Then she changed into riding clothes and informed her parents that she was going riding with Jake Gannon. They had ridden only a few steps when she began to giggle in his ear. "Momma called you Big Jake Gannon."

"Yeah."

She handled herself quite well in the saddle.

"I've been riding most of my life," she said. He enjoyed being with the girl, and especially liked to hear her talk. Her voice was soft and pleasant, and she used the English language much more correctly than himself or anyone else he knew.

They rode past the Arsenal, a colossal thing that Jake had only heard about. Julie knew more, having spent her entire life near it. The Arsenal had been built by the U.S. Army in 1860 and housed arms and ammunition for West Texas forts such as Stockton and Davis. The stables housed the mules that pulled supply wagons, and were built with red cypress imported from Louisiana through the port of Indianola. The walls of the Arsenal were more than four feet thick.

They rode the outlying area for three hours. Returning the horses to the livery, they found a shady spot beside the river, where Julie sat with her feet dangling in the water. She looked like a young schoolgirl to Jake.

Lazily, he said, "Julie Mackey . . . pretty name."

"My name is not Mackey," she said. "My father was John Moore. He died in California, and I did not change my name when my mother remarried."

"I see," he said. "Julie Moore." Sitting beside her with his own feet in the water, Jake laid out more of his life history than he had ever told to anyone. He told her of his ranch on the Brazos, and his house beneath the Studying Tree. She listened attentively to the Jody Stewart story, crying softly all the while. He described Jody's killers, and how he had hunted them down one by one. He added that the men he was hunting now were of the same stripe as the men who had killed her, and deserved the same fate.

"You're not hunting them for the money?"

"The money is the least of my reasons."

"I believe you, Jake," she said, wiping her eyes with her sleeve. "If there is any way I can help you, I will."

"There just might be," he said. "Let me think on it."

For the next several days, both Jake and Julie separately walked the streets in opposite directions. Alone, she was more likely to be approached by one of the wanted men. While Jake visited the saloons and bawdy houses, Julie talked with street entertainers, showing the pictures. She got lucky on the seventh day. A young trumpet player said that he had seen Mack Todd only yesterday, coming out of the general store.

She quickly told Gannon of the news. They entered the store together a few minutes later. Holding up the picture, Julie questioned the Mexican storekeeper in his own language. Like most men who fear getting involved with a manhunt, he answered all her questions in the negative. She turned to Jake, shaking her head.

Gannon grabbed the front of the man's shirt, jerking him halfway over the counter. Drawing back his ham-sized fist, he signaled the girl to continue her questioning. The man spouted an excited staccato of Spanish that lasted half a minute. Julie told Jake that the storekeeper had come up with the right answers.

Outside the store, she interpreted the conversation. The storekeeper had suddenly remembered that he had indeed seen Mack Todd, who had only yesterday bought flour, beans, bacon, several sacks of durham and a box of forty-four shells in his store. He believed that Todd was camped along the river somewhere. Jake squeezed Julie's hand. She had played her part to the hilt. The day had been a long one, and it was almost sundown. They ate beefsteak and potatoes at a small restaurant, then headed for the hotel.

As Gannon had expected, the following morning brought a tearful separation. When Jake announced that he was going hunting along the river, the girl pleaded that she be allowed to accompany him.

"Please, Jake," she said, tears running down her cheeks and falling on his boots. "Please let me go, I'll stay out of the way."

"No," he said softly. "It's simply too dangerous." He kissed the top of her head. "I want you to go home. Stay there until you hear from me."

Wiping her eyes, she nodded. "I will, Jake," she said, "and I will be counting the minutes. I . . . I love you so very much."

Jake felt like saying the same thing, but the words would not come. He kissed her again, then she was gone.

After saddling the gray and roping his pack horse at the livery stable, he rode to a place of business that sold bait and other fishing supplies. He was soon riding south along the river. His pack horse brought up the rear, a fishing pole attached to its packsaddle. He rode at a leisurely pace, keeping his eyes open for any kind of movement. A narrow trail ran parallel to the river, close to the water's edge at times, then as much as fifty yards away, with dense vegetation blocking his view of the river. He rode thus mile after mile. He had not expected Todd to camp close to town, and thought that he might be as much as twenty miles downriver.

At sundown, he picketed his horses a hundred yards from the river, placing his bedroll in a small thicket nearby. He would ride a few miles farther south in the morning, then ford the river and travel north on its east bank, continuing to offer the appearance of a fisherman looking for a likely spot to drop his line. After eating cold food that he had bought at the supply store, he rolled into his blanket. He was asleep quickly.

He awoke at sunup with a start. He had been dreaming of Julie Moore. Not Jody Stewart, who had often invaded his dreams in the past, but Julie. In his dream, he could almost feel her shapely body, her blue eyes dancing as he led her to his bed. Then she was standing on the deck of a ship. The sea breezes ruffled her hair and the loose-fitting dress she wore, as the big vessel abandoned its moorings and slowly moved away, leaving Jake standing at the wharf.

Kicking off his blanket, he built a fire for cooking

breakfast and making coffee. He made no effort to hide the smoke; perhaps it would bring out the man he was searching for. Gannon wanted to be seen.

An hour later, he was back in the saddle, carefully picking his way south along the river's west bank. He had just ridden out of some dense vegetation and into a clearing when he saw an old army tent about a hundred yards ahead and close to the water. He could see a faint curl of smoke from a dying campfire. And though he could see no sign of life, he believed that someone was watching him.

He dismounted nonchalantly, wrapping his pack horse's lead rope around his saddlehorn, then tied the gray to a bush. He walked to the river's edge, peering into the water as if trying to determine its depth.

Moving about leisurely, and watching the tent out of the corner of his eye, he retrieved his fishing pole from the pack horse. The box of worms he had bought yesterday were still alive. He weighted the line and threw it far out into the deep water. Then he sat down on the bank.

Jake had not wanted to actually catch a fish. But his offering had barely sunk to the bottom when he felt a sharp tug on the line. Moments later, he landed a four-pound catfish. Extracting it from the hook, Jake ran a string through its gills and placed it back in the water, tying the string to a root that protruded from the bank.

Gannon had just rebaited the hook and thrown it into the water, when he had company. A man had come from somewhere beyond the tent, and was now walking in his direction. Jake could see even from this distance that the man was Mack Todd. Dressed in Levi's and a brown shirt, the man wore no sidearm, but carried a Henry rifle in his right hand. His left hand held a cigarette, from which he took several puffs before reaching Jake.

"Saw ya ketch 'at fish," he said, his voice a nasal twang, "so ya must be doin' sump'm right. I been fishin' this whole side o' th' river fer more'n a week, an' ain't had a damn nibble."

"I guess I just got lucky," Gannon said, amazed that a man wanted by the law could be so careless. Jake knew that he could draw his gun and kill Todd before the man could bring his rifle to bear, but the shot would be heard for miles, and he had no idea where Red Wills was.

"I just fish for the enjoyment of it," Jake said. "I never eat them. I'll turn that one loose when I'm through fishing."

"Turn 'im a-loose?" Todd shook his head. "Why, they ain't nothin' as good as broiled catfish. Let me have 'im if ya ain't a-gonna eat 'im."

"All right. Just take it off the stringer there and it's yours." As Jake had expected, Todd laid his rifle aside to untie the knot. It would be the last act that he would perform in this world.

With a silly grin, he held the fish admiringly for a moment, then turned to climb back up the bank. When he bent over to retrieve his rifle, Gannon's knee caught him squarely on the chin. Unconscious, Todd landed flat on his back in the shallow water. Jake was on him immediately. Pushing Todd's head under the surface, Gannon stood on his throat until there was no sign of life.

He dragged the body into some underbrush, then rode around the area, studying the tracks. He found Todd's saddled horse a hundred yards from his camp. Dismounting and securing his own animal, he approached the tent cautiously, his Colt drawn and cocked.

Inside, he saw no evidence that more than one man had been living here. There was only one bedroll, and only a few other things that could not be eaten.

After convincing himself that Red Wills was nowhere in the area, Jake led Todd's horse to the river, minus its saddle. He wrapped the body in Todd's own blanket, then hefted it aboard the big black, tying it securely with his rope. A few minutes later, after taking as much of Todd's food as he cared to bother with, Gannon tied the black to the harness of his pack horse. He was soon headed north. He would deliver Todd's body, or whatever was left of it in this hot weather, to Sheriff Grady Lee at Coleman.

Twenty-five

"How in the world are we supposed to know that this is the body of Mack Todd?" Sheriff Lee asked, when Gannon delivered the body six days later.

"Because I say it is," Jake said sternly. He felt no tolerance for argument after six days in the saddle without a decent meal.

"It's him all right, Sheriff," Deputy Hobson said. "See that long, stringy hair? Them yellow buckteeth?" Two men unloaded the corpse and carried it to the sheriff's office, where they laid it on a table. Removing the blanket, Sheriff Lee began to explore the body. "Where did you shoot him?"

"I didn't shoot him, Sheriff. I beat him to death."

The lawman's face changed colors instantly, as he quickly moved to the other side of the table.

"All right," he said, "all right. If you say it's Todd, then bygod that's who it is. I'll have your money within the hour."

Jake had decided to stay in town for a while, for his horses desperately needed the rest, and the weather was very hot. The moon would be full a few days from now, then he could travel at night, resting the horses during the day.

An hour later, Gannon collected the two-thousand-dollar reward. The sheriff said that Coleman had no hotel, though there was a woman at the edge of town who rented rooms by the week. He directed Jake to the building.

"Three dollars a week for a room," the woman said. She stood almost as tall as Jake, and was at least a hundred pounds overweight. "And four dollars more if you take your meals in the dining room. I ain't got many rules here, but the ones I got might as well be carved in stone: no whiskey, no women, no fighting, no loud noises. The rent is payable in advance."

"Yes ma'am." Jake laid three dollars in her hand. She showed him to his room. Bolting the door, he stretched out on the bed.

The sun had already passed over the horizon when he awoke, and the small amount of light coming through the window told him that the day was coming to an end. He was very soon out of the house and onto the street.

He ate his supper in a small restaurant, then walked around the town, visiting one saloon after another. He spoke to no one, except to order a beer, and by ten o'clock he was sleepy again. He returned to the rooming house and slept the night away.

He awoke the following morning feeling a few years younger. He was just about to walk through the back door when the lady of the house called to him.

"You might as well have some coffee before you go

traipsing around," she said, motioning toward the kitchen. "There ain't no charge for that."

"Well, thank you, Miss Wheeler," he said, smiling, "I believe I could use a cup." He followed her to the kitchen, where she pointed to a table with two chairs. Pouring two cups, she then opened the door to the oven.

"Baking a little extra bread this morning," she said, "bread pudding for supper."

"You just talked me into having supper right here," he said, chuckling.

She sipped her coffee as noisily as any trail hand. He concentrated on getting her to talk. It turned out that all he had to do was listen.

Over several cups of coffee, she laid out much of her life history. She had lived in the area all of her life, and knew everybody. She had never married because there were no men worth having. The dirty ranch hands, who worked for little more than the food they ate and the whiskey they drank, were poor choices, as were the gamblers and the crooked businessmen of the town. Never willing to settle for anything less than a well-read man who knew something of what was going on in the world, she had remained her own woman, making her own way. The shelves in her parlor contained two hundred books, of which she had read more than half. Not once had she seen any man in this town reading a book.

"Simplest reason in the world for that, Mister Gannon," she said. "The poor devils can't read." She took her bread from the oven, placing the loaves on a metal table to cool. She poured more coffee.

"Take this fellow you've been hunting," she said, "this Doby Wills. He can't read anything except his own name, and I doubt that he can write it. Everybody calls him Red, you know. He's spent many a morning in this kitchen, sitting right where you are now. He always wanted to talk about his problems, but never about the one that got him into the most trouble."

"Who says I'm hunting him?" Jake asked, pushing the remainder of his coffee aside.

"Who says?" She waved her arms and shrugged her massive shoulders. "A better question would be who don't say it. Everybody in this town knows why you're here, and I believe that most of them wish you good luck. That includes me, too. I've known Red for a long time, fed him meals whether he had money or not, and I know just as well as if I'd seen it that he's guilty. Everybody in this county knew John Wills, and knew him to be a truthful man. He accused his nephew with his dying breath, no less. I say it would be a fitting end to a bad situation if you found Red Wills, Mister Gannon."

"Perhaps you can help me."

The lady produced two letters that she had received from Wills while he was in prison, written for him by another inmate. In both letters, he expressed a desire to wear a military uniform, saying he would probably enlist in the army when he was released. The lady believed that Wills had done so, once his plot to extort money from his wealthy uncle had fallen apart.

Red Wills in the army? The idea had not even occurred to Gannon. That the army would take almost any man was a well-known fact, with the only criterion being that he be able to walk, talk, see and hear. How would a man go about finding out who was or was not in the army? Jake had no idea. A lowly civilian stood no chance of getting cooperation from the Department of Defense. And the secretary of the army, who was himself a civilian, was unlikely to sift through the mountains of paperwork, even if asked by a law official. Anyway, would Wills enlist under his true name? Hardly. If he was in the army, he would be serving under whatever name he chose, as did countless others. Asking after the man under his true name would be useless.

He left the table with his course of action firmly in mind. He would travel from one army post to another, showing Wills' picture and asking questions. Two nights from now, he would head for Fort Concho. In his room, he trimmed one of the wanted posters so that only the picture remained, which was all anyone being questioned would ever see.

His visit to Fort Concho was short. He had barely begun to canvass the soldiers when he was accosted by an army captain. Accused of interrupting military procedure, Gannon was ordered to leave at once. An hour later, at a saloon in San Angelo, Jake was sitting at a table with a young man who said he had been in the army for four years. The soldier assured Gannon that he had never seen the wanted man. He added that most recruits were sent to godforsaken outposts with few amenities. Saying that Fort McKavett, a two-day ride to the east, was just such an outpost, the young man suggested that Gannon seek information there.

The soldier had described Fort McKavett well. Located in west Menard County, it was indeed in the middle of nowhere. Established in 1852 as Camp San Saba, it had later been renamed for Captain Henry McKavett, who had died during the Battle of Monterrey. Abandoned during the Civil War, it was reoccupied by Colonel Ranald S. Mackenzie in 1868. By 1876, stone barracks for eight infantry companies had been built, along with officers' quarters, a hospital, guardhouse, magazine, bakery and post office. Stables and storehouses had been erected, as well as a large headquarters building.

As he rode near, Gannon could see that many areas of

the fort were in a state of disrepair: after 1874, when the Army offensive against the Indians produced several major victories, including Mackenzie's wholesale rout of the Comanches at Palo Duro Canyon, the army had begun to question the necessity of maintaining the frontier outpost.

Though the fort was home to only a skeleton crew of personnel these days, it was still largely self-sufficient. The usual hangers-on were in evidence, small merchants with little to sell other than whiskey, and a few others who were forever inventing ingenious ways to separate the soldiers from their pay. Jake had also noticed a few homesteaders who had gardens growing along the banks of the San Saba River, men who would be around long after the fort was gone.

Gannon was soon fanning flies away from his beer in what passed for a saloon. The shutters on the windows of the dilapidated shack were tied back with short pieces of rope, allowing the flying pests to come and go as their instincts dictated. The front portion of the building had been floored with rough planks. The rear section, and the area around the potbellied stove, had been left to bare earth.

The bartender did not recognize the man in the picture, saying that he had seen virtually all of the men at the fort at one time or another and did not believe that Wills was among them.

"You can ask the soldiers yourself, though," he said, "if you want to stay around for twenty-four hours. Tomorrow's payday for the military."

"Thanks, I'll do that." He drank a straight shot of the man's rotgut, then headed for the door.

"See you tomorrow," the bartender said.

Half an hour later, Gannon was riding along the river, searching for a camping spot. He finally selected a small area between two trees, only a short walk from the water. He picketed his animals on the tall grass nearby, then placed his bedroll where he could see a quarter mile in every direction. After scrounging around for an armload of wood, he soon had a fire going.

Placing a pot of beans and bacon on the fire, he sat down to wait, his back against a tree and his mind on his quarry. He knew next to nothing about the workings of Red Wills' mind. Miss Wheeler had said that he was illiterate, but being able to read and write had little to do with being smart. Was the man even in the army? Having no better idea, Gannon had to assume that he was. Jake could think of no better place for Wills to hide than a military outpost, using whatever name he had picked out of the air.

Jake would speak only with enlisted men tomorrow. He had dealt with military officers before, many of whom seemed to hold contempt for civilians. And he would not be chased off the fort this time, for he would not be out there. Staying in the area of the saloon, he would question a number of the soldiers, then move on to another outpost.

But a favorable reaction came from a twenty-year-old recruit the following noon. Gannon had bought the young man a drink and invited him to sit at his table. Jake saw instant recognition on the soldier's face as he gazed at the picture.

"Redhead?" the recruit asked.

"Uh-huh."

The young man sat quietly for a while. Taking another sip from his drink, he finally asked, "Well, what's his name?"

"Uh . . . he changes it a lot. I think maybe he's trying to hide out from his former wife." Jake waited for the man's reaction.

"You mean that you're hunting a man whose name you don't even know?"

"No, no," Jake said quickly. "His name is Bill Bryan. I just don't know for sure what name he's using now."

"What are you hunting him for?"

"His rich uncle died."

"Well, now," the young man said, beginning to smile for the first time, "that's a horse of a different color. I guess he's got something coming to him. Right?"

"Right," Gannon said, "and the folks back home want to make sure that he gets it."

"Me and him enlisted on the same day down in San Antonio. He's using the name of Will Downing now. His luck must have been a little better than mine. They sent him straight to Fort Clark, while I wound up in this hellhole. Fort Clark ain't far from the border, you know, and a willing woman ain't hard to find. A fellow probably wouldn't even have to go to Mexico. Brackettville's right there at the fort, and I hear that them women go plumb wild over soldiers."

"I'll bet they do," Jake said, getting to his feet, "especially young soldiers like yourself." Gannon had learned as much as he needed to know. He bought a bottle of whiskey for the soldier, then said good-bye. He straddled the gray moments later, and was soon headed south.

Jake could think of few places more uncomfortable than West Texas in late summer. He followed the Llano River for a while, then picked up the Frio two days later. On the fourth night, he camped on the Nueces River, then followed it to its junction with the West Neuces. He rode along the south bank of the West Nueces into Kinney County, then deserted the river and rode through the arid countryside to Brackettville, only a few miles to the west.

He rode straight to the livery stable. The horses were tired, hot, hungry and thirsty, and Jake himself was in no better condition. The hostler rubbed the animals down immediately, and Gannon stood by until they had been watered and fed. Then, throwing his saddlebag over his shoulder, he sauntered down the street.

A man did not have to see the courthouse to know that Brackettville was the county seat. People were rushing to and fro in all directions, with some of the men dressed in town suits and carrying briefcases. Gannon felt sorry for any man whose job demanded that he wear a coat and tie on a day like this.

He walked up one side of the street and down the other. The town had been laid out well, put together with foresight. The buildings would definitely be around for a while. It seemed a friendly town, for every man he passed either spoke or nodded a greeting. He ate his dinner in the largest restaurant in town, then selected a two-story hotel on the corner near the livery stable. As was his custom of late, he slept the afternoon away.

He awoke after sundown. He had been touching the extra pillow and running his hand along the opposite side of the bed, feeling for the body that was not there. He had been dreaming again, feeling the shapely form of Julie Moore as she clung to him. He refused to open his eyes even after he came fully awake, for he could see the girl's full red lips and raven-black hair just as clearly as if she were in front of him. He lay still until the dream faded, then sat on his bed, shaking his head. He could think of only one way to rid himself of these empty dreams. When this thing with Red Wills was over. . . .

Twenty-six

Brackettville had been established as a supply village for adjacent Fort Clark in 1852, and had later become a trade center for surrounding ranches and irrigated farms. In the early days, the settlement had been entirely dependent upon the fort, for both protection and economic survival. Though the town did have a marshal these days, the job of keeping the peace occasionally fell to the army, whose ideas of justice varied widely from one year to the next, depending on which commander was in charge.

Seth Ringling, the young town marshal, usually let the army handle disputes involving military personnel, although he had shown the people of Brackettville on more than one occasion that he had plenty of sand in his craw. Only last year, he had shot a gunslinger dead in the middle of the street. The man had disobeyed Ringling's order to leave town, and chose to make a fight of it. Word had soon spread that the lawman tolerated no nonsense, and most outlaws gave the town a wide berth. The muscular twenty-five-year-old marshal had been raised in the area, and most of the town's residents called him by his first name. Standing six feet tall, and weighing a solid two hundred pounds, the blond-haired young man had sent more than one undesirable packing using only his fists.

A few minutes after dark, Gannon was standing in the doorway of the hotel, trying to decide which saloon would be his first stop. When he heard heavy footfalls on the boarded sidewalk, he quickly moved away from the lighted doorway. A few moments later, the marshal appeared.

"Good evening," the lawman said. "Nice night, huh?"

"Yes, it is," Jake answered, "and good evening to you." He stood watching as Ringling left the sidewalk and crossed the street, passing in and out of the glow of several lighted windows. Gannon supposed that the thick-chested marshal would be a handful for any man, and his quick, deliberate movements suggested that he would not be slow in getting his low-hanging Peacemaker into action. Jake waited till darkness swallowed the lawman, then turned his own footsteps up the street to the nearest saloon.

It was the typical Texas watering hole, with the bar running almost its entire length. Jake ordered a pitcher of beer from one of the bartenders, then selected a table close to the rear wall. From his seat, he could see all of the action throughout the room. About forty men were present, and so far he had seen no women. Perhaps they would wait till later in the evening before starting to ply their trade.

The third saloon he visited was no better than the first, only bigger. It was nearing ten o'clock when he stepped inside, taking a seat at the far end of the bar. He had just begun to sip his beer when a loud shoving match broke out between two off-duty soldiers. The pushing soon turned to blows, and one man was already bleeding at the nose when Marshal Ringling appeared. Placing one hand on the chest of each man, he pushed them apart with a force that sent them both to the sawdust floor.

"Get out of here, Trump!" he yelled, pointing his finger at the larger of the two. "I've had trouble with you before. I don't give a damn how much you throw your weight around out at the post, but it won't work here." He took a step toward the man, who had made no effort to get up. "Move!" The man scrambled to his feet and made a bee-line for the front door. The marshal calmly walked out behind him.

Gannon sat sipping his beer. He had watched the law-man closely, noticing how his right hand hovered near the butt of his Peacemaker as he ordered the man named Trump to leave the building. It was almost as if he were inviting the man to make a move toward his own gun. The young marshal had sand, all right, and Jake decided to have a talk with him tomorrow. He finished his beer, and headed for the hotel.

"I've heard so many Jake Gannon stories that I feel like I know you already," the marshal said, when Jake introduced himself the following morning. "What brings you to Brackettville?"

"I'm looking for a man, Marshal," Jake said, releasing Ringling's hand. The marshal crossed the room and filled two tin cups with coffee, offering one to Jake. Then, after pulling up a chair for his visitor, Ringling took his own seat behind his desk.

"Want to tell me about it?" he asked.

Mentioning no names, Gannon told the story of two men starving and torturing an old man to death in his own house in an effort to extort money from him. He said that he himself had already brought one of the men to justice, and had reason to believe that the second was right here in this town.

"In Brackettville? Hell, I thought I knew about everybody in Brackettville."

"I didn't mean the town itself," Jake said quickly. "I believe he's at Fort Clark."

Ringling was on his feet in an instant, walking around the room and cursing. "That sounds about right to me," he said, wringing his hands. "If the truth be known, half the sonsofbitches out there are probably wanted somewhere. You got a wanted poster on him? Some kind of proof?"

"Got a poster, but I'm not ready to show it."

"I don't want to see it," Ringling said, " 'cause then I'd be duty sworn to make a play for him myself the first time he comes to town. He's your man, you take him. You've already done all the hard work, anyhow."

"Thank you," Jake said, getting to his feet. "I just wanted you to know why I'm here." He walked to the door, then said over his shoulder, "I'll just wait him out, and try to make sure nobody else gets hurt."

The marshal nodded. "I know your reputation, Mister Gannon."

Jake eventually began to wonder if he really knew what he was doing. He had been in town for more than a week, and had seen nothing to suggest that Red Wills was in the area. From early morning till late at night, he walked the streets or sat in saloons. Even some of the townspeople had begun to view Gannon's actions with suspicion. After all, this was a small town, and most of its residents had seen him dozens of times during the past week. Jake had also noticed that Marshal Ringling had developed a keen interest in keeping up with his whereabouts. While walking the streets, Gannon had several times noticed that the lawman just happened to be loitering nearby.

Jake had learned from reading notices posted around

town and from talking with men in saloons that a large
crowd of people would be in town next Saturday.
Brackettville would be celebrating the twenty-ninth anni-
versary of its founding, starting with a parade down Main
Street that had become an annual event nine years ago.
Races between some of the area's fastest horses were
scheduled for the afternoon. The army would participate,
making a loan of several horses and wagons for the parade. Gannon hoped that the gay festivities might bring his
man out.

At ten o'clock Saturday morning, Jake sat on a bench
outside the hotel. He could see the parade forming at the
far end of the street.

Half an hour later, as the sound of a brass band signaled
the start of the parade, Gannon stepped up on the bench
and leaned against the building, a position that gave him
something akin to a bird's-eye view. Pedestrians quickly
lined both sides of the street, shouting and laughing.

The procession moved down the street slowly, for there
were several oxen involved, as well as dozens of happy
handshakers. As the band passed the hotel, Gannon paid it
no mind, for his eyes were glued to the riders immediately
behind the musicians. There, riding matching blacks in
perfect formation and cadence, were three uniformed soldiers. The man who rode in the middle was none other
than Red Wills.

"Red'll be right on Main Street," Deputy Hobson had
said. Well, this is Main Street, and there's Red, Gannon
was thinking.

Gannon walked along beside the procession, careful to
keep a distance between himself and the soldiers. This was
neither the time nor the place for gunplay. He stood by
helplessly when the parade broke up at the end of the
street. The three soldiers intermingled with other army

personnel, then, in a tight bunch, rode straight back to the military reservation.

Jake reseated himself on the hotel bench. Wills had gotten away, all right, but that would be temporary. The conscienceless sonofabitch had been putting on a show. Standing in his stirrups, bowing his head to and fro and waving his hat to people on both sides of the street, a smug expression of self-importance on his face, Wills had emitted an air of complacency usually reserved for celebrities and politicians. Gannon had a bad taste in his mouth. Getting to his feet, he spat in the dust and walked down the street.

He watched the races in the afternoon, barely cognizant of which horses won. His mind had been totally occupied with thoughts of his quarry. Deputy Hobson had said that Wills had something approaching an addiction to whiskey and women. Fort Clark had little of the former and none of the latter, yet Wills had failed to visit any of the places in town where both could easily be found. Perhaps the matter had been taken out of Wills' hands. Jake supposed that it was possible that the man had been restricted to the post for some infraction of the rules, and that the restriction had now been lifted. He walked back to the hotel, having no way of knowing how correct his supposition had been.

Gannon's long wait ended the following morning at ten. He had taken his horse for an early morning workout and was just returning to town when he spied a rider moving down the street from the direction of the livery stable. As nonchalantly as possible, Jake turned his horse toward the hitching rail of the town's leading saloon, where he dismounted and tied the animal. Still standing behind his horse, he moved his Peacemaker up and down a few times, making sure it was riding loose in its holster. He had al-

ready determined that the man riding the slow-walking
black was Red Wills.

Riding on past Gannon, Wills tied his horse at another
hitching rail, a few paces away. He had just stepped onto
the plank sidewalk when he suddenly stopped in his
tracks. There, less than thirty feet away, and already assuming the gunfighter's crouch, stood Jake Gannon.

"Remember John Wills?" Gannon called, his hand
hanging loosely above his holster. The redhead was fast!
He had just cleared his holster when he took a shot in the
chest that sent him staggering into the street. Following,
Jake sent another shot into him. Though dying on his feet,
Wills had still not fallen, or dropped his gun.

"Don't leave no damn cripples ta creep on ya later,"
Uncle Jesse had always said. Gannon sent a third shot
through the redhead's open mouth that sent him sprawling
into the dusty street. He was dead.

Marshal Ringling was beside Gannon immediately.
"Saw the whole thing," he said. "I had a feeling that he
was your man. I've had problems with him myself, barred
him from coming into town two weeks ago. His suspension was up yesterday. His name is Downing."

"Not exactly," Gannon said, walking to his horse and
getting the poster from his saddlebag. He handed it to the
lawman, who glanced at it, then smiled.

"You've got your man, Mister Gannon," he said.

"I'd appreciate it if you'd put that in writing. I'll leave
plenty of money for his burial."

"Be glad to." The marshal motioned Jake toward his office. An hour later, Gannon was headed north. He had
some unfinished business in San Antonio.

He first tried the restaurant, and was told that Julie
Moore no longer worked there. He found her at home,
where he'd told her to stay until he returned. As he dis-

mounted, she ran from the house, stopping a few feet away.

"I was beginning to think you weren't coming back," she said, "that maybe you thought I was too ... too ... easy." Tears ran down her cheeks freely, as she began to wipe at both eyes with her hands.

"Come here," he said, opening his arms wide. She ran to him. Holding her tightly, with her arms around his neck, he kissed her firmly on the mouth, then brushed the moisture from her cheeks with his hand.

"I was hoping you might want to take a ride to the Brazos," he said.

"You mean ... are you asking me—"

"Yes," Jake interrupted. "We'll be married under the Studying Tree."

WESTERN ADVENTURE FROM TOR

☐	58459-7	THE BAREFOOT BRIGADE *Douglas Jones*	$4.95 Canada $5.95
☐	52303-2	THE GOLDEN SPURS *Western Writers of America*	$4.99 Canada $5.99
☐	51315-0	HELL AND HOT LEAD/GUN RIDER *Norman A. Fox*	$3.50 Canada $4.50
☐	51169-7	HORNE'S LAW *Jory Sherman*	$3.50 Canada $4.50
☐	58875-4	THE MEDICINE HORN *Jory Sherman*	$3.99 Canada $4.99
☐	58329-9	NEW FRONTIERS I *Martin H. Greenberg & Bill Pronzini*	$4.50 Canada $5.50
☐	58331-0	NEW FRONTIERS II *Martin H. Greenberg & Bill Pronzini*	$4.50 Canada $5.50
☐	52461-6	THE SNOWBLIND MOON *John Byrne Cooke*	$5.99 Canada $6.99
☐	58184-9	WHAT LAW THERE WAS *Al Dempsey*	$3.99 Canada $4.99

Buy them at your local bookstore or use this handy coupon:
Clip and mail this page with your order.

Publishers Book and Audio Mailing Service
P.O. Box 120159, Staten Island, NY 10312-0004

Please send me the book(s) I have checked above. I am enclosing $ _____
(Please add $1.25 for the first book, and $.25 for each additional book to cover postage and handling.
Send check or money order only—no CODs.)

Name _____
Address _____
City _____ State/Zip _____
Please allow six weeks for delivery. Prices subject to change without notice.

MORE WESTERN
ADVENTURE FROM TOR

☐	58457-0 **ELKHORN TAVERN** *Douglas Jones*	$4.95 Canada $5.95
☐	58453-8 **GONE THE DREAMS AND DANCING** *Douglas Jones*	$3.95 Canada $4.95
☐	52242-7 **HOPALONG CASSIDY** *Clarence E. Mulford*	$4.99 Canada $5.99
☐	51359-2 **THE RAINBOW RUNNER** *Cunningham*	$4.99 Canada $5.99
☐	58455-4 **ROMAN** *Douglas Jones*	$4.95 Canada $5.95
☐	51318-5 **SONG OF WOVOKA** *Earl Murray*	$4.99 Canada $5.99
☐	58463-5 **WEEDY ROUGH** *Douglas Jones*	$4.95 Canada $5.95
☐	52142-0 **WIND RIVER** *Dick Wheeler*	$3.99 Canada $4.99
☐	58989-0 **WOODSMAN** *Don Wright*	$3.95 Canada $4.95

WESTERN DOUBLES

☐	50529-8	AVALANCHE/THE KIDNAPPING OF ROSETA UVALDO	Grey	$3.50 Canada $4.50
☐	50547-6	FRONTIER FURY/WHITE MAN'S ROAD	Henry	$3.50 Canada $4.50
☐	51617-6	KIDNAPPING OF COLLIE THE YOUNGER/ OUTLAWS FROM PALOUSE	Grey	$3.50 Canada $4.50
☐	50542-5	LONE WOLF OF DRYGULCH TRAIL/ MORE PRECIOUS THAN GOLD	Drago	$3.50 Canada $4.50
☐	50544-1	THE LONGRIDERS/THE HARD ONE	Prescott	$3.50 Canada $4.50
☐	50540-9	LOOK BEHIND EVERY HILL/ THE BIG TROUBLE	Frazee	$3.50 Canada $4.50
☐	50536-0	PROSPECTOR'S GOLD/CANYON WALLS	Grey	$3.50 Canada $4.50
☐	50532-8	RED BLIZZARD/THE OLDEST MAIDEN LADY IN NEW MEXICO	Fisher	$3.50 Canada $4.50
☐	50526-3	THE RIDERS OF CARNE COVE/THE LAST COWMAN OF LOST SQUAW VALLEY	Overholser	$3.50 Canada $4.50
☐	50534-4	THAT BLOODY BOZEMAN TRAIL/ STAGECOACH WEST!	Bonham	$3.50 Canada $4.50
☐	51316-9	WILD WAYMIRE/GUN THIS MAN DOWN	Patten	$3.50 Canada $4.50

Buy them at your local bookstore or use this handy coupon:
Clip and mail this page with your order.

Publishers Book and Audio Mailing Service
P.O. Box 120159, Staten Island, NY 10312-0004

Please send me the book(s) I have checked above. I am enclosing $ _____
(Please add $1.25 for the first book, and $.25 for each additional book to cover postage and handling.
Send check or money order only—no CODs.)

Name _____
Address _____
City _____ State/Zip _____
Please allow six weeks for delivery. Prices subject to change without notice.